ALANA SAAB

Please Stop Trying
to Leave Me

Alana Saab is a literary writer and screenwriter. She holds
a master of fine arts in fiction from The New School, a
master's degree in psychology from Columbia University,
and her bachelor's from New York University in the phe-
nomenology of storytelling. She lives in New York with
her partner. *Please Stop Trying to Leave Me* is her first novel.

Please Stop Trying to Leave Me

Please Stop Trying to Leave Me

A NOVEL

Alana Saab

Vintage Books
A Division of Penguin Random House LLC
New York

A VINTAGE BOOKS ORIGINAL 2024

Copyright © 2024 by Alana Saab

Library of Congress Cataloging-in-Publication Data
Names: Saab, Alana, [date] author.
Title: Please stop trying to leave me : a novel / Alana Saab.
Description: First edition. | New York : Vintage Books, a division of
Penguin Random House LLC, 2024.
Identifiers: LCCN 2023040446 (print) | LCCN 2023040447 (ebook)
Subjects: LCGFT: Psychological fiction. | Novels.
Classification: LCC PS3619.A236 P57 2024 (print) |
LCC PS3619.A236 (ebook) | DDC 813/.6—dc23
LC record available at https://lccn.loc.gov/2023040446
LC ebook record available at https://lccn.loc.gov/2023040447

Vintage Books Trade Paperback ISBN: 978-0-593-68678-2
eBook ISBN: 978-0-593-68679-9

Book design by Steve Walker

vintagebooks.com

Printed in the United States of America
1st Printing

for frishta
who stayed

The truly creative mind in any field is no more than this: A human creature born abnormally, inhumanly sensitive. To [her] ... a touch is a blow, a sound is a noise, a misfortune is a tragedy, a joy is an ecstasy, a friend is a lover, a lover is a god, and failure is death. Add to this cruelly delicate organism the overpowering necessity to create, create, create—so that without the creating of music or poetry or books or buildings or something of meaning, [her] very breath is cut off from [her]. [She] must create, must pour out creation. By some strange, unknown, inward urgency [she] is not really alive unless [she] is creating.

Pearl S. Buck

CONTENTS

OCTOBER

NOVEMBER

DECEMBER

JANUARY

THE END

Please Stop Trying to Leave Me

THE STUDY OF OBLIVION

Brown bookshelf. On bookshelf, creepy wooden robot.

Two windows facing Central Park West.

Five gold rings. White veiny hands.

Are those really what my hands look like?

White walls (always white walls).

Tan couch. On the couch, three god-awful, neon-colored textile pillows.

Wait...

Why am I not sitting on the couch?

Norma?

I look up. Brown hair. Hazel eyes. Black dress. Yellow ballet flats on black footrest.

Norma, what are you thinking about?

My old therapist told me to label things by color and object when I feel oblivion, so I was just doing that in my head.

She almost smiles, showing no teeth. The wrinkles on her middle-aged face remind me of lines in a notebook. When her almost-smile finishes, she says, so where would you like to start?

I think, well now that we've got a setting and two characters, we should dive into the conflict.

JUNE

Ask not what oblivion can do for you, but what you can do for oblivion.

John F. Kennedy

THE STUDY OF OBLIVION

seven weeks since breakdown

How long is this thing?

It's two hours.

Is it always going to be this long?

No, this is just a consultation to see if it makes sense for us to work together.

Work together? Like collaborate?

Like if it makes sense for me to take you on as a client.

Ohhh, so this is like a pitch.

My new therapist looks at me and blinks twice. I explain further:

Like you're an agent deciding if you want my manuscript and maybe by the end of this, you'll sign me.

She smiles, but by the way her mouth shifts, it almost looks like she's just eaten something sour. She says, where would you like to start?

With oblivion. Obviously.

My new therapist says, what's oblivion? She says this nonchalantly as if oblivion was a dog I had during my childhood who I should not still be mourning at the age of twenty-seven.

I say, well, let's begin with its etymology.

> Oblivion. Noun. Fourteenth century.

> State of forgetting, forgetfulness, loss of memory.

> Directly from Latin. *Oblivionem.* Forgetfulness; a being forgotten.

A being. *Forgotten.*

According to the Online Etymology Dictionary:

> *Oblivion* is supposed to have originally stemmed from the break-down of *ob-* and *lēvis.* Together meaning: to even out, smooth over. However, linguists ("de Vaan and others") say:

> a semantic shift from *to be smooth* to *to forget* is not very convincing.

This quote is followed up with:

> However no better explanation has emerged.

Also from the Online Etymology Dictionary:

> For sense of oblivion's evolution, compare *oblivious* and *obliterate.*

I never understood the relationship linguistics is trying to draw between these words, so let's continue:

I began calling it oblivion when I was twenty-four. Three years ago, and long after it began. Of course, the word had already been famously used in John Green's novel *The Fault in Our Stars*, but I didn't get the word from there. In fact, when I learned that oblivion had been used in that book, I almost changed the name. But then I didn't, because I'd been calling it oblivion for so long, and I'm lazy.

She doesn't laugh.

Anyways,

Oblivion began when I was much younger. Four is my earliest memory of it. And it is the second memory I have of my entire life.

My first memory is me at two and a half. Looking at my father and saying:

I. Two a half.

I don't remember why I started calling it by the name oblivion three years ago, but that's the only word that came to mind. And I needed something to refer to it as instead of just that thing that happens to me, so I settled on oblivion. And so far:

No better explanation has emerged.

That said, my new therapist seems to have one and will tell me in approximately forty minutes.

I think I was writing at my desk when the word came to me, but I can't really remember. Oblivion tends to mess with my memory. It messes with a lot of things.

Like my life.

You see, oblivion didn't creep in, like most things do. It didn't slide under the weathering foundation of my life, dripping, accumulating, like a slow leak. There are mixed metaphors of water and gas here, but it wasn't, isn't, and won't ever be an element nor a property. In a similar respect, it can't be found on the periodic table or located in a lab. However, it can be, with language, pointed to, like a person with no eyes trying to point at a flying, silent, bird. In this way, it also cannot be pointed to, but still I can try. This is one of my many attempts:

A tarot reader once walked with me along Henry Hudson Parkway. She told me that animals, after they are traumatized, or chased to be hunted down, or if a dog does something "embarrassing" (these are all forms of trauma according to her), shake their bodies viciously for a moment as if trying to shed themselves of the memory. Or, she also offered, as if they are moving the trauma through their animal bodies so it doesn't create blockages in consciousness.

Another man who was not a friend but someone who wanted to have sex with me (though he explained it as wanting to hold me) once said he believed consciousness lived not in the brain but in our fascia.

That's the first time I heard the word.

The word *fascia*. Not oblivion.

what is fascia? About 90,000,000 results (0.65 seconds)

Fascia is a thin casing of connective tissue that surrounds and holds every organ, blood vessel, bone, nerve fiber and muscle in place. Fascia has nerves that make it almost as sensitive as skin.

Johns Hopkins says related searches are hypnosis, Chinese medicine, and imagery (whatever that means).

Fascia, like the brain, confuses scientists and doctors, so they often don't talk about it.

My second memory is of the world emptying. I was in my parents' bedroom when it happened. I'm not sure where they were, but I know I was walking to the bathroom. I blinked my eyes and then they stayed shut. And in that moment when my eyelids wouldn't open, I saw my family home. My parents, in the middle of whatever they were doing—washing dishes, fixing a light bulb, fighting in the kitchen—suddenly vanished. Where they were, a haze for a moment, *a poof*, and then just and only the background. The room, empty. Then I was in my sister's room and she vanished too. Then the vision zoomed out to my town, and everyone there was suddenly gone. Then it zoomed out again, like a camera lens. All the humans in the country, vanished. Zoom out again. Then all the humans in all the continents, gone. All the homes once so violently lived in were empty. Only place and nature left. I was still unable to open my eyes from the blink when the homes disappeared too. Then every structure on earth, small or large, gone too. Then the animals.

Then the vision zoomed out for a fourth time, and I saw the entirety of the spherical earth with obsidian space in the background. From there, I watched as the grass and trees disappeared; the water, dried. The once green-and-blue earth, which I had only ever seen in photos, was gray and desolate. The earth became a bald mass. Not desolated by existence but just that every trace of life disappeared from the planet as if it never existed in the first place. All color drained. All life, void. Then the blackness came. The sun I knew, disappeared too, burning itself once and for all. In the utter blackness of space, time ceased to exist; there was nothing to keep time. There was no sun. Then the vision zoomed out again, and I saw our whole solar system. There, every planet, not just earth, was devoid of any life. Though still spinning. Spinning because that's all there was left to do. Then the vision zoomed out one final time, and I saw a chunk of the universe with its hundreds of galaxies, and in each of those hundreds of galaxies, only empty planets spinning and spinning and spinning.

Oblivion confuses me, so I have to talk about it.

Unlike scientists or doctors, I have nothing to prove.

Oblivion has gotten much worse recently.

Which is why I began to see this new therapist. I mean you.

When I say much worse, I mean I used to ebb in and out of oblivion. Now I'm just stuck here. And I can't stop crying.

When my eyes finally opened, which they did only a second after they closed (it all happened so fast and yet simultaneously infinitely), I came down from space and found myself back in my parents' room. I continued my walk to the bathroom. I had to pee. As I sat on the toilet, I couldn't get the vision out of my mind. And unlike an animal, I didn't shake the memory off; I didn't know I needed to. Instead, I sat on the cold porcelain, unable to feel the chill on my bottom, and I thought about the spinning planets.

If my family didn't have money, I surely would be in a state institution right now. If my family didn't have money, I also wouldn't have been able to take time off from my part-time job after oblivion took over. I also, for the past four years, wouldn't have been able to only have a part-time job at a nonprofit, which provides me with enough income to pay a ninth of my rent while I pursue my dream of becoming a writer, if my family did not have money. In summary, if my family did not have money, I would not be able to pursue any type of dream or have the luxury of a jobless mental breakdown, because this is the type of world we live in. Sidenote: my parents are immigrants who still believe in the American Dream.

My girlfriend doesn't like oblivion very much. From the look on her face right now, neither does my new therapist. However, my old therapist liked it very much. Sometimes I think he even loved me for it.

My new therapist says, does your relationship with your old therapist remind you of a relationship from your past?

When I say love, I mean sometimes my old therapist looked at me like he wanted to take my clothes off. Which means sometimes he looked at me like that guy who told me about fascia. Which means sometimes he looked at me like every other guy I've ever met. Every. Other. Guy.

My old therapist also told me oblivion was my connection to the divine. Which means, according to my new therapist, my old therapist could have made oblivion much worse.

I tell my new therapist, maybe the relationship was reminiscent of something, but I can't remember. I am forgetful. Remember?

For years, I thought of my second memory. And in this way my second memory became my third and fourth and seventh and hundredth and thousandth memory. I still hadn't shaken it off. Why? Because I was not an animal. But really why? Well, because when the last lonely human sacrificed herself to the elements, when the last flower had wilted into dried soil, when the last animal still fought against death, limbs kicking into the air, despite knowing there was nothing to live for (of course, I didn't see all of this, in my mind they just *poofed*, this is me hyperbolizing because that's what people do), the planets still turned. I watched them spin for nothingness. And while the empty planets spun, the galaxies did not mourn the lives lost on their children of mass. They did not cry. They did not feel sadness. The universe still existed despite life, within it, not. Still, you may be wondering why this bothered me so much.

You see, when every person, place, thing, even light, even time, disappeared in front of my closed eyes, I saw the emptying of existence, life completely disappearing, except one thing remained. *I* was still there. I didn't join the rest of life in the act of vanishing, the consolation of not existing together, and through that togetherness, the joint venture of it all, somehow, somewhere, existing. Despite trying, I couldn't make myself disappear like the rest of you. I was trapped there alone, watching the bald planets in every lonely galaxy spin for nothingness.

My new therapist repeats: so where would you like to start?

I need to finish my manuscript.

how to finish a manuscript: About 23,100,000 results (0.71 seconds)

NY Book Editors: Finish Your Manuscript! 8 Productivity Hacks for Writers

1. Just Start Writing. Don't let something as silly as writer's block stop you from actually writing.
2. Write a Lot. I mean, a lot.
3. Give Yourself a Deadline.

My new therapist says, can you say more?

So I say, well I had a mental breakdown and now I'm stuck in oblivion, which wouldn't be so much of a problem if I could still write, but I haven't been able to because oblivion just keeps deepening and there's this pain in my chest too, which isn't what oblivion usually is, so I came to you, I begin to finish my point, because I need to finish my manuscript and my girlfriend found your studies online. She said you've done studies on people who think the world is unreal. And she said that sounds like me, because when oblivion takes over, I say, nothing is real. Like literally nothing except me and I created this whole world and I'm stuck in it.

My new therapist doesn't say anything, so I continue:

So yeah, I'm stuck in oblivion, kind of like a character is stuck in a book but the character also wrote the book but now they can't escape from the book.

My new therapist doesn't move. She's frozen.

And that's all fine, but an agent is waiting to look at my manuscript and I can't finish the last story in my manuscript, which is a story about my girlfriend. And I can't finish it, because I don't know how our story ends.

Are you writing a memoir?

No. I write fiction.

I pause and realize how quickly I'm talking, but I can't stop talking because it's the only thing that pacifies the pain in my chest. I continue: But if you're asking about genre, which I think you are, I don't know what genre my book is because I haven't finished it yet. It may be a psychodrama. Or a horror story. Or a disillusionment plot (a change in worldview from positive to negative). Or an *educato* plot (change in worldview from negative to positive). Or a war story. Or a woman's story. Or a mockumentary. Or maybe science fiction.

I wasn't asking about genre, but it seems like you're concerned about the genre?

This should be a statement, but she says it like a question, which makes me want to itch my neck.

My new therapist continues speaking very slowly: if it *is* fiction, then why are you writing a story about your girlfriend?

Oblivion clouds the room in a haze and I wonder why I made this lady and her tan couch and her awful textile pillows. But mostly, I wonder why I created her to be wearing ballet flats. And why, if I created her, I'm so scared of her. And why, if I created this whole world, it seems so terrifying. Then I remember I'm trapped within it, and I don't know a way out. And even if I *did* know a way out, I'd be alone on the other side anyways. I think all of this but I say:

So think of yourself like my writing professor.

I wink at her and I know how weird that is but still I do it.

My new therapist doesn't say anything.

I push out my bottom lip and twirl the gold ring around my middle finger.

Silence.

Silence.

Silence.

Soooooooooooo, I say.

My new therapist chimes in, saying that my not having written in four months, which, accompanied by my not having slept, my panic attacks, my crippling anxiety, my thirty-pound weight loss, now putting me at what, no more than one hundred pounds?, makes her think, in her expert opinion, that I am severely depressed, amongst other things.

To her it seems obvious.

I just need to finish my manuscript.

To her it is odd that my old therapist never told me I was severely depressed.

I tell her, he didn't believe in labels. He was more spiritual.

What does that mean?

I shrug and say, I'm spiritual too.

What does that mean? And when she asks me this, a taxi honks outside.

That's what I mean.

She says, what is what you mean?

It means that I see signs everywhere.

Can you give me an example?

I point to the window.

She says, huh?

So I say,

Most buildings in New York City skip the thirteenth floor.

And that means?

She doesn't get me. Maybe I should be the one worried about signing her. Maybe I'm the agent after all. Maybe I've got the all-discerning eye.

Norma, can you explain the signs you're seeing that are bothering you most?

God keeps telling me to break up with my girlfriend.

Can you give me an example?

Like she's Muslim and I'm spiritual. She has lots of friends. I have one or two. She likes to cook and I hate cooking.

Hmm.

I know, right?!?

Then my new therapist asks, do you have any examples of signs that don't have to do with your individual preferences?

Well, I should start at the beginning. We met the first day that New York City went into Covid lockdown. We spent the pandemic together, and Covid was a sign that we were meant to be together and meant to fall in love. That's why Covid happened.

A global pandemic happened for you to meet your girlfriend?

Well, it happened for an individualized, specific, spiritual reason for everyone. Mine just happened to be her. Other people got divorced. Other people quit their jobs. You know dolphins came back. Like, everywhere!! And carbon emissions were so low. So yeah, there was a spiritual reason for Covid. Just like there's a spiritual reason for everything. That's obvious.

Is it?

…

Can you give me an example of other spiritual reasons for events?

I want to say, like that frizz in your hair. There's a spiritual reason for that, but I don't know you well enough to know what it is.

Instead, I say,

Like Kim Kardashian's sex tape so she could become famous and make big butts in style.

Any others?

Like my sister, who broke her leg and couldn't go into work at her shitty corporate job and then her husband knocked her up during her medical leave and then she quit her job and now she's a stay-at-home mom, and she's so much happier, if you can even call what my sister feels happiness.

Others?

I try to think of another example, but my thoughts go blank.

Oblivion tends to empty my thoughts and put my mind into high speed at the same time. Yes, simultaneously. It makes no sense. But that's oblivion for you.

Anyways, yes, I say, there is a spiritual reason for everything.

My new therapist just stares at me, blankly.

So, I say, I should continue about the signs because I can tell I'm not explaining it well. That was back then, but this is now. Like this morning, I was scrolling on Instagram and this quote came up about letting things go that no longer serve you and that was god, you know? Talking about me and my girlfriend.

My new therapist furrows her eyebrows and tilts her head to the side like a good, curious dog and asks, Was That God Or Was That Just An Instagram Post?

I can feel the judgment in her voice and so I aim to make my case by saying (please read this part very quickly for full effect):

Well, god's plan for me was that I needed to be with my girlfriend back then, but now that the world is opening again and Covid is just mutating into these little baby viruses, I'm getting all these signs that it's time to leave her. Like yesterday, I was listening to my relaxing playlist on

Spotify and I was trying to meditate in bed and my girlfriend was sleeping next to me, covered in white sheets, and she looked so beautiful even though she was kind of snoring, and then one of my favorite songs came on by Seinabo Sey and it's called "I Love You" and I could breathe easier for a moment because I thought it was a sign that we are meant for each other despite her love of cooking and Allah and extrovertedness, but then, like I had never even heard the song before, the chorus said *if you love somebody, set them free,* and again *if you love somebody, set them free,* on repeat over and over again, and it was so obvious then that god was trying to give me a sign.

My new therapist's eyebrows are stuck furrowed for good, I'm sure of it.

My new therapist is very quiet and wrinkled and then she says, so you believe that God is coming down from wherever He is—

Oh no, no, no, no, no, no, nooo. My god isn't a he and it's not capitalized.

Okay. So you believe god is coming down from wherever *it* is and going into your Spotify and Instagram to send you, *specifically,* a message that you should leave your girlfriend?

Well, yes. Suddenly I feel insane, so I keep talking while I twirl my rings around my sweaty fingers: but god does that for everyone. Not just me. And as I say this my right leg shakes, and now, like my new therapist, I'm also a dog, but I'm the dog who has to pee, and I think that's much worse than the inquisitive dog.

Still furrowed, she says, through Instagram?

Well, and I can't write. That's the biggest sign. Oh, and my lucky number is seven. And I usually see the number seven everywhere and that means I'm on the right path. God sends me the number to say GOOD JOB! KEEP IT UP! But lately all I've been seeing are eights everywhere. Eight here. Eight there. And no sevens!

She writes something down and doesn't say anything, so I give up and say, look, I'm spiritual, okay?

She says, That's Not Spirituality. That's Seeing Signs.

unfurrow

Finally.

Okay okay okay. I'm still not explaining it well. Here's another thing: my girlfriend loves mainstream novels. Always some sappy love story. And I hate that shit.

You're just explaining your various likes and dislikes again.

I can barely hear her because I'm trying to make a point. Sometimes she even writes poetry. She leaves these little poems around the house for me like little love notes. But here's the worst part! SHE WRITES ON A TYPEWRITER. Can you imagine, A TYPEWRITER?! You can't type nearly as fast as you need to on a thing like that. And the WORST part—I lunge forward as if I could grab my new therapist by the neck— there's no Google on a typewriter!! NO GOOGLE!

I'm waiting for my new therapist's reaction, so I lean back again, think- ing I may have scared her and that's why she's not reacting.

Then I repeat: A typewriter! That's crazy, isn't it?

My new therapist clears her throat as if a jawbreaker is stuck in it, and her throat makes a terrible sound, which makes me think of that '90s movie where that popular clique kills their friend on the morning of her birthday by faking a kidnapping and putting a jawbreaker in her mouth.

My new therapist says, can you tell me why you think it's important to be able to write fast?

How else are you going to get it all down?

But what are you trying to get down and why does it need to be done so quickly?

The story. And because the story comes at me fast. The stories are everywhere. I'm everywhere, and I need to catch everything and write it all down. Don't worry. I'm used to this.

When I was born, god scattered me endlessly across the universe. I often find myself in notepads and sticky notes, in the margins of used novels and in the scribbles of bathroom stalls. When I recognize a piece as myself, I am delighted. And no matter how odd or unsettling I find the new fragment to be, I braid it into myself without a doubt that it belongs to me. Like the Tumblr post I saw in high school that said *I'm so glad I was raised Catholic so sex will always be dirty.* Mine. Or that chalk written on the sidewalk on Fourth Avenue that said *your reality is a dream.* Mine. Everything mine mine mine. In this way, my life is always a hunt, a game of give-and-take, better yet, of hide-and-seek. I remember playing this game when I was a child. In plain sight, I would stand not far from the seeker with my eyes closed. Palms tight against my eyelids. I thought that if I couldn't see them, I couldn't be seen. Sometimes I still feel this way.

You're worried the story will escape you?

Of course it will. You don't get it. You're not a writer. You're just a therapist.

I realize that sounded mean. I feel myself turn red and I'm reminded that I have a body.

I'm—I'm—I'm sorry. I didn't mean that.

My skin is burning hot and I can feel a drip of sweat rolling down from my armpit, which I forgot to shave this morning and yesterday morning and every morning for a month.

My new therapist says, mean what?

And now I'm confused.

So Norma, she kinda half smiles at me, adjusts her ass on the chair without removing her feet from the footrest, and then says very seriously and slowly as if I don't speak English:

In My Expert Opinion, it seems like you have Textbook Major Depressive Disorder with at least four bouts of Extreme Depression in Your Short Lifetime, which Predisposes You To Worsening Bouts of Depression for the Rest Of Your Life. You also suffer from Depersonalization and Derealization Disorder, which most likely has worsened recently Due To Your Depressive Episode. You also experience Immense Anxiety, which Further Worsens the Dissociation. And your Obsession with seeing everything as A Sign From God, more so as God Trying To Tell You Something, which I understand you don't perceive as a male god, but an omniscient god, seems to be *You* Projecting Meaning Onto Your External Environment so that You Do Not Have To Do The Internal Work Of Reflection. All of this is most likely a result of Significant Trauma. And you're entering into Another Bout Of Derealization And Depression, which, if we don't stop it, May Get Much Worse Than It Already Is.

In her "expert" opinion.

I want to ask her for the SparkNotes version of what she just said, but I decide I can google it later.

> major depressive disorder: 48,200,000 results (1.13 seconds)

> A mental health disorder characterized by persistent sadness and/or low disinterested mood that causes significant impairment in daily life. Causes can range from biological, psychological and social factors or a combination of these sources.

Boring. Everyone is depressed.

depersonalization derealization disorder: 282,000 results (0.55 seconds)

Otherwise known as DPDR, which reminds me of DDR, which I've always hated. However, Augusta Health dot com, who is paraphrasing from the Mayo Clinic, who is paraphrasing from god knows who, assures me that they are not the same thing.

DEPERSONALIZATION: feeling like *you* are unreal.

- Feeling that you're an outside observer of your thoughts, your feelings and your body (I'm the narrator.)

- Feeling like a robot or that you're not in control of your speech or movements (I'm a character.)

- The sense that your body, legs or arms appear distorted, enlarged, or shrunken (Magical realism.)

- Emotional or physical numbness of your senses or responses to the world around you (I'm an omniscient narrator.)

- A sense that your memories lack emotion, and that they may or may not be your own memories (Again . . . I'm just a character.)

DEREALIZATION: feeling like your *external world* is unreal.

- Feeling that you are unfamiliar with your surroundings (Like I've been transplanted into a novel.)

- Feeling emotionally disconnected from people you care about, as if you were separated by a glass wall (Feels more like Saran Wrap to me.)

- Surroundings appear distorted, blurry, colorless, two-dimensional or artificial, or a heightened awareness and clarity of your surroundings (Uh, these are opposite. Seems like they can't make up their mind with this one.)

- Distortions in perception of time, such as recent events feeling like distant past (Isn't that how everyone feels?)

- Distortions of distance and the size and shape of objects (My new therapist's yellow ballet flats take up the whole room.)

You know...

I say to my new therapist, my gynecologist's "expert" opinion is that the deepening oblivion is premenstrual dysphoric disorder (PMDD), and just two weeks ago, when I sobbed uncontrollably in her office without my underwear on, my gynecologist put me on birth control that jacks me up with both estrogen and progestin.

And told me to see a psychiatrist.

Premenstrual dysphoric disorder (PMDD) is a severe form of PMS that causes extreme mood shifts of unprompted severe sadness, rage, anxiety and sometimes suicide. Symptoms often begin at the start of ovulation and last two weeks or until a period begins. PMDD can damage relationships and impede work.

People also ask:

- Is PMDD considered a mental illness?

- Does PMDD get worse with age?

- Does PMDD go away?

PMDD reminds me an awful lot of female hysteria. And so, I don't necessarily believe in it. I'm a feminist.

My new therapist is staring at me like she's waiting for something or like she's very bored.

And my neurologist's "expert" opinion is that the deepening oblivion could be a side effect from getting the Covid-19 vaccine and he's seeing this with a lot of his patients lately. And he really doesn't think it's a brain tumor but will send me to get my head checked anyways.

And also told me to see a psychiatrist.

I tell my new therapist, who is also my new and first psychiatrist, that I appreciate her opinion but it's not depression.

Or derealization

Or depersonalization

Or anxiety

Or PMDD.

It's oblivion.

My new therapist asks me what that word means to me.

("That" word. Not "this" word. As if she doesn't want the word. As if she's disgusted by the word. As if the word is my plate of food that she's eyeing from across the table at the restaurant, leaning over to inspect it, and it, obviously, has beets in it and she hates beets.)

Apparently gray oblivion doesn't match my new therapist's tan couch and textile pillows. However, it does match the armchair that she has placed me in.

I'm offended by her use of language but I'm pitching to her, so I say:

My second memory is of the world emptying.

She asks me what this has to do with oblivion.

I say everything.

She asks me what this has to do with depression or derealization.

I say nothing. That's what I'm trying to tell you.

The wooden robot on her bookshelf stares at me.

My new therapist tells me Oblivion Is Just A Symptom.

A symptom: a sign of a disease.

A sign.

That my girlfriend and I can't be together or else I'll never finish my manuscript. I knew it.

And so did Instagram and Spotify.

My new therapist says, You Can Get Better.

My new therapist says, You Can Get Better by talking about your past: remembering what happened, how you got here, and then integrating your memories and feelings into the present with self-awareness and self-reflection.

Like writing nonfiction? Or a lyrical essay?

But First You Have To Admit Where You Are.

But I write fiction.

Which makes me think maybe oblivion isn't just a symptom. It's a state of not remembering or of not being integrated.

A being. Forgetting.

A being. In fragments.

Some would even call it autofiction.

My new therapist says, Remembering and Integrating our traumatic memories are often the key to our current distresses. The past distorts our present.

remembering a memory: 155,000,000 results (0.67 seconds)

National Geographic: The human memory—facts and information:

Enter your email address to continue reading. Already a subscriber? Sign in.

Thanks for signing up! You have three free articles left this month.

For a short-term memory to become a long-term memory, it must be consolidated for long-term storage. To store a memory, individual nerves must modify themselves to talk to their neighboring nerves differently. That remodeling alters the nerves' connections in the long term, which stabilizes the memory.

I once had a neighbor who lived in the building across the street from me and every night for two years, he stood at his window naked and jacked off to me walking around my apartment.

But the memories are unstable, skewed.

Sometimes he even danced.

My new therapist says, I Promise You Can Get Better.

But the memories are remembering the memory on top of remembering the memory on top of remembering the memory and so on and so forth.

I hated flipping the shades up and down from day to night so usually I just let my neighbor do his thing. It didn't seem so abnormal.

Also, some memories are locked away. And I don't know where I threw the key.

And what was the spiritual reason for that neighbor?

Well obviously it was time for me to move.

And did you?

Yeah. Two years later.

> Recent work has shown that some memories must be reconsolidated each time they're recalled. So, the act of remembering something makes that memory temporarily malleable—letting it be strengthened, weakened, or

Otherwise Altered.

From this I gather that memories are useless.

The three colorful textile pillows on my new therapist's tan couch, which are spread out unevenly across it, are also useless.

What is useful? What does it mean for something to have utility? What's the point in asking my new therapist questions if she never has an answer and only asks a question back?

One time in a state of drug-induced oblivion back in college, I wrote twelve pages of maps, diagrams, lists, and scribbles of what value was and what it meant for something to have value versus to be valuable.

My new therapist says, what were you trying to figure out with all of this?

I think: I was trying to deduce whether anything in life was worth saving.

Or if life itself was worth living.

At least this is how I remember it. And I've remembered it many times, so it may be tainted by improper consolidation. Stable yet false. I should call the infinite man.

I think all of this, but I say to my new therapist, well obviously I was trying to figure out if my mother's diamond jewelry is actually valuable or if the value just exists in her head.

I think I was also trying to understand oblivion even back then, before I called it oblivion.

My new therapist tells me I've been in oblivion for so long that I could benefit from antiobliviants.

Of course she doesn't use the word *oblivion*. She's much too concerned to indulge in my delusion.

And she's seriously curious as to why I haven't considered medicine before because It Could Have Saved Me From Many Years Of Suffering.

I remind her that I'm spiritual. And ask her if I should break up with my girlfriend so I can finish my manuscript. That's really all I want to know. I'd rather get it over with now.

She says we will discuss that at a later time when we haven't gone thirty minutes over our scheduled session.

Wait . . . so you're signing me?

And also that I can pick up my prescription at the pharmacy. Most likely in twenty minutes.

Oh also, she says, you should start writing again. Maybe not about value or about your girlfriend, but just writing.

Ta-daaaaaaaaa.

THE STUDY OF OBLIVION

eight weeks since breakdown

I told my girlfriend, my new therapist thinks it's a symptom.

My girlfriend said, *of what?*

The bedroom lamp was shining purple on my girlfriend's skin and I wanted to take a picture of her, but I didn't know where my phone was.

So I said, did you know that there's more carbon dioxide in our atmosphere than at any time in human history? And scientists have injected human embryonic stem cells into the brains of fetal mice still in the womb, believing with this study they can advance research on human brain disorders and improve testing of experimental medications. And did you know that pig bladders are being used to regrow human limbs? And the FDA has approved implantation of radio-frequency identification chips in humans, meaning soon the government and corporations will use the chips to track people's locations, medical history, and literally everything about them. Correctional facilities are already monitoring inmates' behavior and location with this thing. Tracking behavior, can you imagine? And average wildlife populations have dropped by 60 percent in forty years, which is exactly why I'm vegan even though I know that makes me annoying to go out to eat with. And scientists are working hard to bring extinct animals back to life, starting with a twenty-first-century woolly mammoth using well-preserved ten-thousand-year-old blood, even though like so many species are going extinct right now because of humans. All of this and they haven't figured out how to merge two eggs together so that lesbians can reproduce, and this feels like they're trying to stop us from taking over the world.

I hear my new therapist say, I thought the world wasn't real? Does any of that feel real to you as you say it to me?

So then I shrugged at my girlfriend and said, this new therapist makes me feel like I'm insane. The way she looks at me. It's like I've completely lost it. My girlfriend reached over to my side of the bed, took my hand in hers, and said, *we know you're having a hard time but you're not crazy.*

For further proof, I called my best friend, Felix, and asked him if I looked crazy at dinner the other night. He said of course not. And as he responded, my girlfriend looked at me with a face that said, *see, I told you so*, and then I thanked Felix and hung up.

Then my girlfriend said, while walking to the bathroom to wash her face, her voice slowly trailing off as she entered the other room, *are you nervous about taking the medication?*

And I said: I don't want to but then again, I've tried kambo, psychedelics, Reiki, craniosacral therapy, shamanic healing, neurofeedback, Osho dynamic meditations, mindfulness meditations, chakra meditations, holotropic breathwork, L72, 5htp, naturopaths, hundreds of dollars' worth of herbs, acupuncture (Korean and Chinese style), self-help books, EMDR, tapping, lucid dreaming, kanna ceremonies, and crystal healing and nothing has helped, so maybe I should just take the pill.

This morning I took the pill.

When I took it, from the other side of the kitchen counter my girlfriend told me, as if in passing, that her friend from high school who has been on antiobliviants for years told her that it will get worse before it gets better.

I said, it can't get worse. It can't. It can't.

She said, *it might, but I'll be here.*

And then I collapsed onto the floor like a terrible theater actress and screamed, It can't It can't It can't It can't It can't It can't! over and over again.

But my girlfriend's friend from high school is right. It has gotten worse.

My new therapist says, you are certainly not able to feel the effects of the Prozac yet. It's too early, but You'd Be Surprised At How Strong The Placebo Effect Is.

I look around the room and find my eyes on my new therapist's three, awful textile pillows that are still not arranged symmetrically on her tan couch, which makes me think she actually likes them this way. I should explain why they're so awful. First of all, they are too colorful and happy for such a depressing place: a mix of pink, orange, yellow, and every other abrasive color. Second of all, one big pillow is on the far end, another smaller one is in the middle, and the other, another big one, is on the final three-quarters of the couch. I want to stand up, run over, and smush the two larger pillows behind the smaller pillow right in the center of the couch. Then I want to look at her and say Jesus! How much better is that! How easy was that!

Truly, I couldn't stop thinking about her pillows all week. Every night when I tried to sleep, they were all I could see, but every time I rearranged them in my dreams, they would just magically *poof* back into their original awful places. I decided on the subway ride over here that I would fix them today. But now, from my armchair (I'm still confused as to why I can't sit on the couch—my girlfriend says that I should ask), I resist the urge because my new therapist is more intense than I remember.

Instead I say, I feel like I'm on Molly but not in a good way. Like you know, when you take too much Molly and wish you hadn't.

We'll start to see how the Prozac Really Affects You in about four weeks. Let me know if any of the symptoms become too stressful to handle.

I go to open my mouth and repeat that I feel like I'm on Molly because my new therapist just really isn't getting it today, but then my new therapist places her hands down on her clipboard and says, we're out of time, but I did want to mention one thing before we end:

I Think With Your Current State We Should Meet Twice A Week.

THE STUDY OF OBLIVION

nine weeks since breakdown

To start our session, I tell my new therapist that I thought it through, and I cannot meet twice a week.

Is it the cost?

No, my trust is paying for therapy. My nonprofit job can't cover your expensive ass.

I skip the last sentence.

So then why not come two days a week?

Because I have a manuscript to write.

She says, I thought you weren't writing.

I'm not.

But then I correct myself:

I'm trying to.

Anyways, I reach into my purse and hold up a piece of paper, I brought this in today to show you my initial findings from the study of oblivion. I started this before I met my girlfriend and before oblivion took over, back when it would just show up sometimes. It was easier to study when I was in and out of it.

Really I brought this paper in to prove to her that what's happening is *not* her psychological diagnosis and it *is* truly oblivion.

She says, okay, would you like me to read it?

And I say, no I'll read it to you, because it's always better to hear someone's work read out loud in their own voice.

P.S.: if you know oblivion well, I suggest you skip this part.

But I know my therapist doesn't know oblivion at all; therefore, it won't trigger her, so I read out loud:

> Questions to be studied: Do I exist? Am I transient? Can I and this world disappear at any moment?

> This study began not out of scientific ambitions or interests, but rather out of necessity. In order to survive oblivion, she became curious about it.

Sorry to interrupt, but who is *she*?

Me.

I continue:

> To begin, I would like to offer the realized properties of oblivion. All information comes from her experience.

> Properties of oblivion when it appears (not all perceived at the same time, though many have been experienced in combinations, though also sometimes independently):

EXPANSIVENESS OF OBLIVION:

1) You become wider than your own body
2) Or have no body at all

EVER-PRESENT NATURE OF OBLIVION:

1) You experience timelessness
   a. Past and future collide into the present, and there exists no before or after

COLLAPSIBILITY OF OBLIVION:

1) You feel that life could collapse in on itself at any moment
   a. You, and only you, are responsible for both the collapse and the continued creation

UNIFICATION (UNFRAGMENTED SELF) OF OBLIVION:

1) Your personal self disintegrates
   a. You are everyone and, simultaneously, you are not anyone or even yourself
   b. You are nothing but also you are the entirety of existence (including the nail salon)

My new therapist interrupts me: the nail salon?

Well I discovered *that* property of oblivion while I was getting my nails done.

You had an episode of derealization during a manicure?

We're talking about oblivion.

My new therapist scribbles something down on her clipboard as I continue:

> 2) Feels kind of like you are already dead
> 3) Or you were never alive in the first place

SPATIAL WARPING OF OBLIVION:

> 1) You lose sense of geographical space
>   *a.* Hard to compute up, down, left, right
>   *b.* Hard to know how close or far an object is

LINGUISTIC DISSOLUTION OF OBLIVION:

> 1) Language disintegrates into sand and you struggle to speak
>   *a.* Words lose meaning

My new therapist is still writing. Is she even listening?

MEMORY DISSOLUTION OF OBLIVION:

> 1) You have trouble with memory recall
>   *a.* Including remembering numbers, dates, scheduled activities, what you did yesterday, how you felt yesterday, and so on and so forth

VERBAL WARPING OF OBLIVION:

> 1) Speech is altered in every way
>   *a.* When someone speaks to you, it feels like the sound is coming from inside your head
>   *b.* When you speak ...
>   *i.* it sounds as if your words are siphoned through an echo chamber or coming from outside yourself

    ii. it feels like you aren't actually saying the words
   iii. it feels like you are watching yourself speak but
       don't have control over your speech

Silence.

Silence.

Silence.

So what do you think?

My new therapist looks at me with her head cocked to the side in her typical doglike manner and says, is that it?

It?

IT?

IT?!?!

I spent over two years gathering those findings. I feel my face get hot somewhere outside my body by her bookshelf.

Yes.

My new therapist says, it sounds like you're just describing the felt phenomenological experience of derealization and a little bit of depersonalization. People who suffer from this will usually experience one more persistently than the other. It seems as though you lean toward derealization.

I stopped listening after she said, you're *just* describing.

JUST?!?!

AS IF MY WHOLE LIFE ISN'T OBLIVION.

AS IF OBLIVION ISN'T GOING TO SPIN THE ENTIRE UNIVERSE INTO EMPTINESS, LEAVING ME BEHIND.

AS IF I'M NOT *JUST* A CHARACTER IN A BOOK I WROTE WITH NO SAY IN THE PLOT.

JUST. JUST. JUST.

She's still talking:

All of that just confirms that it *is* DPDR. Now we have to understand why dissociating became your natural response to the world.

THE STUDY OF OBLIVION

ten weeks since breakdown

I start by saying, I wrote this week.

She looks surprised. As surprised as a Freudian psychotherapist can be.

She asks me about what.

I tell her I was so disappointed when I showed what I wrote to a fellow writer yesterday who I sometimes exchange work with, and he said, *wait!*

Were you inspired by David Foster Wallace, and I said, no, why? I've never read him. And he proceeded to tell me that that was shocking, because my story reminded him so much of DFW's book *Oblivion*, not just by way of topic but also the voice. I was disappointed because I was under the impression that no book had ever been named "oblivion." I was also disappointed that my voice sounds like it's copying someone else's. I tried to hide my disappointment, which was easy, because I'm used to masking whatever is going on inside of my head. For example, the fact that I seemed completely coherent during this lunch yesterday.

I like to think my straight-across bangs help me hide what's going on behind my forehead, like they're some sort of shield. I got the bangs a week before my breakdown, which should have signaled me to the fact that I was about to have a mental breakdown.

It was so obvious.

I missed that sign.

Then again, it's not important because none of this is real anyways.

So you wrote about oblivion?

My new therapist is wearing her yellow ballet flats again today, and her feet are up on the footrest like last time. I wonder if this is her only pair of shoes or perhaps just her favorite pair.

I'm also disappointed after yesterday's lunch with this writer person, because to complete my study of oblivion, it seems necessary to read the book he mentioned but I really don't want to.

I don't like reading.

I once read a book about screenwriting that said someone who doesn't like watching movies should definitely not write a screenplay. I remember feeling like I should stop writing books then.

Yes, I wrote about oblivion.

I am even more disappointed when I discover many writers have written books called *Oblivion*. One is a six-hundred-page fantasy novel, which is the fifth and final book in the Power of Five series. Which sounds very intense. One is a masterful novel and epic literary attempt to examine a very troubled Russia. One is a heartbreaking, exquisitely written memorial to the author's father, whose criticism of the Colombian regime led to his murder. Which sounds impossible to live up to. One is a hotly anticipated follow-up to a mega-selling Lux series. Which sounds very sexual. And DFW's 329-page book comprises short fiction, so now it truly does feel as if I am attempting to mimic him.

Anyways, this will probably be my first and final book and now I will most likely not call it oblivion.

I should note that I have not read and will not read any of these above-mentioned books.

My new therapist says, well I guess it's progress that you wrote this week.

I don't like reading. Therefore, I shouldn't write.

My new therapist thinks that I spend too much time thinking about oblivion to read.

My new therapist says I don't know what she's thinking.

And that I have a Tendency To Project My Thoughts Onto Her when I do not want to hold them as my own. And that I do not want to hold them as my own thoughts because Ambivalence Is Concerning To Me.

I nod and google what ambivalence is when I leave the office.

   ambivalence: 101,000,000 results (0.30 seconds)

   the state of having mixed feelings or contradictory ideas about something or someone.

My new therapist says, before I leave and before I google what ambivalence means, that my Being Weary of Ambivalence is why I have a hard time with both loving my girlfriend and being skeptical of love lasting and distrusting those who say they love me, and perhaps this is also what catapulted my recent episode.

Stephen King once said, If you don't have time to read, you don't have the time (or the tools) to write. Simple as that.

I wonder what my new therapist spends so much time doing that she cannot fix the chaotically arranged textile pillows on her tan couch.

I can't finish our story, The Last Story. Not *our* story, I point back and forth between me and my new therapist, but me and my girlfriend's story. Or is it I and my girlfriend's story? Or mine and my girlfriend's story? Oh my god, how am I supposed to be a writer? I don't even know proper grammar!

My new therapist ignores my grammatical meltdown and says, I know. You told me you couldn't finish the story. But you also said that it's not a memoir.

I hear myself say, my girlfriend is like my best friend in the whole world.

The words echo.

That's good.

Yeah. But.

But what?

In the echo, I say, the signs.

Do I see suffering as sacred?

I ask myself this, not my new therapist.

Perhaps Because You're Not Suffering In Your Relationship, You Don't Think It's Love.

Can my new therapist read my mind?!

And Perhaps The Depression And Derealization Is Self-Punishment So You Cannot Experience Love.

If it's not painful, it isn't love.

And Perhaps You're Scared To Actually Find Out What Love Really Is Outside of Suffering now that your girlfriend is offering you that, and perhaps your breakdown, as you call it, is Your Unconscious Having A Difficult Time Reconciling What Love Is.

So, I was right. I gotta get rid of her. It's her fault that I can't write.

I didn't say that.

Please don't cry. Oh gosh. Come here let me hold you. I'm so sorry that I brought you here. I know, I know. I knew it was going to be painful. I knew it wasn't safe. I knew what they would do to you, what *I* would do to you, and, still, I did it. I'm sorry, my darling. I'm sorry, my daughter. I wish I could take it all back. I wish I could undo what I've done.

What I imagine my mother saying to me one day about my being born.

What I imagine my mother never saying to me, because she never will, but maybe she thinks it. Sometimes. Anytime. Maybe even just once would be enough.

In fact, I Don't Think Your Inability To Write, Your Depression, Your Derealization, or Your Anxiety Have Much To Do With Your Girl-friend At All.

So it's not her fault. Are you sure?

I really don't think she's to blame.

Are you sure?

I already answered that.

Do you want to know about my birth? I ask my new therapist this as if she cares about my birth.

As if she's Stanislav Grof.

She lifts her eyebrows in what seems like a sarcastic way, but which also gives me the go-ahead to keep speaking.

Well, I didn't come to this world, the world came to me. My mother's umbilical cord was wrapped around my neck twice and after twenty-four hours in labor they decided to cut me out of my mother or really cut me a break. Ha! Do you get it? Cut—me—a break. Anyways, so they cut my mother open and untangled my neck from the umbilical cord (twice) and told me to cry. To cry meant I was alive. To cry meant I was human. But I didn't cry, so the doctors took me out of the room and I don't know the rest of the story because my mother and father weren't there and my first memory is at two and a half.

Nowadays, I cry a lot. Sometimes I scream. Sometimes I tell my girl-friend I want to die, like two days ago when we were in the elevator heading up to our twenty-fourth-floor apartment. We were sweating from the eighty-degree New York City heat, and when I told her this (not about the heat but about my sudden inspiration to die), she hugged me and that made me want to die a little more. And every time I tell my girlfriend this (no, this wasn't the first time, and she's the only per-son I tell because I'm smart enough not to share that information with too many people), I imagine myself walking into lava and disintegrat-ing completely. I have chosen Kīlauea on the Big Island of Hawai'i for the event. I visited there once when I was twenty-four and ended up staying longer than anticipated. It was my first time traveling alone.

I walked barefoot in the grass. I chanted with hippies. I woke up for meditations by the cliffside. God sent me a sign in the form of a lizard by the black sand beach that said I was in the right place. The lava had erupted not long before I arrived and almost destroyed the entire town, so a new friend and I took a boat out at four in the morning and went to see where the lava was pouring into the ocean.

It was the most beautiful and terrifying thing that I've ever seen in my life. Later that day, when the new friend tried to sleep with me, I let him because he had shown me the lava.

A year later, when I was back in New York, I was living in an egregious duplex apartment by myself (my mother approved of the luxury since I had broken up with the guy who looked like a skeleton and who she hated, though I'm sure now she regrets encouraging me to break up with him because at least he had a penis). That afternoon, I decided to open my laptop and watch an old home video from when my mother was pregnant with me. I wanted to know what my family looked like before I was alive. It was their last trip before me. A cruise. A ship. The tiny little room. Then it's my mother standing at the top of Kīlauea in a white blouse rubbing her belly. My stomach dropped. I began sweating into the brown couch. My love for that volcano, that place, suddenly made sense.

Later on in that same video, I am born and my father says my name over and over again to my tiny reddish face that can't even see or hear yet. Then he says I'm going to love you forever, and so then grown me on the couch started to cry, and I couldn't stop crying, and my best friend, Felix, who was upstairs taking a poop, came into the living room and saw me sobbing on the couch in front of my laptop and asked me what was wrong. Then Felix told me that his family didn't take any videos of him when he was young, and then I started to cry even more. Pretty quickly after that, I stopped having sex with men.

Why do you think your father's voice made you so emotional?

I think I just have a lot of tears.

My writing professor in college once said it's cheesy when characters cry in a book, and readers just glaze over at the mention of crying, so you should reserve tears for the most climactic moment in the story. Even then, tears probably will feel cliché. So, the professor said, try to avoid them as much as you can.

I always found this rule to be troublesome since humans don't just cry in climactic moments, but like all the fucking time. And shouldn't literature be reflective of the society it's writing to?

But I also get what that professor meant because by now, in this story, I'm already tired of seeing the word *cry* and tears on the page. Still, I've got to be truthful to the facts.

And to humanity.

And so somehow in my mind, it only makes sense to go out by way of lava.

When I close my eyes, I often see myself walking into the lava. And when I see this, I think that I'm kind to kill myself in such a way that no one would have to find my skinny dead body or have to deal with moving it later. I also think I'm kind to have such a niche suicidal fantasy, which would require at least fifteen hours' worth of travel, meaning my girlfriend doesn't have to worry about me when she goes to work or out to the grocery store. She still worries, though.

Now that I cry a lot, I wonder if I'm more alive, more human, than I was even at my birth.

You know, I say to my new therapist, this whole breakdown could just be my Saturn Return. Maybe I should just suck it up. Wait it out. You see, my Saturn, my Sun, and my Jupiter are all in Leo and all very close together in my natal chart. The sun, which rules me, and the planet of rules and the planet of pleasure are lying side by side, almost on top of one another, which is never a good thing and signifies something like *I have cages around my fun*. Of course, the astrologist explained it more gracefully than that. So obviously, I am in oblivion. It says so right there in my chart. The planets and stars aligned as such when I was born that I will forever question or, rather, restrict my happiness. It's def just my Saturn Return.

Def.

Didn't Anne Carson have something to say about volcanoes?

My new therapist says, I don't know who Anne Carson is, but I do know it's highly unlikely, and Actually More Like A Fantasy, to fault the planets in our solar system for your Current State, however, I *am* curious as to what was going on in your life before you had this mental breakdown.

Oh, you want the backstory?

Sure.

Sure? Does she or does she not want it? What's with these mixed messages?

I would hate to date my new therapist.

Dragon Island happened, I say, Dragon Island.

Dragon Island

There is a place called Dragon Island that no one can find on a map.

Dragon Island: A pseudonym. A sanctuary. Some would call it a paradise, but there were no palm trees and it wasn't always warm. In fact, for a quarter of the year the bay froze over and the island was covered in snow. During this time, the ferry didn't run and Dragon Island was abandoned. But in the summer, gay men migrated to the island like families to Disneyland. There, the evenings were neon, no candlelight, and the mornings were sun and sex and sheets that desperately needed to be washed. To my surprise, there were no cars on Dragon Island. Instead, everyone walked the wooden pathways or biked on the one sand road that spanned the entirety of the island. On the boardwalk, there was one small grocery store called the Pantry, but it was more like a bodega. Next to it there were two restaurants: one that served pizza and the other, things like burgers and tacos. When newcomers like me came to the island they searched in the moonlight for food, but nothing was open after eight. Newcomers, at first, did not like Dragon Island. After all, they were hungry. It was only in the sunrise of the next day with lovers coming out of their houses, with naked bodies and half-naked bodies burying themselves in the sand, that newcomers came to see Dragon Island for what it was. Eventually, they learned the ways of the island. They learned that the Pantry on the boardwalk was barely a grocery store, and yet it was enough. They learned that hunger can be filled in different ways. Like skin. Like salt drying under their fingernails. Like the arrival of a ferry carrying someone you can't wait to hold in your tanned arms.

A week before I stepped on the island for the first time, we were lying in bed in an apartment that used to be mine but three months ago had become ours. Under the starless sky of New York City, I asked her why they called it Dragon Island. She said it was because the heat there, independent of the season, was fiery, brutal.

But why call it something other than what it is?

To that, She just smiled:

You're gonna love it.

I turned my body away from her. With her warm belly against my low back, I bent my legs behind me like a mermaid and sandwiched my cold toes between her calves. No matter the season, She was, in the midst of both heat and freezing cold, whatever was needed. By this I mean when I was too hot, my body curled into hers and her skin, like an ice pack, cooled me down, and when I was shivering, I'd wrap my limbs around her and wait for the warmth. She and I together reached equilibrium.

Days later, I stepped off the ferry with my duffel bag pulling at my shoulder. Dragon Island would be our first vacation together and I wasn't sure what to expect. At the end of the dock, I saw her lit by the morning sun. I walked quickly toward her with my face morphing into a smile that I was still getting used to. A smile that had come into my life when She did almost a year earlier. When I reached her, I fell into her arms and kissed her to the sound of men in leather Speedos eating lunch with one another on the boardwalk. She whispered something in my ear, but I couldn't hear exactly what it was. Maybe She said:

Welcome to Dragon Island.

Or maybe:

Welcome home.

She grabbed my bag and threw it around her shoulder. Then She reached for my hand and walked me past the Pantry, past the two restaurants, and toward the bamboo-lined wooden sidewalks that led to our Airbnb. That first day, we walked the beach, debated between tacos and pizza, settled on smoothies, kissed in the one carless sand street, and then lay by the pool at our rental home. I had forgotten my AirPods, so She read her book out loud to me as I sweated into the lounge chair, dipped into the water, and lay back down in the blazing sun.

Sometimes I'd stop her:

That's a good line.

Really good.

And then She would dog-ear the page.

That afternoon, as I showered the salt and chlorine off my skin, She rushed over to me with damp hair:

Hurry hurry! We're going to miss it!

Miss what?

Together, we ran down the bamboo-lined walkway. At the boardwalk, dozens of men were gathered at the dock, waiting to watch the sunset. I had never witnessed so many humans stopping everything—their Zoom meetings, their fucking, their drinking, their arguing—to revel at the sun performing its daily duty. She squeezed between a beefy group of men, plopping herself down on the old wooden dock, and motioned for me to sit beside her. I apologized to the muscled man on my left as I sat down. He replied, revealing a perfect set of white veneers:

It's okay, honey. Enjoy. It's gunna be a good one.

I swung my bare feet back and forth over the bay like a child while She took a photo of the waning sun. Behind us, there were white boats decorated with rainbow flags and string lighting, also posted up for the event. On them, men were dancing to the glow of the setting sun.

I turned back around to face her:

You know how people say, blah-blah-blah is "like watching paint dry."

Yeah, when something's boring.

Well, I think watching paint dry would be fun. Like having the time to sit there and watch something turn from a liquid into a solid. That sounds like a good day.

Should we do that one day? Just watch some paint dry?

Yeah. We shou—

But before I could finish my sentence, everyone on the dock starting shouting in unison:

Ten! Nine! Eight! Seven!—

They were counting down to the exact moment that the sun would disappear completely beyond the horizon: a vanishing sliver of orange making way for an unending sky. We joined them:

Three! Two! One!!!!

And then all the men in muscle tees, booty shorts, and jockstraps turned to one another, kissing and hugging as if it was New Year's Eve, not a random Tuesday in May. She looked at me and said, as if it was my birthday:

Happy first sunset on Dragon Island.

As the sunless sky shape-shifted into neon colors, the muscled, veneered man to my left began gently crying, wiping away his tears with his large hand. His fingernails were painted a bright pink. I remembered then how my sister once told me that my nieces couldn't comprehend how adults cried out of happiness. Children know tears to be evidence of only sadness or pain. But I knew this shirtless man whose biceps were the size of my head was crying not from pain but from the lack of it. From joy. Right before it happened, I remember wondering: why, when we grow older, do we evolve to cry from happiness?

Then a droplet on my cheek. At first I thought it was sweat, but when I went to wipe it away, another tear fell from my right eye. As if reading my mind, the man next to me nudged me, a steady gaze in his glistening eyes:

I'll tell you something about this place. Here, you have no choice but to be happy. So be happy. You're here. You've made it.

She smiled at me:

Yeah we have.

I reached over, held her hand, and asked the man:

We've made it. But now what?

He laughed:

The day before you leave, take some G. That's the best advice I can give you.

She chimed in:

G? As in GHB?

He nodded, and She said:

Why would we give ourselves a date rape drug?

You have to numb your mind so you can forget about the morning ferry back.

He pointed across the water at the mainland:

So you can forget that the world on the other side of the bay hasn't tried to keep us all apart. Parents. Religion. The government. Pretend, for one final night, that you'll never lose each other because of these things.

The man turned away from the mainland and toward the sunless sky. As if speaking to the pinks, purples, and blues, he said quietly:

Out of all the things that can tear us apart, it's memory that scares me the most.

I didn't know what he meant. On that perfect Dragon Island day, I didn't feel the past. Instead, the present lingered in the sand and encroached the wood pilings that held up the dragon homes.

The front doors, mouths. The bodies that passed through them, fire. She reached her arm around my waist and kissed my almost-sunburned shoulder. The tenderness on my skin only a warning to what could have happened had I not lathered myself in sunscreen at three. Almost burned. Almost pain. Almost.

If what the man was saying was true, then—in the midst of the world, in the world of time (beginnings, middles, and endings), in the world of space (here, there, and elsewhere)—Dragon Island was an island of almosts. But that didn't make sense to me, because on Dragon Island, watching the sunset, everything seemed complete. And because of this, I felt as though nothing, especially memory, could tear us apart.

She said:

> Well I don't know about G, but my girlfriend here really wants to know why you guys call it Dragon Island.

He smiled, showing all his bright white teeth, and looked at me again:

> We call this place by another name, so that no one in the outside world knows where we exist so freely, so happily. They'll look on a map, but they'll never find it. It's how we keep this place sacred. This old lady who owns the Pantry named it decades ago. She used to be a lesbian, but now she's married to a guy on the mainland.

She added:

> You can't "used to be" a lesbian.

But at the same time, the words rushed from my mouth in a panic:

But if it's a secret, how will people know it's okay?

Know what's okay?

Umm . . .

I felt my cheeks get red, my mind go blank:

I don't know. I mean . . . I guess I meant . . . how will people who need it find it?

He shrugged:

You found it.

When the sky faded to black, She and I parted ways with the man in one large, muscly embrace. Back at the Airbnb, She grilled us dinner on the porch while I read to her. When the chapter ended, She said:

I think we should add this to our bucket list: read ten books together. Oh, and watch paint dry for a day.

I agree. When we get back, remind me to add it in the notebook.

I will. And then we can check off Dragon Island. Number one on the list.

She came over to me with a spatula in her hand and bent down to kiss me. When I lifted my chin and met her lips with mine, I felt my mouth tremble, and my skin, despite the heat, transformed into a canvas of goose bumps. Though we had been together for months, She felt different than before. In a place unlike anywhere else on earth, a place we called by another name, She felt like home. Not the starless-sky city I called home or the one a state away, but a home like an island where everyone was safe and nothing bad could happen.

The next morning, I woke up before her, not with a headache, but with my head revving its engine like a sports car. I couldn't make out any thoughts; I could only feel the force of them rushing in all at once. Leaving her beneath the sheets, I quietly got out of bed and went outside for fresh air, but with every step I took, the more my consciousness awakened and the fuller my mind became. Sitting by the pool, I tried to meditate, to sift through the racing mind-chatter, like sand. But nothing gave way. Instead, the thoughts multiplied exponentially, each thought screaming something different into the back of my eardrums, each thought screaming at another thought, and my chest, on fire, began to burn. The island wind was blowing on my skin, but I couldn't feel it. The men next door were still party-ing from the night before, but I couldn't hear them. A blue dragonfly danced on the pool water, but I couldn't see it. I checked my phone; two minutes had passed since I had woken up. Only two minutes. It felt like an hour. My chest burned brighter, deeper; aflame. With every second—no, millisecond—no, some measure of time even smaller and more infinite all at once, the larger my mind became: at first larger than the lounge chair I'd sweated into yesterday, and then the pool that cooled me down, and then the carless sand street where we kissed and the boardwalk and bamboo sidewalks we ran on and any and all of the food there could ever be on Dragon Island, and then my mind grew larger than the island ocean and all the granules of sand, in fact larger than the whole entire sunset sky with us and all the yachts watching and all the planets in the Milky Way watching too—the pinks, the purples, the blues—and before I knew it, my mind was very large and I was very little and Dragon Island was teeny, teeny tiny, miniature and plastic, not like the Bar-bie Dreamhouse I used to play with, but more like an architectural model of a Barbie Dreamhouse made for Barbie, but it also wasn't a Dreamhouse; instead, it was a Barbie Dragon Island House, and this miniature model of the Dragon Island House was displayed within the actual diptych Barbie Dragon Island House that Barbie was, through a plastic case, staring at, with another Barbie—two Barbies. And then Dragon Island shrank even smaller than that, a white blip in a photograph hanging in a one-inch pink plastic frame in real Barbie's real Dreamhouse; a photograph of the two Dragon Island Barbies looking at the miniature model of the Dragon Island House inside their Dragon Island House, and a real Barbie is staring at the photograph on the wall, looking suspiciously at the Dragon Island House and Dragon Island Barbies, and real Barbie hears the first Dragon Island Barbie say, *this is my home and a model of my home in my home in a picture that's in your real house which isn't even real so you have to fucking run just run just go now, now!,* and if you were there, you wouldn't even be able to hear her say this, because it would just be a little white thought bubble drawn next to Dragon Island Barbie, but you also wouldn't be able to read it because the words don't make sense—

JULY

The city is redundant: it repeats itself so that something will stick in the mind.

Memory is redundant: it repeats signs so that the city can begin to exist.

Italo Calvino

THE STUDY OF OBLIVION

eleven weeks since breakdown

My new therapist is wearing black ballet flats today (which means she owns more than one pair of shoes). I stare at the bottoms. They are pristinely clean, as if she's never walked on them before, which makes me wonder if she even *can* walk. I've never seen her feet on the ground or anywhere except up on her black footrest. Maybe she has a wheelchair. Maybe she has a husband who wheels her to work every day and picks her up and puts her in her armchair and then hides the wheelchair so her clients, like me, won't know.

I was wondering, my new therapist starts, if Dragon Island is a real place?

Yes, I told you I went there before my breakdown, but no, I won't tell you the real name because that's the whole point. But if you really want to know, I'll tell you.

I didn't understand the end of the story, my new therapist says as if she's judging my writing abilities.

Well, neither do I, I say defensively, I told you I can't finish the story about me and my girlfriend, and now you see why.

Right.

I also know the ending seems cliché, because it talks about Barbie and now they're making a Barbie movie, which might turn this whole story stale, but in actuality, Barbie was like my whole childhood and I have rights to her too. I'm also conflicted about this upcoming film because what if they ruin Barbie and, therefore, my whole beautiful, magical childhood? Can we trust Greta Gerwig to write the script? Because I don't know if G.G. breaks glass ceilings for women or just taps on them, like *tap tap*, hey patriarchy, I'm here. But what about the rest of us? Actually, never mind. Forget what I said. I'm just being judgy like you now.

Silence.

Silence.

Silence.

This weekend I went to a July Fourth party that my girlfriend's friend was hosting in Williamsburg, and we were on the roof in the blazing sun. My girlfriend was socializing by a table of sweaty food that had surely already gone bad in the heat. I was sitting near the corner of the roof on a lounger with my phone open to Notes, and I was writing. When my girlfriend came bouncing over, she asked how I was doing and if I wanted to meet this girl she went to high school with. I said no thanks, I'm just working. I mean writing.

She sat beside me, threw her arm around me, and kissed me on the cheek. She said, *my little writer.* And I couldn't help but think how we're exactly the same height and wear exactly the same shoe size. When we first started dating, we even wore the same size shirts and pants, but now, from my weight loss, every pair of pants is baggy on me and almost shows my coochie when I walk. So now I've resorted to wearing crop tops and harem pants like the hippies. Yes, even though I'm mentally unstable, I still wear crop tops. I still wear hoop earrings. I still put on mascara. I still plaster on foundation, but only around my jawline to cover up the acne that has come, like a dictator, to overthrow my face in the past few weeks. Hormonal acne, the gynecologist told me. Further proof of PMDD. My girlfriend said, *baby are you okay? Do you want to go home?* I said, no it's okay, I know you're a Libra and you need this time to talk to people other than me. And I truly meant what I said but I was also butthurt, because I'm a Leo and why can't I be enough?

My new therapist says, what are you thinking about?

I say, what my character wants.

I say this so automatically, as if part of my brain is truly thinking about this.

So then she says, what character? The one from Dragon Island?

I say, no, my new one.

And why are you thinking about that?

My undergrad professor at NYU once said that your character has to want something to give the book meaning. Like a story is nothing if a character doesn't have a desire that they are actively trying to reach. My professor didn't exactly say that, but something like that. I can't fully remember.

That one character's pursuit of her objective creates unity of action; the story, then, follows the character in pursuit of her goal.

That same professor, when I told him I wanted to be a writer and eventually a professor, said: definitely don't be a writer or a professor. Do something that can actually change the world. Something that's actually important. Like politics. Or medicine. Which was very confusing because he *was* a writer and a professor, and I realized he must have very bad self-confidence and that made me sad. Anyways, when I asked him to write a letter of recommendation for an MFA program I was applying to when I was twenty-three, he emailed me back in all caps: DO NOT GET AN MFA. DO NOT BECOME A WRITER. I'M SERIOUS. DON'T DO IT.

My new therapist says, what do you think your character wants?

I broke up with my girlfriend yesterday.

Oh?

But after, she said that I was just having a bad day and begged me to stay. So I did.

How many times have you done this?

Many. And she always makes me stay.

She doesn't make you stay. You choose to stay. Isn't that right?

My new therapist just checked me, checked like in chess. I can feel it in my bones.

I adjust my body. I suddenly have a nasty headache.

All the signs say to leave.

Maybe You're Projecting Your Fears Onto Reality.

I want to say, reality isn't real anyways.

But instead I say, and why would I do that?

Because I'm truly curious as to why I would project my fears onto an unreal reality and why my brain, if that was true, would therefore be, literally, my worst enemy.

My new therapist says, I'm not sure.

At this point, I really don't get the purpose of therapy if she can't answer my questions. So I say:

But, you see, I fucking hate my girlfriend sometimes. Especially when she tries to take care of me. How could I not break up with her when she's being so lovey-dovey and I feel like this?

It seems like, my new therapist says, You're Mad At Your Girlfriend Because She Threatens Your Dissociation And Depression. Do you want to explain what happened yesterday?

Well, the signs were coming at me so fast yesterday. The summer rain was a sign that god was crying for me. The full trash can in the kitchen was proof that my girlfriend and I are not meant to be together. Her social needs at Fourth of July were evidence that we're incompatible. So last night, I rocked back and forth on our faux leather couch and my girlfriend held me. And I said, the medication is going to kill me! I can already feel it! It's going to kill me and the keyboard! The *N* is stuck! The *S* has doubled itself! My writing is dead! I can feel it already! I was extremely melodramatic but in my head it felt real.

It always feels real.

I think before that, I was thinking about Kanye West and how he doesn't take medication, because he says it kills his creativity.

What happened earlier that day that made you feel so unsettled?

Well, in the morning, my girlfriend left the house for work. She builds pop-ups around the city. And before she left, she said I should distract myself today. Keep my mind busy. *Maybe go outside.* So after she left, I went to Google. By Google I mean I went onto my laptop and looked into Four Ultimate Concerns of Existential Psychology Theory, which are:

1) death
2) freedom to make choices
3) isolation
4) meaninglessness

Isn't it interesting that one of the primary existential concerns of life is the freedom to make our own choices?

When I asked my girlfriend this exact question later at night (before I started rocking back and forth on the couch), she said, *that's not what I meant by distracting yourself.*

Free will is a burden.

What did you do after you googled the existential concerns?

Well, after my existentialist research, I decided to go outside like my girlfriend recommended, but as soon as I got downstairs I realized I forgot my keys. So I asked the doorman for the extra set but they were already in the apartment (I hadn't returned them last time I had forgotten. And all I do is forget these days). So, I called my girlfriend crying, and she said that she would come let me in. I waited out on Sixth Avenue (but there were so many homeless people and blind people and it made me so sad so I just kept crying) until my girlfriend had a break from work and she took an Uber from Brooklyn to Manhattan.

When she got there, let me into our apartment, and went back to work, I felt oblivion taking over, and the only thing that kept me from disintegrating completely was typing on my sticky keyboard. I counted the seconds by counting the words. Of course I don't count the words myself. I use that feature that counts them for you. And I knew that in a few more tens of thousands of words, she would be home again and I could apologize for ruining her day. Just keep writing. You are the timekeeper now. You are the black-hole clock bender. You are not going crazy. You are not an illusion. You are not poison. That's what I was saying to myself. And my girlfriend was looking at me from the other end of the couch, and she said you'll start to feel better soon and I wanted to tear off my skin.

I thought you said she went back to work?

She did. This was later. Then my girlfriend squeezed my foot and smiled crookedly, but her smile told me that she doesn't know if I will actually feel better soon and that she misses who I was before all of this and she hates that earlier she had to Uber to the city to let me into the apartment because I can't remember shit these days. And then the signs were coming at me faster. So then I broke up with her.

It sounds like maybe you were feeling guilty that she came to let you into the apartment.

Duh. But it didn't end there. Later, it was dark outside. The rain had stopped. But then a sign appeared on the TV show that we were watching. The show was about a toxic couple who part ways despite their immense sexual attraction, and I knew it was about me and her, and I started dry heaving. My girlfriend held my hollow cheeks and said breathe with me, honey. To which I said, I am a black hole and I am infecting the atmosphere. I am. I am. I am. And all of the animals are dying and there are so many homeless people on the street. And the bald planets, I'm going to suck them all in. And when that happens, the universe is going to collapse and I am (I am. I am.) going to kill you or myself and I haven't even finished my book and I can't write our story and you don't deserve this and I can't do this. And she said, it's okay you're just having a bad day.

If a planet orbits a black hole, life can theoretically survive on said planet. However, due to the black hole's intense gravity, time as we know it would stretch. One year on this planet would be the equivalent to thousands of years on Earth, and an ominous darkness would fill half the sky.

Would you say your girlfriend gets you? My new therapist picks a piece of thread off her red blouse.

Well, yeah. I guess she gets me more than anyone else in the world.

My new therapist says, that's very nice. She rolls the piece of thread into a ball and reaches over to place it in the trash can without moving her feet from her footrest. And do you love her?

Huh?

Are you willing to love her?

I don't know what that means.

Are you, at least, willing to let her see you?

She sees me every day. I even let her read my stories.

I mean beneath the words.

You mean show her what's between the lines?

My new therapist doesn't say anything.

I can't be both a writer *and* have a relationship. It takes up too much of my headspace.

Which does?

Well both, and they're competing. And writing has to win.

My new therapist pretends to be curious even though she knows the answer: According To Whom?

To these words. Isn't it obvious where all my attention is going? Besides, maybe I'm not gay.

Is there a reason why you keep rubbing your eyes?

Well they're really, really itchy. I'm going blind from the Prozac.

The itchiness could be from that or from anxiety.

I say, or the Prozac.

She says, or anxiety.

I realize we're bickering, so I stop and say, I really feel like I'm going blind. And going blind is my worst fear.

There's a blind school around the corner from my apartment. Right in the middle of Manhattan. So there's a lot of blind people in the neighborhood. Fifty percent seeing persons and fifty percent blind. On the intersection there's even a sign: BLIND PEOPLE CROSSING. It's like this little hub in the center of the city where those who can't see migrate. Going blind has been my worst fear since I was little. More so living in the dark, which reminds me of the attic in my childhood home and the spinning planets all at once. And each day when I walk outside and see the blind treading through puddles that no one has warned them are there, because no one knows if it's polite to warn them (at least that's what goes through my mind), it reminds me that my worst fear hasn't come true yet. It reminds me—

One time about a year ago, I saw two blind persons with walking sticks bump into one another pretty aggressively on my block. And the woman started yelling at the man, saying, Hey! Watch where you're going! And he said, Watch where *you're* going! And the woman said, Can't you see that I'm blind?! And the man stumbled for a second and then called back: Hey! I'm blind too! And then the two of them apologized to each other awkwardly and swiftly. Oh sorry. Sorry. Sorry. And kept... Sorry!... walking.

I wish it was that easy to solve all conflicts. Like: Hey, why'd you do that? Hey, I'm just human. Oh, me too. Sorry, sorry. Sorry. And then we go our separate ways with no animosity toward one another, only general annoyance at space and time and gravity and the atoms and nuclei and bacteria that make us, us.

Sorry, sorry. Sorry for being alive.

Being alive is Sorry hard. Trust me Sorry I know.

THE STUDY OF OBLIVION

twelve weeks since breakdown

When I walk into her office today, I am immediately overcome with the urge to take off my shoes and place my feet on the footrest in front of me. Unfortunately, I'm afraid my new therapist will think that's rude (I'm also scared my feet will smell or that she'll judge my unmatching socks). Then again, my new therapist always has her feet on her footrest. And when I say always, I'm not being dramatic. Whenever I enter her office, she is already sitting in her chair with her feet up. She never even stands to greet me which is very rude. She must have a buzzer next to her armchair that lets me in, which makes me wonder if she is lazy or if this is further proof of the wheelchair theory or if this is just part of her therapy, a game to see how long it takes me to snap at her. Should I say something about her lack of manners? Should I say something about her awful pillows? Would it be useful to my Getting Better? I decide I shouldn't waste our (expensive) time today because I've got more pressing issues at hand, like

I have no sex drive anymore and I can't cum. I'm starting to think I'm not gay. Like what if I actually want to be with a guy?

Do you want to be with a man?

No.

She blinks at me as if she's just solved world hunger with a snap of her fingers.

Okay.

I pick at the dirt under my nail. I always know how mentally unstable I'm feeling by how my nails look.

> Painted, no chips: DOING GREAT.
> Painted, slightly chipped: STILL LIVING.
> Painted, almost all chipped: UH-OH.
> Completely bare: BAD BAD NEWS.

My nails, if you're wondering, are completely bare today.

Wait. That didn't help. My head keeps saying I'm not gay.

Well that's why I asked you directly if you wanted to be with a man or not. A Direct Question Can Often Bypass The Anxiety Mind.

But the thoughts aren't stopping.

Norma, how have the signs been?

Oh, they're everywhere and they're talking to me. Instagram keeps showing me singles events and Facebook too. Every time I think I'm safe. *Bam.* There it is. I keep telling god to send me the signs in another form so I can prove to you that it's it (it, god), but they just keep appearing to me on social media. Would you like to see one?

She looks down at her clipboard and says, you know your phone listens to you and serves you ads based on what you've said recently? So if you've been telling your girlfriend you want to break up with her then that's probably why you're receiving those ads.

Or maybe it's a sign.

Is my phone listening to me? 584,000,000 results (0.60 seconds)

In short, yes. For one, when certain apps like Instagram request your phone's microphone, and when you tap *allow*, you're giving them permission to hear you. This makes for effective advertising that seems accurately geared to you or what you've already been searching for.

Very effective.

Should I be worried about my phone listening to me? 660,000,000 results (0.69 seconds)

Not necessarily, unless you have a really bad oblivion problem.

So you're saying that not only my old therapist but also my iPhone is making me crazy?

I'm saying that you're being target marketed.

I'm saying that I'm being brainwashed.

Well that's one way to look at it.

I just need to be able to write again.

Aren't you writing a new story?

Yes. But I don't need that story. I need The Last Story. And the new story is a fucking mess. Sorry for swearing. Besides, nothing will come of it. I've been writing for almost ten years, and nothing has come of it. So fuck it. Sorry again for swearing.

You're allowed to swear here.

Oh. Then I should probably just fucking give up fucking writing al-fucking-together.

I think of lava.

My new therapist says she wants me to start thinking in terms of who is talking. For example, is it you, your derealization, your depression, or your anxiety talking.

You mean "what"?

What?

Derealization, depression, and anxiety aren't people.

But I try not to be too difficult. So then I say, I get it. I heard Maggie Nelson talk about it in her book. She says, *That's my depression talking.*

My new therapist asks me what I've been reading lately.

I say nothing. I told you I don't like to read, which is why it's surprising I read Maggie Nelson.

Maggie Nelson is a genre-busting writer defying classification.

People also ask:

How old is Maggie Nelson?
Where did Maggie Nelson go to school?
How do I contact Maggie Nelson?

That's when I find out that Maggie Nelson has a new book out so I order it.

I used to like reading when I was a little girl. To which my new therapist responds, then what happened?

When I started having sex, I stopped reading books. I never saw the two as related, but it's true that they happened around the same time. It's true. Wow. I've never thought about that before. That's interesting. Maybe therapy is actually working.

Silence.

Silence.

Silence.

In the middle of my revelation, my new therapist goes, this week we're going to up your dose of the Prozac.

What?! Why?!

We talked about this.

Oblivion makes me forgetful.

We need to up your dose because ten milligrams of fluoxetine Doesn't Treat Depression Of Your Kind, and you'll need something more like twenty to sixty milligrams.

But what if I go crazy?

Well, you're tolerating the medicine well so far.

Am I really though?

THE STUDY OF OBLIVION

thirteen weeks since breakdown

Norma, how are you feeling today?

Yesterday, I was good, but today, I am a bird locked in a cage. A parakeet, a rosella. But with fading red and blue. I have stopped singing. I have stopped screeching for a key. I am half asleep and my eyelids are coated with dream goo.

My new therapist says, your body may just be adjusting to the new dosage. Some days will be better than others.

I'm starting to become desensitized to my new therapist's *justs*.

It's not some days. It's some minutes. Sometimes even some seconds. One minute I feel better. Other minutes I feel much worse. For example, my fish died yesterday and then I couldn't stop thinking about how everything in this world is going to die. For example, yesterday I took a walk in the park and saw a squirrel burying a nut, and I laughed. For example, yesterday I thought again that I wasn't gay after I told my girlfriend for the second time this week I wasn't in the mood to have sex, and then I couldn't stop shaking.

I thought you had a good day yesterday?

I told you it's not about days. It's about minutes. Seconds. I don't know if you're familiar with it, but there is a clock in Union Square Park that ticks down, to the second, the time we have left until climate change is irreversible. It reads, EARTH HAS A DEADLINE. And when it says *deadline*, all I can see is the word *DEAD*. Other people pay little mind to the clock. Even the mothers with strollers. Most people don't even know what the six years and so on are counting to. When I walk by the clock, I try to keep my head down now so I don't look at it and completely lose my mind.

Silence.

Don't you think it's weird that we are living and simultaneously dying? We count our age up while counting down the time we have left, assuming we'll live until seventy, eighty, a hundred. Like I'm twenty, eighty years to go. Something like that. When really any of us could go in the next hour, the next day. And all that time we spent counting down to a faulty end date are minutes we'll never get back. And yet, some people say time doesn't exist. Should we listen to the quantum physicists? Or the gurus? Or the philosophers? Or the scientists? Should we listen to anything at all except the beating of our own hearts?

Anyways, it's like I am seesawing on the edges of emotionality, with each sway slamming against the ground only to bounce and bang back to the other side.

What's on either side?

Oblivion and that clock in Union Square.

You mean reality?

You know, I used to hate seesaws as a kid. Hate them! But my sister loved them. So she tossed me back and forth on the playground outside our childhood church and I screeched with my fancy dress catching dirt on the bottom. It was utter terror and yet, somehow, at the same time still fun. This isn't fun like that, and I worry I've gone completely insane, but sometimes I do feel much better. You know, I didn't always sound so crazy. People used to tell me I sounded so Zen, so calm. I think it's my voice. Sometimes people still tell me this. Those people who don't witness me here or inside my house pacing around or crying on my girlfriend's lap. This is just a recent thing. I swear.

I can see my new therapist's attention drifting as if I'm not telling the truth and so none of this is of interest to her so I say, but good news! I've been writing a lot. Working on that new story.

My new therapist asks me if I'd consider bringing the story in next week so she can read it.

I say, I'll show you my manuscript when I'm done.

I ask her if I can use her as a character.

She says, no.

Then: I'd Rather You Not.

I don't tell her that I can't take her out of the narrative or else it won't make sense anymore and I'll have to start all over.

Instead I tell her, you're the one who gave me the meds.

Or you're vital to my Getting Better.

Or you're the enemy of oblivion and therefore my antagonist.

Or okay, I understand.

Then I say, I don't know if I'm the one writing or if oblivion is writing.

(I'm trying to prove to her that I am using her methods. That she is helping me. But truthfully, I don't care whether I or oblivion is writing. At least there's something on the page.)

At least I think I say this, but then she asks if I've gone to the eye doctor yet for my itchy eyes?

NO, I want to shout, IT'S THE FUCKING PROZAC'S FAULT.

But instead I say, I have an appointment next week, because they're still unbearably blurry and itchy. Even worse than before. And slimy. I want to stick my fingers inside of them and pull out the gunk. Sometimes I do. This makes them more itchy and more blurry. The words on my laptop are a haze. The buildings outside my window are undefined.

Blurry vision prozac: 75,600 results (0.45 seconds)

Drugs for the Mind Affect the Eye—Review of Optometry
Keeping an Eye on the Ball: Visual Problems on SSRIs
Fluoxetine-induced blurring of vision: A rare ocular side effect

PMDD blurry vision: 678,000 results (0.55 seconds)

Surprising Impacts Your Hormones Have On Your Vision
6 Surprising Side Effects of PMS—*Good Housekeeping*
These Weird Period Symptoms Will Seriously Surprise You

Surprise! During the first week of menstruation the typical elevated estrogen level can cause blurred vision, trouble focusing, and watery eyes.

Maybe my new therapist and my neurologist are wrong, and it *is* PMDD.

Then I say to my new therapist, don't worry, I'm not going blind.

She says, I'm not worrying. Are you projecting again?

My eyesight was better on oblivion.

I realize as I finish my sentence that I make oblivion sound like a drug. It's not a drug.

She says, we'll see if your eyes worsen over the next few weeks.

I tell her I could go blind in that time. I actually tell her this.

She thinks I'm dramatic.

I don't actually know what she's thinking.

Maybe my gynecologist, new therapist, and neurologist are all wrong, and *I'm* right. It *is* the meds and I'm perfectly fine and oblivion needs me and I gotta go.

I say, I read about it on the internet. It's called Unilateral Sudden Loss of Vision (SLOV).

She says, That's Catastrophic Thinking And Part Of Oblivion.

She, obviously, doesn't call it oblivion.

So then I say, I also can't orgasm anymore. I don't know which is worse. The feeling of going blind or the feeling of not feeling.

   Prozac sex help: 5,180,000 results (0.47 seconds)

      Antidepressant fluoxetine lowers sex drive
      Managing Antidepressant Sexual Side Effects

Will Antidepressants Wreck Your Sex Life?—Depression
   Center

I ask her why she put me on the anti-obliviant that is most likely to
cause sexual dysfunction and if she's trying to ruin my relationship or
if this is just another sign that my girlfriend and I shouldn't be together.

I don't ask her this.

She says, great. Well, we're out of time for today.

GREAT?!?

BUT MY EYES AND MY PUSSY!

THE STUDY OF OBLIVION

fourteen weeks since breakdown

I step onto the crowded subway car going uptown, and I am immediately greeted with the smell of metallic blood. There is a homeless man lying horizontally across the blue subway bench sleeping with bare feet that are bright red with open sores. I take in the details of his humanity as if I'm building a character for him. He has a beard like a jazz musician. He also has a FreshDirect bag filled with other plastic bags, which means he cares about being prepared. He's probably forty, though the lines on his face may be deceiving, and for this, if he wasn't homeless, people would call him wise. With my prying eyes, I realize I'm probably intruding on this man's sleep. To stop, I look around the subway car and calculate the ratio of readers to cell phone users. This is an activity I partake in often. When my girlfriend asks why I do it, I say, research. You see, the subway is the only place left in existence where there could, possibly, be the same number of people reading as there are staring at a screen. This gives me hope. Yes, the underground transport system, where people are pushed onto the tracks in front of an oncoming train, where homeless people lie with their open sores and are never tended to, gives me hope in humanity. Unfortunately, today is not a day that gives me hope. Only two people are reading. One older woman and one man wearing a Canada Goose jacket who keeps looking up at the homeless man as if he's mad at the blood smell and cannot, because of it, concentrate on the prose in his book. I look toward the subway screen to see how many more stops until Eighty-seventh Street and guess what I see next to the screen? There is one of those horizontal skinny ads with a stick-figure smiley face that has a mask over its mouth and nose. The text reads, THIS IS YOUR SIGN. I almost laugh out loud.

I still can't cum with my girlfriend. It's definitely a sign. The subway told me so.

My new therapist says, don't you think this is Most Likely Because Of The Prozac?

I'm not gay.

She repeats:

—Most Likely Because Of The Prozac?

Did you know Prozac is associated with a twofold increase in the odds of developing some form of dementia? One study shows.

My hands start to shake. She repeats with less patience this time and more *umph*:

Don't You Think Your Inability To Cum Is Most Likely Because Of The Prozac And This New Idea That Perhaps You Are Not Gay Is Just Your Anxiety Talking And Another Form of Self-Punishment, So You Don't Have To Experience Love?

I saw a commercial about children with cancer yesterday. And you know how I think there's a spiritual reason for everything? Yesterday I'm watching TV and I'm like: what the fuck spiritual reason does a kid get cancer? Or what spiritual reason does a Black person get shot in the back every fucking week? Or what spiritual reason is the man on the subway homeless and literally rotting, while I'm here talking about unconscious self-punishment in your cushy Central Park office?

It Doesn't Really Make Sense, Does It?

No. It doesn't at all.

Italo Calvino's second memo for the next millennium exists in his collection called *Six Memos for the Next Millennium*, which actually contains only five memos because he died before he wrote the sixth (Why did the publishers still call it the six memos? To remind us that we'll all die with unfinished work?). In it, Calvino says: As for the writer, success is in the felicity of verbal expression, which can sometimes be achieved by a flash of inspiration but which normally entails a patient search for the mot juste, for the sentence in which no word can be replaced, for the most efficient and semantically dense arrangements of sound and ideas.

This reminds me of Maggie Nelson's patient labor, which I just read about in her new book that I ordered.

Maggie Nelson: When I was younger, "feeling free" through writing felt totally on the menu. Whereas now it feels like a forced, daily encounter with limits, be they of articulation, stamina, time, knowledge, focus, or intelligence. The good news is that such difficulties or aporias do not determine the effect of our work on others. In fact, it increasingly seems to me that the goal of [a writer's] patient labor is not our own liberation per se, but a deepened capacity to give it away, with an ever-diminishing attachment to outcome.

My new therapist says, patient labor. That's very interesting.

Very.

I say this sarcastically, even though I do think it's very interesting also.

Then I say, did you know that since 2014 the United States has averaged more than one mass shooting a day? And 97.2 percent of those shooters are male? Doesn't this seem like not only a gun issue but also a male issue? And right now, about 30 percent of adults in this country haven't got the Covid-19 vaccine because their body is a temple. Not like they're not all on Prozac or Viagra or McDonald's or Fox News or Facebook or Amazon anyways.

She didn't know this statistic.

Did you know that 35 percent of human traffickers are the victim's immediate family, 27 percent are their boyfriend, 14 percent are friends of the family, another 14 percent are employers, and only 9 percent... *ONLY 9 percent of human traffickers are strangers?*

She didn't know this either.

And did you know 60 percent of mammals on earth are livestock, 36 percent are humans, and only 4 percent... *ONLY 4 percent of mammals are wild animals?*

She didn't know this either. I wonder what she does know.

Then she says, It's Interesting, Isn't It, That You Would Care About All Of This When The World Isn't Real, According To You? Isn't It Also Interesting That You Would Be So Concerned With The Question Of Whether Or Not You Need To Break Up With Your Girlfriend, Again, If The World Isn't Real? These Things Are Contradictory, Aren't They?

I'm not sure if any of what she said is interesting except for how many questions she just asked in a row. But now as I stare at her pillows, I feel an ice-cold rush travel in slow motion down my body, from the top of my head all the way down to my toes. It's so slow and precise as if it's one of those futuristic scanners from a sci-fi movie: a neon green light that scans a body wanting to enter some secret room.

Now, I'm ice-cold and fully scanned. And my vision goes real, real hazy. Like Saran Wrap.

I think, fuck.

I also think, ahhh, oblivion again. My old friend.

You're dissociating, aren't you?

Her voice sounds like it's coming from inside my head.

I nod. Because what else am I supposed to do when I'm covered in Saran Wrap.

It's okay. Those Contradictions I Just Pointed Out Must Have Caused You A Lot Of Anxiety, And Because Of The Anxiety You Had To Dissociate.

And with that, someone cuts the Saran Wrap, the haze ends, and my body feels normal again.

Oh whoa whoa whoa. That was crazy! I just felt it happen! It was like this laser beam going all the way down my body and I got so cold. That's never happened like that before and—

She interrupts me by saying, the medicine is working. You feel safe enough to come back from it now.

And then I burst out in tears like a little baby. And all I want to say to my new therapist is thank you thank you thank you I'm back. And I want to hug and squeeze her little stationary body and kiss her ballet flats. And pay her extra. But then...

My new therapist looks toward the clock and says, well, we're almost out of time and I wanted to talk about your weight. I can tell you've lost more weight, which may not be your fault. Prozac is known to curb hunger, so I'm going to need you to buy a scale because you can't afford to lose any more weight.

And before she says all of this, she doesn't even offer me a tissue or ask if I need a minute because I'm still sobbing. She's just staring at me, waiting for me to leave like my time's up and my problem is no longer her problem.

And this is probably how everyone in the world will feel once that clock in Union Square gets down to zero.

So you'll buy a scale? she asks.

Suddenly I hate my new therapist again. And her wooden robot. And her pillows.

While snorting boogers up into my brain, I say, I don't believe in scales.

She says, what do you mean you don't *believe in* scales? Actually, we don't have time to go into that. We can revisit the topic next time.

Can I at least have a tissue?

They're right next to you, she says without moving an inch.

Oh.

I stand up, grab a tissue, and blow. Before I walk out of the room with my dirty tissue, I say, you should know that I never cried when I was a kid.

She tells me that's impossible.

I say, no, really.

She repeats that that's impossible.

So I repeat, no, really.

Then I say, I'll show you a story I wrote about this. It's supposed to be the first story in my manuscript.

She says, Make Sure You Send The Story Before Our Next Session So That I Can Read It Prior To Our Session. That Way, We Can Talk About It Next Time We Meet.

I think: do I have to pay you overtime for that?

But instead, I want to hurt her feelings like she hurt mine, so, with my hand on the doorknob, I say viciously:

You know, when you speak I just think of what letters you're meaning to capitalize.

And she says, oh, that's nice.

Home

With every one of my mother's high-pitched screams, the wooden ladder shakes under my legs and the book in my hand quivers. It would be a shame if I lost my footing, fell off the ladder onto the library's oriental carpet, and split open my chin: blood pouring out of my head. A whole wall of books just staring down at my prepubescent body as I die with my favorite book dashed on the floor—binding open, pages creased—beside me. And all because my mother is yelling at my father in the kitchen for drooling at the waitress's boobs during our Friday night family dinner.

The thought of dying with a good book beside me sounds like a great ending to a tragic story, but this is just the beginning of my story. I steady myself. I tighten my grip on the ladder. I feel the wood press against the palm of my sweaty left hand, while my right hand, which is just as damp, squeezes *Bridge to Terabithia* as if it's the American flag, which cannot, under any circumstances, hit the ground or else I will have to burn it (at least I think that's the law?). When I was little, I secretly started putting my books in the library downstairs. I don't put all my books here. Only important ones. Like *Are You My Mother?* and *The Velveteen Rabbit*. I thought, at first, that my parents might find the books, read them, and finally stop yelling. But they haven't. I think this used to make me sad, but now, after what happened yesterday, it makes me happy.

If this ladder wasn't so wobbly and old, then this probably wouldn't be so hard. But the ladder, like this house, is ancient. And if *Bridge to Terabithia* wasn't so important, this also wouldn't be so hard. But it is important, because this is the first book that has ever made me feel like life is beautiful and sad all at once, like we're all going to leave this world someday, it's just a question of how and when, and whether someone will care when we go. It's also the first book that has ever made me cry, and I usually don't cry. I'm not even sure I know how to.

Like: I have this teddy bear that one of my parents' friends gave to me when I was a day old, because when I arrived here, everyone was worried that I would die, or, like my mother says:

We were worried you wouldn't make it.

When I was supposed to, I wouldn't budge from my mother's stomach. So the doctor cut her open and untangled me from her umbilical cord. My face was purple. And when I took my first breath, I was silent, not a sound, not a wail. The nurses took me away, and eventually, in another room, I cried. That's actually the beginning of my story. Not this ladder. Not this bookshelf.

But that's not what I meant when I said I don't cry. I was talking about my teddy bear. One day my older sister came into my room, walked toward my teddy bear, plucked one of the bear's eyes out, and then left with the eye. Before she left, she said:

I love you.

It's a rule in this house that any goodbye or good night must be followed with an "I love you." No matter what happened that day. No matter the screaming. No matter if my sister just blinded my teddy bear or, like this morning, violently undressed me in the kitchen, grabbing at the cotton of my pajamas, in front of my parents, who were eating breakfast. All because I was wearing her bra. Once, I asked my mother why we always have to say "I love you." She said,

Just in case something bad happens.

Anyways, when my sister took my bear's eye, I didn't cry. Actually, I didn't say or do anything. I just watched as the whole thing happened. Kind of like when I was born. When my mother saw my eyeless teddy bear, she asked me who had done it. My sister typically cries when my mother yells at her, but I knew that as my mother yelled, I would just imagine what outfits my Barbies wanted to wear tomorrow; so I said I did it. And sure enough she screamed, and, sure enough, by the end, when I still hadn't shed a tear, my mother said:

You're so stoic, so strong, just like me. My strong girl.

I'm not sure if my sister still has my bear's eye. I'm not sure where she hid it or if she just threw it away.

A door slams, the one between the kitchen and living room. My toes contract to grip the ladder, which, to my surprise, makes it wobble even more. I can tell by the specific tone of the door slam that it is my father. And I can tell, without ever hearing a word from him, that he is finished with the screaming match my mother is having with him. I know it's my father, because the door went with a *whoosh* and slammed at the same pace. Whereas my mother's hinges more slowly and then *bangs* with a concentrated force into the door frame. My sister's is a *whoosh*, then a quick catch and then a soft *click*. If she and I did anything other than a click, there would be hell to pay. Not the real hell that my mother talks about, but this house's own version of hell, like the one happening in the kitchen. It's weird, I know, but the doors in this house speak. Or, rather, we speak to each other through the doors.

Other people used to live in this house before us, used to open and close these same doors. Did you know that? I didn't for a long time. I only discovered the two previous owners' existence when flipping through the books in the library on a day similar to today when my parents were preoccupied by their fighting. When I found the owners' names written in pencil on the first page of each book, I couldn't believe, firstly, that they had written in their books (I'm not allowed to); secondly, that someone else had lived in these rooms before; thirdly, that my parents hadn't been here since the beginning of time. I think, honestly, I learned about time—the passing of it— and death—the ending of all time—from these owners, from their books and the way they just sat there unopened and unknown but known before. If that makes sense. That day, I also discovered that my parents don't read books at all: my father is a doctor, and my mother is a mother who often takes girls' trips with her friends and forgets to pick me up at school. They only bring me to the bookstore so that I'll stop playing Barbies. They're worried I will be twelve soon and that I'll still play with dolls. They think I'm too attached to them, but little do they know the books aren't so different. It's all just stories and made-up characters. Same thing, different medium.

My parents may not have any books in the library, but they exist on the door frames. But I'm only allowed a click and my mother doesn't measure me against the wall, marking my height and age, because, she says:

   I never want you to grow up.

So how will anyone know I was here? That I existed in this place too? That's when I started scribbling my own name in my important books and placing them in the library.

Another step up the ladder and, thankfully, only one more to go, but then the same door swings open again, and I hear my mother's footsteps, heavy and haphazard, searching. Shit. I know I'm not supposed to say that, but it's the only thing I can say as I scurry all the way back down the ladder and crawl under the library desk as fast as I can. Shit. Shit. Shit. It's not a good hiding spot, but based on the noise, my mother is coming fast and I don't have time to run upstairs. You see, in the house, like the doors, our footsteps speak. They announce who is coming and going and if someone is coming to yell at you or just say good night I love you. The thing is, though: when I walk, the floors don't creak. My footsteps are too light. This is how I see everything and no one notices. One day, my footsteps will make a sound too. At least, I think they will.

Under the desk, I try to slow my breathing. I wipe my sweaty hands on the carpet, but instead of the dampness disappearing, lint from the rug clings to my skin. If I didn't have to put this book on the second-highest shelf of the library, I could have finished by now. But I have to because of what happened yesterday. I have to because if I don't, my parents might find my book, place it in a storage container, and bring it up to the attic. Or worse.

I try to avoid the attic at all costs. Up there, there's no ceiling, just wooden beams and the belly of the roof to keep out the Connecticut snow, and the air feels dense with ghosts or some other imaginary entity that will, if I stay up there, consume me. When I tell my mother this, she says my imagination is too wild and that I should stop reading books. This confuses me because she's the one who bought them for me. My dad says ghosts aren't real and when we die, we just die: zilch dead nada. My mother always scolds him after he says this, saying we live in a Catholic household and Heaven is our promised land even though we are and will always be sinners. She reminds me of this every night when we pray together, begging God to protect us. Protect us from what, I want to ask. The ghosts in the attic?

From under the desk, a pounding echoes through my body, but then I hear my mother's footsteps pivot from the library entrance and retreat. Her feet storm into the living room, where my father is probably sitting on the yellow couch, watching TV under the chandelier. The china in the curios shakes as my mother moves closer to him. I hear her voice again, louder this time. It always surprises me how loud it can get.

I take a deep breath and emerge from under the desk. I have to start all over again and this time I have to go faster. Time is running out. The pages of *Bridge to Terabithia* tremble as I grab the ladder with my lint-ridden hands. I take a deep breath in and out to steady myself. I know I'm being dramatic (this I get from my mother, according to my father), acting as if placing this book on the bookshelf is a matter of life and death. But in some ways, it is.

You see, a week ago, my mom and I were setting up the Christmas tree in the living room. She asked me to go to the attic and bring down a box of ornaments. First, I tried to protest, then I tried to stall, but nothing worked. I walked up two flights of stairs and shivered all the way up. My nipples got hard. These days I have puffy nipples, which my dad calls ant hills. I am almost ready for my cell phone. My sister got hers when she was thirteen. When I got up there, I was looking for the ornaments and trying to do it fast, because it was so dark up there and my nipples felt like knives. I heard something flap above me, so I quickly pushed some boxes out of the way. Suddenly I was standing in front of a painting: a white canvas with a woman's face on it. Behind that painting, there were more canvases. All with the same woman's face. It looked like my face. Dark brown eyes. Large eyebrows. Small lips. The woman wasn't smiling in the paintings so I'm not sure what her teeth looked like and if they looked like mine too. I stared into the paintings, and I wasn't scared of the attic anymore. I stood there, looking at the woman, until I heard my mother call my name from downstairs. That night, I wrote about the woman and the paintings in my diary.

The next day when I got home from school, my mother was standing in the front hallway with my diary in her hands.

What were you doing snooping around in my attic?

You told me to go up there.

No I didn't.

I bit my tongue.

If you need to know who she is so badly, that woman is your grandmother. Your father's mother.

What's her name?

She handed my diary back to me:

Rose. She was an artist.

But I knew I would never use the diary again:

That's so cool.

No, it isn't. Rose wasn't well in the head.

I wanted to ask what that meant, but then my mother put on a fashion show with the clothes she'd bought that day. As she modeled for me, I sat on the hallway floor, thinking about the woman in the attic.

Later that night, I heard my mother in her bedroom, telling my father about what I had found. If I was allowed to have *NSYNC and Britney Spears posters then I would have stared at them as I listened to their muffled voices. But instead I stared at my teddy bear. As I looked into the bear's empty, black eyehole, I heard my father tell my mother about the paintings:

We should really get rid of those things.

But that was a week ago, and this is now, and now, my mother is saying to my father in the living room, her voice shrieking:

I should have gotten rid of you years ago!

I have two more steps to go and now my bare feet have turned damp too and they're sliding on the ladder. I rub the sole of my foot against my other calf and try to drown out the noise. If I wasn't so stubborn like my father (that's what my mother always says), I would just place this book on the bottom shelf of the bookcase. But my mother is right: I am stubborn. Though only about certain things. Like undressing my Barbies when I'm done playing with them for the day, because they may not like that particular outfit tomorrow. Like jumping into bed before the lights turn off, because under my bed there is a black hole that wants me inside of it. Like placing this book on the second-highest shelf in the library.

Last night, after I finished *Bridge to Terabithia*, I wanted to tell the woman who looked like me about the book, about the way life was beautiful and sad at the same time, about the way words had the ability to make someone smile and then laugh and then cry. I put on my sister's push-up bra that I had stolen earlier that day. I knew if my nipples were to survive the attic cold, I would need a shield. With hollow humps on my chest, I walked out of my bedroom, down the hallway, and climbed up the stairs to the attic. My mother and sister were in their rooms. My father was downstairs watching something on TV that moaned. In the attic, I went looking for the paintings, but they weren't in their original spot. I searched everywhere for them, but they were gone. They had disappeared.

That's when I realized the truth about this home: how easy it is to be erased if you ask the wrong questions, if you write something that doesn't fit into the story someone else is trying to tell, if you don't have a good hiding spot. And that's when I decided to put my books on the highest shelf that I can reach in the library. Do you get it now?

The books on that shelf are from two hundred years ago. They belonged to the first owner of our house, who died in my parents' bedroom from a broken heart, but:

> *Of course, that's not true, because scientifically that's not pos-*
> *sible. He probably had a heart attack.*

That's what my father said when he told me the story. My mother, however, said a broken-heart death is completely possible. My parents' stories always conflict, so sometimes I have to make up my own. Hence, the Barbies. This man's books stayed in the library when they auctioned off the house. The following owner, the second owner, also died here. He used to have a gun collection in this very library, and, polishing his guns one day, he accidentally shot himself in the leg. He tried to run out of the house for help, but he died at the front door. This owner's books are on the lower shelves, but they're boring, because he didn't write in the margins of his books or leave letters tucked into the pages.

One time I found a letter in the first owner's copy of *Don Quixote*. The letter was signed: *with all the love in the broken universe, Mario.* Sometimes I imagine Mario was the owner's secret male lover, which also means that he was gay. I learned this word from my sister after I told her that when Princess Jasmine came on TV, I felt a weird tingling in my private parts. She said that means I'm gay and never to tell Mom or Dad, because if I did, it would break their hearts. And then, according to my mother, my parents could die. After she told me what gay was, I asked my sister if Santa was actually real, and she swore on her life that he was. Obviously he's not, so I'm not sure what is real or true anymore.

My right foot, finally steady enough, takes the second-to-last step toward my destination. I'm still not tall enough to reach the top, top shelf in the library, even with the ladder, so I'm not sure what's up there. I'm not sure who those books belong to or if they could make me cry or if they could make me feel anything at all.

What are you doing?

I jump, and *Bridge to Terabithia* jumps from my hands, crashing onto the floor. My heart races. My two hands grip the ladder as it shakes under my bare feet, almost toppling over. I almost let out a scream but then I remember where I am. I look toward the library door. My sister.

To the sound of my parents yelling in the living room, a game that my father has now joined, shouting back:

Well maybe if you weren't screaming all the fucking time!

I look at my sister, put my pointer finger to my lips, and plead:

Shhhh.

Without another word, my sister walks over to the fallen book and hands it to me. Then she holds on to the sides of the ladder and whispers:

Go.

I look down at my sister, surprised. She must be in a good mood. I think to ask her about my teddy bear eye. But then I realize the teddy bear is not part of my Barbie stories or my books, and that I really don't care. So instead, I look up and lift my right foot. Finally on the top step, I stand up tall. It's not as scary with my sister holding the ladder. With my hands, I part the sea of old books and squeeze *Bridge to Terabithia* amongst the first owner's books. I smile, pleased.

Hurry.

As if my sister knew what would happen before it came, I hear another door slam and my mother's footsteps coming to find me and tell me how awful my father is. Quickly, I climb down from the ladder. Back on sturdy ground, I put my hand up to give my sister a high five, but when I do this, she's already gone, and it's just me in the library again.

With my silent footsteps, I scurry into the foyer and upstairs to my bedroom. I decide I'll pretend to be sleeping. I jump into bed to avoid the black hole and slip under the covers. I close my eyes and think about the day when I'll finally be able to reach the library's top, top shelf. I don't know what I'll find there. Maybe it will be a teddy bear eye or a hidden set of paintings. But anyways, I hope whatever it is, it's good. And I hope it has notes in the margins.

AUGUST

I know words. I have the best words.

Anyone who thinks my story is anywhere near over is sadly mistaken.

Donald Trump

THE STUDY OF OBLIVION

fifteen weeks since breakdown

My new therapist is wearing yellow ballet flats again. They are definitely her favorite pair, which makes me wonder if yellow is her favorite color. She looks like someone who would love the color yellow. I wish I actually knew personal facts about my new therapist so that I could make her a full character free of clichés. Unfortunately, my new therapist is as cliché as therapists in New York City come. She works in the Upper West Side. She's middle-aged. She's got brown hair that's cut medium-length like all the other middle-aged women. She's just like any other person.

Except when I google her, compelled to show my girlfriend a photo of my new therapist who I'm always complaining about, I can't find a single picture of her online. Sure, the studies she's conducted with DPDR patients are all over the internet with her name, but there's not one picture. NOT A SINGLE ONE. When my girlfriend says, *that's not possible*, I say, maybe I made her up.

So today, I was half expecting to walk into my new therapist's office and have it be deserted like in a psychological thriller movie. I imagined I would have to go to the doorman of this fancy Upper West Side building and ask for her, just to have the doorman say, *who? What are you talking about? That's never been a therapy office. It's been abandoned for years.* Now, that would be an exciting Wednesday, but instead I walk into her office and my new therapist is in her armchair with her yellow flats resting on the footrest as always. I want to ask her how she scrubbed the internet clean of her photos. Maybe I'll need that skill one day, but then my new therapist leads the conversation, saying that after my story:

It certainly seems like the character rarely cried in her adolescence, because she pushed down her emotions for the sake of her emotional, seemingly highly narcissistic, mother.

See, I told you.

I smile, content.

But I'm slightly confused, she continues, because I thought your manuscript was fictional.

It is.

But—

I cut her off, because I'm tired of this debate:

Listen. I decided I don't need to buy a scale, because it's okay if I get a little skinnier.

My new therapist says, you're frail. And then stares at me without blinking.

Ouch.

Look, I don't like scales, and it's not like I have an eating disorder or something. I just think I look better thinner. When I'm chubbier, I look like a little girl.

A little girl? She seems intrigued.

Yeah. Like a little, round, happy girl.

Hmm.

Yeah.

Do You Think Maybe Your Desire To Be Skeletal Has Something To Do With Wanting To Look Unfeminine and, therefore, Not As Desirable To Men?

I don't think looking like a little girl is desirable to men.

You don't?

Silence.

Silence.

Silence.

Uhhhhhh, I say.

More silence.

Very awkward silence.

I can sense that even her textile pillows feel awkward; that they want to jump out the window, run into Central Park, and scream FUCKKKKKKKKKKKKK.

But maybe that's just me projecting.

To dodge the awkwardness, I change the subject; I tell my new therapist how yesterday I spent four hours online on a climate change map that shows the flooding predictions by each year in a beautiful, easy-to-read graphic. I tell her how I watched West Chelsea go first. And then FiDi (thank god). And then all the coasts of Manhattan. I leave out the part about how after the map I tried to find her picture on the internet.

My new therapist goes, it seems like you really care about this topic?

Yeah, well, it's a theme.

What do you mean?

She doesn't get me, so I continue,

The water is coming to get us, there aren't enough boats, and Jeff Bezos and three other rich guys went to space just for funsies. We've got random satellites and shit up there too. And for no good reason except we have no more space on Earth to put our junk. I'm desperate to make a metaphor to endnotes here but I'm not sure if it works. And I was looking at archives from *The New York Times* the other day. You see, I've been trying to catch up on what I missed in oblivion all these years. And remember when Donald Trump stopped people in the street looking to deport immigrants on the fly? Or just knocked on their doors and dragged them out? Or put their children in cages and then lost the only way to contact their deported parents? Pretty sure there are still some children in cages.

IS ALL OF THIS REALLY REAL?

And yet, it's not very surprising that the president of the United States intruded upon families and communities, when our entire country was founded on the premise of intruding upon families and communities. Because, remember when we gave the Native Americans smallpox and alcohol as warfare?

WHO WROTE THIS STORY?

Anyways, Joe Biden is supposed to be a better president so maybe we'll turn this shit around. You know his wife died tragically so that makes him a great person. That's what my mother says.

My new therapist hasn't written anything down on her clipboard this whole time, which means I have said nothing of relevance.

So I try again, because I'd like some of this down on paper.

I EXIST.

Remember when the United States bought slaves from the Portuguese, who intruded upon Africa to start the slave trade?

Well, I don't remember that because I wasn't alive for it, my new therapist says.

And I say, oh, and remember just this year and last year and the year before, big oil put pipelines through the minuscule amount of land that we pushed the Native Americans onto? Intruded upon their gravesites for the sake of oil, which is ruining our climate anyways? Think about it, I mean the entire human species has intruded upon all of nature. We've cut down trees. Burned forests.

AUTHOR, SHOW YOURSELF.

My new therapist says, aren't you the author? Isn't everything else fiction?

To top it all off, we've taken the animals and put them in zoos for our sick enjoyment of watching another living thing trapped and pacing between four walls. And in the zoos animals live a life span less than

50 percent of what they would have lived in the wild, probably because they're so anxious and depressed like me. And we drive animals to extinction, then we try to bring extinct animals back to life, also just for enjoyment. And while we do this, we murder animals every fucking day just because we want a burger or bacon, and as long as we don't see the slaughterhouses we're cool with it.

WHERE THE HELL IS GOD?

And you know, when humans replant trees to offset what they've cut down, we usually replant all the same kind of tree in one area. And guess what? That's the worst thing for trees. And did you know, tilling soil literally destroys the soil but that's what most farmers do even though there is no-till machinery they can use? You can look all this up. It's real. I swear it's real.

My new therapist's face is stationary, and I think perhaps she's frozen, her Wi-Fi cutting in and out, but then I remember we're not online and we're actually face-to-face.

And while the human species is intruding upon one another and upon nature, humans are being constantly intruded upon by ads. Everywhere we go someone is trying to sell us something. On social media. On billboards. At the grocery store. We can't escape it. We go outside, we go on our phones, we go on the subway, and bam! Buy this! Do that! Get skinny! I can't take it anymore. I look up and see an ad on a charging station. I look down and see an ad on the sidewalk. I look sideways and see a shop that says sale, buy me, wear me once, throw me out and buy some more, a new me will be on sale again in a month. That's why I've stopped going outside except to see you.

You're not going outside?

Shit.

Well, no. I mean yes, I mean ...

But it's not just because of the ads. I need to finish my manuscript and write The Last Story, so that's what I've been trying to do.

Norma, Maybe You Should Take A Break From Google For The Time Being. I Think It May Be Triggering Your Anxiety And Depression. What Do You Think?

I think you want me to live in the real world but you don't want me to know what's happening in the real world.

Silence.

Silence.

Silence.

Therapists use silence: 5,420,000 results (0.49 seconds)

How to Use Silence in Therapy & Counseling
The Effective Use of Silence | Psychology Today
(AD) Therapy For The Modern Woman—New York City
    Opening

I don't need to know how to use silence myself so I opt for Psych Central:

Done supportively, silence can exert some positive pressure on the client to stop and reflect. Nonverbal signals of patience and empathy by the therapist can encourage the client to express thoughts and feelings that would otherwise be covered up by too much anxious talk.

Sympathetic silence can signal empathy.

I don't think her silence is very sympathetic. It's more ominous.

My 400th memory is of me in eighth grade waiting in line for a ride at the amusement park. It's me, my best friend Tay, Johnny the blond who Tay has a crush on, and Ducky, who is tall and has pouty lips like a girl. Tay and I had convinced our mothers to let us go alone to the park, and there we secretly met up with the guys. Tay says we're on a double date. While we're waiting in line for thirty minutes, the guys challenge us to a truth or dare. Tay says dare because she's fearless. *I dare you to kiss Norma.* She looks at me and smiles. Tay knows what she wants, which is Johnny the blond, and she knows how to get him. With her two hands she reaches toward my face, wrapping her fingers around my ears, and presses her lips against mine. I close my eyes and I can feel her full breasts up against my flatter chest. Everything, her lips, her breasts, her hands, feels like padding on my skin. Like something that could save me from being hurt. Johnny the blond starts to cheer. Tay smiles in the middle of our kiss, then she takes her lips off mine and turns to Johnny, saying, *you liked that didn't you?* And I'm just standing there with no more padding, no more protection, and I feel my skin burning up. Ducky looks at me and says, *Norma I think you're getting a sunburn.*

My 401st memory is of the four of us finally inside the ride, which I learn is just a circular room that we will stick to when it starts. Tay and I find a spot against the circular wall to lean against. We stand next to each other and each of our prospective "dates" comes to our sides. There's no ceiling on this ride. There's just the sky and sun above, shining down on us. A teenager speaks into the microphone: *And off you go.* It's Johnny the blond, Tay, me, and Ducky, and when the ride starts to spin, our bodies smush against the wall. Gravity rolls the fat in my cheeks backward toward my ears as if it's a rolling pin and I'm the dough. It starts to spin faster and faster, and all the people in the room are suddenly no longer people, but wallpaper. *Norma!! Take my hand!!!* From the corner of my eye, I see Tay try to lift her hand. I watch as her limb defies all natural laws and reaches toward my body. For a split second it's the only thing that exists in this spinning room with humans for wallpaper. But then just as quickly as she lifts her hand up, gravity shoves her hand back down, punching it right into the center of my stomach. I think I let out a scream, but at the exact same time, the floor beneath us drops, and everyone is screaming. And I'm there suspended in the air with Tay's hand pressing into my stomach and tears falling out of my eyes as gravity pulls them back toward my hairline.

My 402nd memory is of me with tears blurring my vision, an ache in my stomach, and still spinning and spinning as if there is anything in the world to spin for. The weight of the air conjured up in that circular room with no ceiling makes me feel like I'm lying down in the grass at the end of the world, watching the sky above spin into oblivion. And it feels like at the end of the world, Tay will be by my side with her hand in my abdomen and I'll have tears spread wide across my face and the remnant feeling of her lips on mine and there will be two guys beside us who have no idea what is happening.

I look at my new therapist and say, you know these meds you gave me? All they've done is trapped me in my body. Intruded on my brain. They've sealed up the top of my head so I can't escape anymore. No more oblivion. Or derealization or whatever you call it. I thought these were supposed to be happy pills, but they're more like anxiety pills. Now all I feel is this burning in my chest like a little girl is inside there, and she's scratching, clawing me with her long nails trying to get out. She used to be able to escape through the crown of my skull, so she's climbing up my spine vertebra by vertebra. Up my brain stem. Into my skull. But the usual passageway is sealed off with Prozac, and now she's screaming, and she's clawing at me harder and her nails are growing longer with each minute that she's trapped. And my heart hurts so badly that I want to escape from anywhere possible even if it's through my eyes, which is maybe why they're so blurry and itchy.

What I really want to say is, you did this to me, but instead I say,

I miss oblivion.

You're starting to feel better.

No, I'm starting to feel worse.

Well you're starting to Feel. Period. The derealization and depersonalization kept all emotions at bay. You couldn't feel the positive ones or the negative ones. Now that the feeling valve has been turned on, you're experiencing the negative flood first.

You mean Prozac opened the valve, siphoned oblivion out, and now I'm fucking terrified.

She doesn't say anything.

If this world is real then what the fuck is happening?

THE STUDY OF OBLIVION

sixteen weeks since breakdown

Before I walk into therapy, I decide I will waste today's session, aka I will do anything to not have to talk to my new therapist about feelings because I didn't come here for feelings, I came here so I can finish my manuscript and she really isn't helping. So for thirty minutes, I babble about my plants and how my girlfriend and I repotted a bunch of them last night, then about take-out food and how it's gotten so much worse recently and it's way better to just eat at the restaurant, then about my new sweatpants that already pilled, then about my girlfriend's boss who is a weirdo that makes comments about her bra straps, then about my hatred for bras, but then without realizing it, I've gone through all my preplanned topics so quickly that I've run out of things to talk about. Damn. While I think of something to say, I stare at the collages on my new therapist's walls: the one with the crooked lines and haphazard eyes, the one with the sunflowers in bright blue and neon pink, the one with the penguins. I've never noticed them before. Are they new? No, maybe they were always there, but her pillows were too distracting.

I point to the collages: who made those?

I did, she says.

Oh, you're an artist too.

She laughs and says, of sorts.

Of sorts? I don't know what that means.

On her penguin collage, there's a cluster of bigger penguins on a white diagonal line that I imagine is a cliff of ice. They seem happy over there, all together. At the bottom corner of the painting, below the ice cliff, there's a small penguin who is all alone. It seems wrong that the little penguin isn't with the others. After all, it's just a baby. Then I wonder, is it a baby or is it just a small penguin?

My youngest niece, who is currently obsessed with Baby Shark, has started to call anything of varying sizes Mommy, Daddy, Baby. It could be three pieces of Play-Doh rolled into balls. If two are slightly larger than the other, she'll point to them and in her high-pitched voice say, *Mommy, Daddy, Baby.* I used to do the same thing when I was young, except it wasn't Baby Shark. It was utensils. The fork was always the mother. The knife, the father. The spoon, a baby. I always considered the baby to be me, though I can't remember ever thinking that the fork or knife were my actual parents. But me, I was definitely the spoon. Maybe I felt a kinship with its roundness and curved edges. The way it flipped my face upside down when I looked into it. Maybe I recognized myself in a thing born with the ability (and duty) to hold rather than to puncture or divide. Just cradle the goo and hold steady so you don't spill. Just hold steady. Don't spill.

I wonder if the purpose of my new therapist's collages is for patients to describe what they think they mean, like some projection exercise. Then I wonder if she makes them for that particular reason or if she makes them just because she likes to collage and considers her Upper West Side office to be her gallery. *Then* I wonder if I am paying so much to meet with her in order to keep her gallery open.

Is the lone penguin a sign that I'm supposed to be single?

My new therapist says, Norma, how would you say your anxiety is on a scale of one through ten today?

Three.

Really?

I can feel my new therapist and her black ballet flats and her wooden robot judging me.

Well, maybe eight.

She's more satisfied with this answer.

And depression?

I look at her misplaced textile pillows and feel the familiar urge to run over to them and rearrange them.

Probably a seven.

My new therapist writes my numbers down on her clipboard. At least I assume she does. She may just be doodling.

I add, I've also had my period for twenty days straight.

That's probably from the birth control. Not the Prozac.

Then she asks if I'd like to try a pill that may, possibly, make it easier to orgasm and will also give me energy so I don't have to nap every day at eleven a.m. She says I must take it in the morning, and it may increase my anxiety, but On Such A Low Dose It Shouldn't.

Every time she mentions how low of a dose I'm on, it makes me feel like I'm a lightweight and I want to defend myself like I did when I was twenty-one to all the guys I dated, demanding that in fact, I was not a lightweight. And I would prove it to them. And I did.

And every time I surprised a man, I felt a little more power in my veins. I think all that started when I learned Tay and I could make their jaws drop. (hair flip)

Nowadays I'm sober and boring and my new therapist is surprised that I made this decision two years ago as if I could never have done something so productive for my mental health without her help.

Just so my new therapist doesn't think I'm a saint, I tell her I still smoke and she says, that's okay.

I feel the need to justify myself, as smokers usually do, so I say, I started smoking when I was eighteen because it reminded me of having a pen in my hand.

She almost smiles, uninterested.

But ever since the LEEP (which is also when I stopped drinking), I vape. But the vape still reminds me of a pen. Or a pacifier. Either way it's comforting.

She ignores me and says, would you like to try the Wellbutrin or not?

I hate meds, because I'm spiritual. But I really want to cum again so I say, okay I'll take the sex pill.

She says, it's not a sex pill, and then sends the prescription to the pharmacy.

As I wait for the subway home, I realize I am a rat.

A subway rat running away from arriving trains.

Either that or a lab rat.

Which, I do not know.

But both are simply trying to, against all odds, survive.

Or eat.

THE STUDY OF OBLIVION

seventeen weeks since breakdown

My father has been calling me nonstop.

My new therapist says, oh really?

Yeah. He's bored. My mom is on vacation again.

Does your father know how you're feeling?

I've told him like ten times, but every time I bring up the breakdown I had months ago, he goes, *huh what's wrong? You didn't tell me this.* But I have told him this at least ten times. It's like he erases his memory after every phone call he demands to have with me. So I've stopped telling him and instead have resorted to saying, hi, yes, yes, yes, I miss you too, right, okay, yes, huh interesting, yeah, okay bye. I mean if he forgets every time anyways then what's the point of telling him? I mean my mom remembers. She calls me from whatever tropical place and says, you're doing so great, you're perfectly lovely, but you'll be even better if you moved out of New York City and back home.

Why do you think your parents have a hard time digesting the realities of your mental health?

Probably because it's their fault.

Their fault?

I mean our parents are always to blame. Aren't they?

My new therapist says, I was thinking we could go back to when this episode started?

I say, my second memory is of the world emptying.

No, no. More recently. When you say things got really bad.

Oh, well, I was fine until Memorial Day weekend. My girlfriend and I had just got back from Dragon Island, and we were sitting on the couch with nothing to do. We had been together for a little over a year. She was tickling me. Not those kinds of tickles where you want to punch the other person right in the throat, but the kind that actually feel good. It's a very fine line, but she was perfectly straddling it. And she was straddling me and I was laughing so hard. Then she fell onto my body, took me in her arms, and we lay horizontally on the couch, limbs grasping onto limbs so we wouldn't fall. I tucked my head into her shoulder and everything felt so calm, so good. Without any prior agreement of a midday nap, we fell asleep on the couch this way. I've never done that before. You know, felt so content and silent that I just fell asleep. When I woke up thirty minutes later, she was still sleeping so I just lay there in her arms watching her blood pump through the main artery on the side of her neck, her tanned skin pulsing to the rhythm. I thought about how that same blood had existed inside of her since she was four, five, sixteen, eighteen, twenty-four, twenty-five, thirty. It was the same blood that she had tried, over and over again, to bleed out of herself in high school, wishing that with each letting of her insides, she wouldn't be gay anymore and would make her Muslim parents proud. I lay there watching her blood pump, and I just felt so happy that we were there together. That we had made it past all the shit to be there holding one another and falling asleep accidentally. Everything felt peaceful. Then she woke up. And you wanna know the first thing she said when she woke up? *I have to pee.* She got up from the couch and squirmed to the bathroom, and while she was in there, BAM!!!! Oblivion. By the time she came back, I was saying that we had to break up. Later that day, the signs started showing up.

What do you think happened?

I don't know. And when I say this, I feel the Saran Wrap begin to form like a new skin around my body.

Why Do You Think That Moment, Which Sounds Like You Were *Very* Comfortable And Happy, Scared You?

My parents should have gotten divorced.

What does that have to do with you?

Don't we fall in love with people like our parents? Isn't that what the psychologists say? Or is that *Cosmo* articles? I don't know. But I do know that I'm not like my mother because I don't yell, so I must be my father, which means my girlfriend is my mother, and I can't take two women like that in my life.

My new therapist looks down at her clipboard so she can be silent and not have to look me in the eye, which I think is cowardly. I wonder if she feels like a coward right now or if this is a tactic she learned in psychology school. Maybe she's trying to get me riled up. Maybe that's what her pillows and feet are for too. Maybe it's all part of her plan. What is her plan, anyways?

So what's the plan here?

My new therapist says, what do you mean?

Like . . . do we have an outline?

Huh?

Are we in the middle of our story? The beginning? Close to the end? Where are we headed and how are we going to get there?

She blinks at me. I wonder if they taught her blinking in psychology school too.

I want to Get Better and it's been a while and clearly I'm not Better. So what's the plan?

There's no agenda to our sessions, but do you feel nervous without one?

So we're going the stream-of-consciousness route?

Silence.

Silence.

Silence.

So I say, you know, modernism and postmodernism are over and done with. I think stream of consciousness is pretty outdated. Maybe we can meet in the middle, you know. Millennial meets the Silent Generation.

I'm a boomer.

We finish our session on an awkward note because I just inadvertently and yet very obviously called my new therapist old-looking. And the whole subway ride home I want to die. When I get home and see my girlfriend, I pull my self-loathing together and tell her what happened as if I'm not completely mortified, because I think she'll think it's funny. When I tell her, she laughs, really loudly, so loudly it scares my cat and he rushes into the other room with a bang. Her reaction reminds me of the first time I ever heard her laugh. We hadn't met yet. We were talking on the phone for the first time. The world outside was panicking about the virus, but, listening to her, I was calm. When she laughed through the speaker that night, it took me by complete surprise. Her laugh was deep like the belly of the ocean, raw like an unpolished gemstone, untamed like someone who didn't put cages around their fun. I remember taking a step back. I had been cooking in the kitchen and I just left the fried eggs on the pan to burn. I remember saying, wow I didn't expect your laugh to sound like that. Her voice pounced through the speaker, *WHAT DO YOU MEAN?!?!?* I had never heard someone so animated before. Someone so alive. I laughed and said, I don't know. I just didn't expect it. It's nice. *WHAT DO YOU MEAN NICE?!?!?* With every one of her question-mark-exclamation-marks, I felt myself sink into an unfamiliar feeling. A feeling I can't name but that I can only equate with seeing the sun after a bad drug trip that you couldn't fall asleep from or feeling the sun sinking into your pores the moment you step off an airplane that departed four hours ago from a snowy state. I guess what I mean to say is that she felt like the sun to me. Now she's at the same stove, and she's laughing in a way that reminds me of what it was like back in the beginning, when oblivion was at bay. I'm smiling with her now, but then suddenly she looks straight into my eyes and gets very, very serious and says, oh wait . . . wait . . . that's really fucking awkward. Like really fucking awkward. What are you going to do?

I feel my blood pressure rise.

What do you mean? What am I supposed to do?

I don't know, but you have to do something! You just called her old!

I'm sure other patients have said worse.

I don't think there's anything worse than calling a woman old.

THE STUDY OF OBLIVION

eighteen weeks since breakdown

As soon as I sit down on the armchair, I tell my new therapist that I edited an old short story this week. I start the conversation abruptly so I don't die of embarrassment over calling my new therapist old last week. I practiced doing it with my girlfriend last night and from my vantage point, I'm doing quite well right now. I keep blabbing about the story and how great it felt to edit it.

Sometimes I think I talk for the same reasons that an animal shakes after trauma.

Oh. What was the story about? my new therapist asks.

Not about oblivion.

Okay. Then what?

About rape.

Oh.

I look up "rape" on Goodreads.

The first quote that pops up is from Alice Sebold: You save yourself or you remain unsaved.

I say, and I finally finished Maggie Nelson's new book, *On Freedom*. And all I learned is that writers patiently labor in order to provide liberation (or solace or care) to others.

Writers rip themselves apart to put others back together.

Then I say as if apologetically, I never actually got raped. I write fiction.

Why don't all the quotes on page one of Goodreads contain the word *rape*?

I guess it's not used enough in books.

Or it's not used as much in books as it is in real life.

One of the quotes farther down on the rape page: Oblivion is comfort, but it's still not living. Also by Alice Sebold. Also she doesn't use the word *oblivion*.

Or maybe the rape stuff is censored to keep people from seeing something they don't want to see, but if I'm searching for it, don't I want to see it? Who gets to choose what I see and what I don't? Who is the censor gatekeeper and why can't they filter out racism or homophobia or ignorance instead?

I tell my new therapist that the story probably won't get published and I'll have to edit the rape out.

Why?

Well, it's obvious, isn't it? People don't like to talk about rape. We save it for support groups or social media movements, but never at the kitchen table or on the subway or lounging on the porch or on a family vacation or in bed before you go to sleep.

Keep it out of your mouths and in the streets! I joke.

She doesn't laugh.

Does a book develop consciousness in the same way that AI could?

Actually, I say, Eimear McBride wrote an awesome book, which mostly contains rape and dying. And its form is highly fragmented. And it actually did quite well. But it took her ten years to find a UK publisher. And American publishers were super hesitant to publish McBride's book even after it won a thousand awards in the UK. THAT'S how much America doesn't like to talk about rape and incest.

Incest?

Anyways even with these new sex pills, I have no sex drive whatsoever, and I keep rejecting my girlfriend and I'm pretty sure she's going to cheat on me if I don't give her a little sumpin' sumpin' soon.

My new therapist doesn't even smile.

Why do you think your girlfriend will cheat on you?

Because if you're not fucking, you're not fucking. Right? Now that we're on the topic of my girlfriend, my girlfriend and I were watching a movie on the couch last night. This happened after we practiced for today.

Practiced what for today?

Never mind. Thirty minutes into the movie, I guessed how the whole plot would unfold. My girlfriend said, *no way.* At the end of the movie, I was right, and she looked at me and said, *You're the worst person to watch movies with.* And then she got up from the couch and went to get an ice cream bar out of the freezer. Why? *Because you always ruin the movie. You always guess what will happen.* Well, I guess it because it's obvious. They introduced that friend at the beginning of the movie. It had to be for a reason, so obviously he was the killer. *Well, it wasn't obvious to me. Next time just don't tell me.* And then she walked into the bedroom. I assumed then that *I* had to feed the cat dinner. As the smell of canned cat food penetrated my nostrils, I thought: it's not my fault that plots are so predictable.

So now my girlfriend likes traditional novels and traditional movie plots, so I think we have to break up.

It's okay for couples to argue sometimes and it's certainly okay for couples to have different interests. You know that, right?

But if she likes that type of story, she'll never like mine.

But she *does* like your writing, from what you've told me?

Sure, but that's just because she hasn't seen the new crazy story. And I haven't written The Last Story. She's waiting for it to all wrap up neatly and I don't think it will. But who knows, maybe it will and then the whole thing may be so clear-cut and not worth anyone's time to read it. But, actually, most people are the type to go along for the ride, like she did with that movie even though it was obvious the whole time. She didn't even want to see what was happening. If she did early on, like she could have, it wouldn't be fun anymore. And speaking of, don't you think it's a little odd that our culture loves to watch serial killer movies and rapist thrillers. And I mean there's a whole *Law & Order* series that's been on since 1999 that every week focuses on sexual crimes. Shouldn't it be surprising that women watch these things? Shouldn't it be retraumatizing us? Or is it just desensitizing us? Don't you think there's a little fetish going on? My girlfriend loves those shows. We have to break up.

Silence.

Silence.

Silence.

I think my new therapist is over me, like I'm the worst person to have therapy with, but still, I can't stop talking.

And I've been trying to write The Last Story every day. And every day, my girlfriend comes home from work, gives me a kiss, and interrupts my whole flow.

You have a flow going?

Well, no. But if she stayed at work, maybe I would.

Silence.

Do you want to leave her?

Well if I don't, I may cheat on her.

My new therapist looks like I'm giving her whiplash.

Why do you think you'll cheat on her?

Because I like women and she's the first woman I've ever dated and what if I can't control myself?

Can't control yourself?

Yeah. Like a pussy grabber.

I thought you were worried that you weren't gay? Or that *she* would cheat on *you?*

Now I'm worried that I'm going to cheat on her. It's all I can think about.

This sounds like your anxiety talking again. Why do you think you keep coming up with new reasons to break up with your girlfriend?

I think, IT'S A SIGN! OBVIOUSLY!

I say, I don't know.

She says, maybe it's because you're scared of intimacy. What examples of love did you have growing up?

I say, idk.

I actually say idk. Not I don't know.

Look, I really need you to help me finish my manuscript. The agent emailed me again asking for it.

Why don't you just send her what you have?

Because right now there's no through line. There's no meaning behind it.

You seem very concerned with your manuscript having a meaning.

Shouldn't we all be concerned with our work having meaning?

She cocks her head to the side. That's when I realize she doesn't have any water next to her. Or coffee. Or any sort of cup with any sort of liquid. I wonder if she's thirsty.

Suddenly I hear myself blurt out:

Can I sit on the couch?

She looks at the tan couch and says, during an ordinary time you could, but because of Covid the couch is too close to my armchair. These are precautionary measures.

Oh.

From her remote island of an armchair, she asks, what does the word *meaning* mean to you?

Well I guess, in my head, meaning is kind of like a reason. Like if you know something's meaning, there's a reason it exists. But it's more than just a reason, it's a good reason. Kind of like value.

I look up at the ceiling for a second to help me think.

Why does this help people think?

Yeah, meaning is a reason that has some value to you. Like love or hope.

I'm not sure that I'm following?

How does she not know if she is or isn't following? I'm really starting to think my new therapist is dumb.

I try to explain: If I come to you and I say oblivion is taking over. And I tell you that it started on the couch, and you say the reason it started is that *you have glitchy serotonin from significant trauma and therefore you're chronically depressed and dissociated, always have been and always will be.* You gave me a reason, but it's not a reason with any value to me.

I scratch my jawline, because it's itchy. I can feel my acne breakouts on my fingertips.

But if I said oblivion is taking over and that happened when she asked me to marry her, and if you said, *the reason for that is because you have glitchy serotonin from significant trauma involving relationships and so it makes sense that it was set off when she asked you to marry her and your current journey with me is your spiritual journey back to trusting relationships,* then there's not just a reason for my current state, but there's a *meaning* behind what I'm going through and every single thing that led up to my current state, which is altogether shitty and hopeless without any fucking meaning.

I wonder how my girlfriend still thinks I'm beautiful with all these hormonal pimples.

I don't see the difference between the two scenarios you just offered.

Well one is chronic and unfixable. The other, once I know the narrative, is under my control. I can make it better. I can change the future. It's all part of *the journey.*

What does that have to do with hope?

ARE YOU FUCKING KIDDING ME?!?

Holy.

Shit.

I slap my hands over my mouth and my eyes get really big.

That was supposed to be in my head, but the words land in the room with a thud that shakes the foundation of her office. Will this old war building crumble? Will it take Central Park down with it?

Norma?

Yes, I say, muffled, from under my hands.

Are you okay?

Mm-hmmmmmmmmmmmm.

I stare at her robot so I don't have to look her in the eye. Next to the robot, on the bookshelf, is the *DSM-5*.

Silence.

Silence.

Silence.

Does your fascination with the number seven have anything to do with what you're trying to explain about meaning?

Dear oblivion, please wipe away the past three minutes. I beg you with whatever soul and life I have left in me. In the name of Oblivion, Amen.

I unbind my mouth, hoping I've tamed it with lack of oxygen.

The number seven shows up to say I'm being guided by god in whatever I'm doing at that moment. It's kind of like 11:11 to normal people. So yeah, I guess the number seven gives meaning to whatever action I'm doing at that moment.

But why seven?

I've loved it since I was little, since before I knew it was a special number.

A special number?

You don't know the number seven?

I say this as if she's just said, I've never heard of New York City, or, What's the Bible? Or, Who is the Muffin Man?

My new therapist shakes her head reluctantly, which means she has full awareness that I'm about to go on another rant and she really doesn't want me to.

The number seven......I say longingly. Well, there are seven continents, seven days of the week, seven wonders of the world, seven colors in a rainbow, seven chakras, seven stages of grief, seven celestial bodies visible to the naked eye on earth (Mercury, Venus, Mars, Jupiter, Saturn, the sun, and the moon), seven books in the Harry Potter series (even though Rowling is CANCELED), seven deadly sins, seven virtues, Jesus's seven last words on the cross.

What were Jesus's last words?

Oh I have no idea, but my girlfriend told me that even in Islam, there are seven hells and seven heavens (for each door to hell there is another door to heaven). But mainly, I like the number because seven is the number that symbolizes the world between life and death, which reminds me of oblivion.

Right.

Also there's something called the seven-year itch, which is why I know my girlfriend and I will eventually break up even if it's not right now. So why not just get it over with? The seven-year itch is also why I don't name most of my characters.

What do you mean?

In my manuscript, I don't name any characters that haven't been in my life for more than seven years in at least a supporting character role.

And why is that?

I already explained. Because I may get the seven-year itch. I don't like naming anyone if I don't know for certain that they're going to be there at the very end of my story.

So if someone is in your life for seven years then you feel some certainty in knowing they will be in your life forever. And all of this is because of The Seven Year Itch, which is Just A Theory?

If she wasn't a therapist, I'm certain my new therapist would have said, *and you believe all of this because of the seven-year itch, which is just a stupid fucking theory, are you for real? Like for real for real?*

Yuhhhhhh.

Well, do you name yourself in your manuscript?

I go by a different name.

And is that because you're worried that you won't be there by the end either?

She's trying to be smart with me, and I don't like it. So I say sassily back,

No. I actually have a name. It's just a different one.

Why?

Safety reasons.

Silence.

Silence.

Silence.

But I gave myself a name that is so obviously fake. So anyone reading the manuscript will know it's fictional. Just like everything else in my manuscript.

You want them to think it's fake?

Yes. Because nothing is real, remember? Well, it's more real now because of the blue pill you gave me.

Your Prozac isn't blue.

It's a *Matrix* reference.

Oh.

Anyways, all of this is a waste of time, I just need to know what to write for The Last Story. And I think I'm struggling with The Last Story because that story can't come from memory like the other ones. It's all about the future and I don't know what the future will look like or feel like or even what it will sound like.

And she says,

Okay, well maybe you can reread all your old stories. You may find a through line that helps show you what The Last Story needs to be.

Ehhhhh, that sounds like a lot of reading. I don't like to read, remember?

Do you think it would be useful for our work if you share more of your stories with me?

This is "work"? Does that mean I have a job now? If so, why am I not getting paid and, instead, am paying her?

I say, useful like value?

But she ignores me and says, what story comes after "Home"?

"American Love."

Please send that before the weekend so I have time to read it.

My new therapist looks so pleased with herself and it annoys me. I stare at her orange ballet flats that are lounging on the footrest like always. I've never realized how small her feet are. They're like elf feet if elves were real. Are they? After seeing her tiny feet, I wonder how tall my new therapist is. I look at her outstretched legs and try to measure. Oh, I'm definitely taller than her. Much taller. Maybe that's why she never stands up. She doesn't want me to feel dominant. Women are always so competitive with each other. If it was ladylike to fistfight, I wonder if this story would turn into *Fight Club 2* instead of "which ballet flats will my new therapist wear today" and "will she ever put her feet on the ground." Of course, in the *Fight Club* scenario, I'd be Brad Pitt.

American Love

At the start of eighth grade, boys at school had started to like me. During recess, they said that if God put me and this girl Tay together, her boobs and my butt, we would be the perfect girl. Tay and I had been rivals since the day we met in fourth grade. I'm not sure how we became enemies: maybe it began by us competing for a solo in the school choir or one of us having cooler DC sneakers. I really don't know, but after that day, at the start of eighth grade, Tay and I became best friends, as if we were bonded by the makeshift woman the guys made up in their minds. All school year, Tay raved about her white-shuttered summer house on Cape Cod: how there we didn't need adults to drive us anywhere; all we needed were our bikes, how last summer she met two local boys through a neighbor: one for her and one for me. And so in my last year of middle school, I went directly from playing Barbies to kissing boys behind the trees at recess. Tay said it was all practice for the Cape, as if real life didn't start until we reached the tip of Massachusetts.

In June, the weekend after school got out, Tay's mom and dad drove us out to their Cape house. Tay was right about everything: the firepits, the bikes, the boys. That summer, every other weekend, she said, we would come to the Cape. We would become women. After all, we were going to high school next year. I was excited. Not just because of Tay's plan, but because I liked being around her family. Their house was new and didn't creak. Her parents let us hang out in Tay's room that had posters plastered on the walls, and they never shouted, only discussed in hushed tones. I remember the first time I saw them do this. I said to Tay:

Are they not yelling just because I'm here?

Yell? No, they never yell. They just do this, like all the time.

My mind couldn't make sense of it. It was like I was visiting a for-eign country on the other side of the world, where gravity worked upside down. In the midst of confusion, I decided I would, when I grew up, be like them, like Tay's parents.

This is going to be the best summer of our lives.

Tay promised, and, sitting by the firepit, smoke blowing into my hair, I believed her.

_____

Dear Diary,
Never start a story with fire.
It will burn itself to the ground.

_____

The first weekend of July, Tay woke me up in the middle of the night. She still smelled like sunscreen from our beach outing earlier. Tay whispered:

Come with me.

I got out of bed in my Fall Out Boy T-shirt and followed Tay out of her room, tiptoeing down into the kitchen. Her mom wasn't there that weekend, so there were fewer people to worry about waking when Tay emptied a full water bottle into the sink and then opened the last cabinet on the right-hand side of the kitchen.

If you just take a little from each one, they don't notice.

_____

My father could fix anything: the leaking sink, the testy garage door, the lopsided desk. He was always running around the house fixing whatever needed his hands for a moment. My sister and I sat at the wooden kitchen table and watched him repair the broken parts of our home. When the list of what needed fixing ran out, he fixed the things that didn't need to be touched. He took the TV and got a new high-tech remote. He took the kitchen chairs and put sturdier, taller legs on them. He took the thermometer and programmed specific temperatures that coordinated with the levels of the sun. My sister and I were exhausted by the way he ran around from room to room fixing and tweaking our surroundings. My mother was unbothered. She said:

This is why he's a great doctor, so good at his job.

———

Tay never told me all the details, and I didn't ask. It was, probably, our fifth firepit that summer. Our fifth round of s'mores. I'm making this number up, because, honestly, after our late nights in the kitchen, everything started to blur together: blur into sand and fire igniters and new contacts in our phone labeled by the beach we had met the boys at. Never their names. Just the beach. Tay's dad was inside in the kitchen. Tay kept watch as I pulled the water bottle out of my pink backpack, a bag that, I had explained to her father, I needed to keep with me at all times because I had my period. Somehow, I always had my period when I spent the weekend with them. Her father was powerless against the lie. Tay took a sip of our favorite brown concoction and told me that her dad and some blond woman had become coworkers a few months ago, and like all men, Tay explained, her dad liked cars. He liked trading in one for another. When I responded, saying:

But they don't even yell at each other.

All I could think was how Tay's car metaphor didn't sound like something she would say. It sounded like something her mom would.

I don't know. Maybe yelling keeps the passion alive.

———

When my mother picked me up from Tay's that weekend, I told her what had happened. With her eyes glued to the road as if in a trance, she started to rant about how in some countries, people didn't care about the seemingly greener grass on the other side, because everyone was too busy trying to keep their own grass away from the government.

What do you mean?

My father didn't cheat on my mother until we came here.

She said there was something about America. Something in the air or the water or the land. In America, she said, it was like there were too many binoculars and too many people who had too much time to waste, and so they stared at their neighbors, waiting to be entertained. Plus, homeowners weren't building fences anymore, because Americans didn't care about privacy, didn't care to keep others out. In fact, they wanted them to come in. As if she could hear my thoughts, or as if we had the same ones brewing, my mother said:

Your dad would never do something like that. He may have come to America before me, but he's still not American.

But neither was your dad, I wanted to say, he wasn't American either. But then my mother said:

Besides, I would never let that happen.

———

It was our last weekend at the Cape before high school started when I fell off my plastic chair near the firepit. I was laughing so hard the whole chair flipped backward. My body lay in a heap on the grass, the moon shining on my summer skin. Earlier that day, Tay and I had ridden our bikes to the beach. We never usually drank during the day, but Tay was adamant about it that weekend. This time we both had water bottles. Hers was brown. Mine was clear. We learned our parents liked different alcohol, but we liked both, so we took turns sipping each other's. When an hour had passed, both water bottles were clear as air. Tay approached two guys who were oiled in the sun. They were seventeen and going off to college in a few weeks. We didn't even bother lying about our age. They didn't care anyways. When I hopped back on my bike under the Cape Cod sun, sweat and salt lay on my cheeks like a new layer of skin.

By the time we reached Tay's driveway, I could barely see. Tay said that's how it was supposed to feel. We showered together in our bathing suits and took pictures on our flip phones. Tay sent one to the guys we had just met: one of her, then one of me, and then one of us together. As I got changed for dinner, Tay was looking out the window with a haze over her slow-blinking eyes.

Your dad's gonna know we're drunk.

I don't care.

I pulled on a pair of Tay's jeans. Tay yelped and quickly ducked under the window as if a war had just broken out and bullets were coming through the glass.

What are you doing?!

She's here. She's here.

I walked to the window, and Tay yanked me down to the floor with her. We peeked our heads slowly over the windowsill, and that's when we saw the blue Honda. The blond hair.

That's her.

Tay whispered. Not to me. But to something. Maybe to the Cape house.

Later that night when I fell off my chair in the backyard, we laughed so hard that Tay's older brother stuck his head out of his bedroom window and told us to shut up. Tay said:

Fuck you!

But really we meant fuck that summer and that Massachusetts house. After she screamed "Fuck you" once, she wouldn't stop screaming it, which made me laugh even more, which made Tay laugh even more. I had a cramp in my head, but we liked it best when it felt that way. When Tay's dad came outside with marshmallows and graham crackers, he looked at Tay and said:

Too bad you couldn't show this fun side to our guest tonight.

Tay stopped laughing and grabbed the bag of marshmallows from her dad's ringless hands, tearing the plastic open, just as she had torn into the bread at dinner and then into the blond woman:

Why are you even here? You know, we—

Tay pointed to herself and then to me.

—don't even want you here. You should just leave.

The rest of the night, to the smell of mosquito repellant and burning wood, I toasted sugar that stuck to my fingers, while Tay tried to forget that for the first summer in her life and for the rest of her life, she no longer had a mom and dad.

Now, Tay had a mom, and Tay had a dad.

————

Dear Diary,
Fire itself is not loud. It does not make sound.
What makes sound are the things torn apart by fire.

———

By the following summer, Tay's dad was engaged to the blond. So instead of Tay's beach house, we went to mine in the Hamptons. My parents had bought the ocean-view summer house a few months before. Somehow even with the ocean tempting us, the beach house was quieter. Less screaming. Less door slamming. No creaks. No footsteps. It was carpeted. Something about the house made me feel like we, my family, had evolved to that place where gravity worked the wrong way, though perhaps the right way. Like the house was not only a place, but a home.

My mother knew that nothing she approved of happened on the beach after the sun set and the sand went cold, but she let us go to the water anyway. At sometime past midnight, Tay and I would grab our backpacks and head toward the sliding door. My mom would shout from upstairs:

Don't let the bugs in. Don't leave fingerprints on the glass. Lock the door behind you!

It was all old news. And the way we ran up that sandy hill, old habit. It was dark as space as we reached the peak and began to hear the crashing waves.

When Tay and I finally reached the water, we'd lay a towel down and sit side by side, facing the black ocean. We'd listen to the sound of water collapsing onto the sand while the backs of our oversized hoodies stared at the porch-lit houses past the sand dunes. To warm our tanned skin in the chilly summer nights, we'd pull our sleeves down past our wrists and rub our legs. We stayed this way, listening and warming, until our water bottle was empty, until we had no remaining secrets to empty into the restless waves.

Before heading back over the sand dune toward my white-shuttered house, we'd walk up to the edge of the waves and let the frigid Atlantic numb our toes.

———

I was visiting a college in Syracuse with Tay when I first found out about my father. We were at a Mexican restaurant drinking margaritas and smelling of stale smoke from cigarettes, which Tay had convinced me to try. Tay raised her glass:

Bottoms up to getting the fuck out of Connecticut.

Like she always had, Tay made me laugh. When my mother called me again an hour later, I was already three drinks in. My mother's voice boomed through the phone.

Your dad is a fucking liar. I always told you he was a fucking liar.

She said this as if I was the one responsible for him being my father, for him being her husband. I tried to keep up as my mother recounted the details: a woman a little older than me, caught by an email exchange, how long it had been going on for. I sat there listening, one ear to the blaring mariachi music and the other to my mother's voice giving me a play-by-play of my father's infidelity.

Wait what'd you say?

I pinched my ear and listed closer to the crackling of the speaker:

I said, he brought her to the Hamptons house.

In the middle of the Mexican restaurant, far away from the ocean, my stomach plummeted into my intestines. My veins wrapped tightly around my lungs, while my heart twisted in my chest, pushing outward against my rib cage. The phone slipped from my hands and landed under the wooden table, and I fell to the ground, hyperventilating. Tay rushed to my side and tried to calm me, but I couldn't stop the feeling of drowning; saltwater suffocating my esophagus, sand burying me. Panicking, Tay said that she was going to call an ambulance. I grabbed her by the arm and, gasping for air, I said:

I can feel my heart breaking. God! It's breaking!

———

I don't know if my heart broke that day or if I drowned, the current of the Atlantic finally bringing me to my knees. I don't know if there's even a difference. All I know is that the doctor was too busy giving excuses to revive me: something about a thirty-year-old patient at the hospital being broken, poor, needing to be fixed. My mom screamed:

A patient. You fucking pig!

When I got back from Syracuse, the first thing I asked my father was why he did it. When I said "it," I didn't mean why he cheated but why he brought her to *that* house, instead of this one that creaked. My father responded:

A home is made of happy memories. A house is made of every memory.

It didn't make sense to me, so I responded in the way Tay taught me to:

Fuck you. Fuck you, Dad.

I thought, like Tay's parents, my father would sleep at the beach house that night, banished alone for eternity. But that night he was back in the same bedroom as my mother. She said that she didn't trust him so she needed him close. My sister agreed, but I didn't understand it.

Every night that fall, I could hear my mother crying from my room; she would be yelling not at my father, but at God. I listened for God's response, but all I ever heard was the sound of my father watching TV downstairs. I took another swig from my water bottle, lay on top of my covers, stared into the light, and made my thoughts go blind.

One November night, my phone rang. I picked up:

Thank god, it's you.

My mom's moving.

Moving where?

Tay was slurring her words. I was slurring my words. When she said:

Florida. And my dad's gunna live at the Cape with the blond.

My eardrums fogged:

What about you? It's the middle of the school year!

I don't fucking know. I. Don't. Fucking. Know.

———

They tried. No, my mother, with her loud voice, tried. She tried while my father kept scanning the house for things that needed fixing. He couldn't comprehend that the problem at hand couldn't be found in metal pipes or woodwork, couldn't be fixed with his toolbox or his scalpel or his mind. Every time he spoke, I imagined him breathing into the other woman's neck; every time I stepped into our house by the sea, I pictured him walking that woman up the stairs, opening the sliding door for her, and letting her sleep in between the sheets that my mother had chosen. My father was a problem solver. He could fix everything except his marriage.

It was a Thursday night in March. Tay was in Miami, living in an apartment with her mother. My mother had just sold the Hamptons house to newlyweds. Earlier that day, as I packed my bathing suits into cardboard boxes, I thought I heard the beach house creak. Later, staring at my old teddy bear, I lay, breathing, on my bed in Connecticut with all the lights on. From the corner of my eye, I could see my school notebooks popping out of my pink backpack. If I breathed carefully enough, in through the nose, out and up through the mouth, I could inhale the whiskey-vodka mix on my breath. And if I breathed loud enough, I couldn't hear my mother crying or the TV downstairs. I lay there oscillating between the two methods of breathing.

As the clock was about to strike midnight, announcing my eighteenth birthday, I looked up at the ceiling and saw a fly stuck in my chandelier. The bug was panicking, hitting the frosty boundary over and over again, trying to get out. It banged and banged its body against the glass until finally, right before the clock hit 12:00 a.m., the fly escaped through a narrow crack and flew into the room.

Two days later, I got my college acceptance letters and Tay still hadn't texted me "happy birthday."

Almost a year after my heart broke, I packed my things, got on the train, and moved into a dorm room the size of my parents' bathroom in Connecticut. On a cold fall afternoon, I stood on an East Village rooftop where a fraternity was throwing a Welcome to New York party. Standing away from the crowd with a Four Loko and cigarette in my hand, I looked down from the roof into the neighbor's backyard. A child's bike. Metal chairs. A stone walkway. A firepit that reminded me of how much I missed the sound of the ocean. It was odd for me: to see into a neighbor's yard without glass in between, with a bird's-eye view. I thought, this is how God feels, but I didn't know if God really felt anything. I thought maybe He was unfazed by the things that we did to one another; He just watched us from above with a blank stare. Or maybe, more probably, I thought, He had stopped watching us altogether. Like maybe, God was too busy looking out His own white-shuttered window at a neighbor's world.

Still staring at the unlit firepit, I started to hum my favorite song, but I hated the sound that reached my ears. How can something feel so good at its moment of release and so awful when it returns? I threw my cigarette off the roof and watched it fall twenty stories down to the neighbor's yard. And then I did what I hadn't done since I was a little girl. I began to pray. I prayed for all the flies in the world. For all the wood and the marshmallows. For each wave and grain of sand that crashes against the shoreline. And of course, for all the fences: that they may be taller than ever and unscalable. Then I prayed for God; I prayed that He would turn away from the window and look into the home that He had created. When I finished praying, I heard the words in my head:

> If a body meets a body in thick air like summer, how long does it take for the flashbacks to begin? A week? A year? Is it enough time for the comedown to finally come down? And in that thick air if I see a glimmer on my eyelash, like a nucleus or an amoeba, will I return to a time that I wish I knew now?

I took a deep breath. With the city's air penetrating my nostrils, I waited for an answer to the cryptic questions, but nothing came to mind: nothing except the smell of Cape Cod that summer, hitting me just as intensely as it had that June afternoon when I stepped out of the car and looked at Tay's beach house for the first time. At first glance, I remember never wanting to leave, never wanting to smell anything except the Atlantic Ocean ever again. But by the end of that summer, Cape Cod looked and smelled a little differently, a little bit more like a bottle of alcohol violently crashing into a fire. That summer, I learned that love, like a fire, always burns out. Sometimes you can't even get it started. Sometimes the wood burns long after you've gone to sleep. Or the worst: it fizzles away right in the middle of the night, when you're hungry for your next marshmallow.

Girls started squealing on the roof, and I realized it was beginning to rain. As all the frat boys scrambled to keep the girls from going home, I knew that it was time to leave a lifetime of summer secrets there amongst the buildings, far away from where they were created. The ocean, even with its come-and-go waves, never managed to take the heartbreak away. I hoped that maybe this concrete place could. I looked up toward the leaking sky, the sky that my father probably could have fixed. And then I left the party and walked back to my dorm.

———

Dear Diary,

Fire began and then fire ended. Fire burns to an end eventually but always, and fire and water can't mix (I tried to tell you this from the start). Fire's leftovers, the ash, came here long ago. It descended from the heavens. Circulating in the sky, the ash first settled on airplanes. From the planes' wings, it sprinkled onto the clouds. Rain cradled it in droplets that landed on black and brown roofs. We didn't even know it was there. Ash hid in kitchen cabinets and king-sized beds that were scapegoats for bodies that didn't work: for bad love. It clustered in the corners of white rooms. It turned to clutter, and we mistook it for dust.

But where did it come from?

Ash came from gold, from white, from wood and metal. From tears, excuses, and so-called forgiveness. From a too-friendly neighbor or coworker or patient and a formidable doorway. From wet grass, sandy surfaces, and a sliding door that creaked from the salty air. Ash came not from lack of faith, but from a lack of understanding. From an ill-equipped toolbox and hands that felt the need to keep busy. From mouths that either screamed or moaned but never both at the same time. It came from white-shuttered windows, make-believe, and a man-made hell.

Ash came from love. At least that's what they called it.

SEPTEMBER

I am stuffing your mouth with your
promises and watching
you vomit them out upon my face.

Anne Sexton

THE STUDY OF OBLIVION

nineteen weeks since breakdown

FUCKING FUCK JOE BIDEN.

Why?

You know why! I say viciously to my new therapist as if she is, in fact, Joe Biden in the flesh...wearing green ballet flats.

She sits there so still and blank, like a mannequin in a Chico's store.

Afghanistan?! Hello?! All those children?! Killed with a fucking drone? Biden lied about it. Put his hands up in a shrug and was like IDK HOW THAT HAPPENED, NOT ME. And now my girlfriend is crying, because her family is from there. I told you that before, right? Or did I just say she was Muslim? She's Muslim AND Afghan, which means people fucking hated her in middle school and called her a terrorist. And now I'm trying to console her, but I'm also trying to finish my manuscript. But I've done little writing. Just thinking and thinking and thinking.

I'm walking down six flights of stairs right now, leaving the writers' workshop I recently signed up for so I can finish my manuscript and prove to you that I'm getting outside and living a real life even though I can't go back to my old job, because they let me go and I completely get it. When they called me this week to fire me, I just said, perfect, thank you, thank you so much, you're amazing, so amazing. And, thirty minutes ago, the facilitator of the writing workshop who wrote a best-selling novel was commenting on the new crazy story I'm writing, not The Last Story, and she said, *don't leave the reader guessing or confused for too long, because they'll get bored.* She also mentioned that I'm going to have to *severely edit* the story. Severely. Then a woman in the writing workshop said my character sounds too ill to have a girlfriend so the "story" (yes she put it in quotes) felt not believable. I think she used the words *too mentally unwell*, and I almost laughed out loud, but then I didn't, because it's not funny, and maybe I am too mentally unwell to be in a relationship. And maybe this world is too mentally unwell to have a god because we just fucking killed kids in Afghanistan, a country the United States promised to keep safe after we fucked it up back in the '70s when we jacked up the Taliban with machine guns and told them to kill the Soviets. So they killed the Soviets like we wanted and then took over Afghanistan. So then we went back into Afghanistan with our big guns and machinery, saying we were going to save the poor Afghan people this time. Isn't that the most American thing you've ever heard? And I can't even break up with my girlfriend anymore, because I promised her I would stop after I told her what you said.

Oh, and what did I say?

I want to punch my new therapist, but instead I say,

That oblivion wasn't her fault after all. That there are no signs. That this breakdown has nothing to do with her.

What did she say to that?

She started crying. Then she asked me to please stop trying to break up with her. Actually I think she said "leave" her.

And what did you say?

I told her I would stop.

That's progress.

Then my girlfriend promised she would stay by my side even though things are really hard for me right now. And to be honest at that point, I really wanted to run out of the park and back to our apartment and change the locks.

My new therapist looks down at her clipboard and says, oh? Her promise scared you?

And when she finishes the question she looks up at me with what are supposed to be doe eyes but are actually therapy eyes, which means she's trying to, with her question, ignite a certain part of my psyche that tells me my thought process is flawed.

This look makes me miss my old therapist. Then again I think of our last session when oblivion had just started to fully take over. He said, *oblivion is your connection to the divine.* Twenty minutes later, he and his beard told me, *you're losing your curves from the stress,* and then he too eagerly asked, *are you and your girlfriend having sex?* and then I vomited on his carpet.

So I say to my new therapist, I just didn't like it. Anyways, now that I know oblivion isn't her fault, I've got to take my girlfriend out of the narrative.

What do you mean?

Like she's not a main character in the story anymore. So I've got to bring in another character instead.

You're scratching your eyes again. Are you feeling anxious from this conversation?

The anxiety could be from that. Or it's my lack of writing. Or it's this new cum medicine that you gave me. Or it's walking down these stairs and simultaneously typing. But I did stop taking my birth control and I have a sex drive again so maybe I'm not totally mentally unwell. My girlfriend and I had amazing sex three days ago. Her hands felt so good on my skin that I thought I would cry.

Did you consult your gynecologist about getting off the birth control?

Of course not. I've been stuck in this writers' workshop.

Norma?

Yeah.

Do you feel present today?

What?

I just want to know if you're present here right now. That way I can gauge if what we're talking about is actually going to stick.

What were we talking about again?

About the fact that you slept with so many men despite knowing you were attracted to women for most of your life. I asked you why you did this and then you started talking about Joe Biden.

In undergrad, a professor once asked me: how does your perception of an artist change when you learn new information?

Well, I didn't sleep with all the guys. Well, actually, I slept with all of them except the infinite man.

I'm just trying to understand why you dated men if you knew you were interested in women?

I don't know.

In the same class, the professor said, the story wants to get rid of you as much as you want to get rid of the story.

And when I heard this and whenever I think of this, I see a red apple in my palm.

Then a red apple on a tree.

Then a red apple falling from the tree.

Why the apple is in my palm first, I don't know.

Perhaps it's because my palms are on the keyboard right now.

You know, my dad's mom, my grandmother from the "Home" story, she committed suicide, jumped off a bridge. Apparently she had a mental disorder.

My new therapist says, you didn't tell me mental illness ran in your family?

It doesn't. It jumps.

As if someone told *me* the joke, I start hysterically laughing, slapping the side of the armchair that I am a prisoner to. I laugh so hard I snort. Once. Then twice. I pinch my nose to stop another one from escaping.

My new therapist is not laughing with me. She's probably not allowed to.

I try to contain myself, sighing and saying, well anyways...

My new therapist just stares at me blankly.

I say, still chuckling, yeah so...she killed herself like a month after immigrating to America.

And then I dissociate like a motherfucker.

THE STUDY OF OBLIVION

twenty weeks since breakdown

I still can't fall asleep. I lie in bed and listen to my girlfriend snoring. She's been sleep-talking lately. Last night she said *oh yes baby yes. the country.* I tried to imagine the context of this phrase in her dreamland. Perhaps she was running for president or was an anchorwoman for Fox News. Or maybe she was just reading my manuscript. Anyways she woke up this morning saying she remembered orgasming in her dream. At the start, I didn't take too much offense to this since we've had sex only three times since my breakdown and one time doesn't even count, because we just dry humped on the couch. But then I got to thinking, did I give her the orgasm in her dream? Was she having group sex? Was someone peeing on her? Does she have a fantasy that I don't know about? So then I asked her what her dream was about, and she said she couldn't remember. Yeah right. I think she lied. Because of this, I didn't tell her what I heard in the middle of the night. It's a very personal thing, hearing someone's dream speech. It's like listening to a world that exists on the other side of a wall.

My new therapist says, your bedroom was next to your parents' bedroom, correct?

Why do you insist on making everything psychological?

Of course my new therapist doesn't answer. She never answers my questions. So I continue,

It's like scientists whose reasons for everything are biological. Or economists whose reasons for everything are economical. No…wait… that's not the right word….

I stutter trying to find the right word and then she goes…

Before, didn't you, as a spiritual person, have a spiritual reason for everything?

My jaw drops. Well at least it does in my mind. Sometimes I forget she has a sassy side too.

My new therapist asks if my manuscript has a title yet.

I say, yeah, it's called please stop trying to leave me.

She asks why I chose that name.

I say, well it was a tie between please stop trying to leave me, please shut the fuck up, please put a lock on my door, please please please do anything except what you're doing, please help someone please fucking help. I decided the first option was the least aggressive and the least desperate, and no one likes aggressive or desperate women.

But why did you choose that name?

I don't know.

You don't know?

I mean I could probably find a spiritual reason for it, but I'm not allowed to do that anymore.

Silence.

Silence.

Silence.

You know once upon a time I wasn't spiritual. I was an atheist.

Oh really?

Yeah, I'll send you that story next.

My new therapist smiles insincerely and says, great, and well, we're out of time. See you Friday?

I want to say, see you never. But instead I nod and gather my leather jacket and purse from the carpeted floor. As I place my purse around my shoulder, the strap falls down and the whole bag bumps against the chair. The impact makes my jacket do a little jump and my ChapStick falls out of my jacket pocket. I lean over and pick up the ChapStick from the floor, but when I do this my purse goes upside down, and of course it's not zipped. My phone falls out of it and lands right side up on the carpet and the screen goes bright. Four missed calls from my mother, which makes my heart drop into my stomach, which makes me drop my ChapStick for a second time. Then I have to pick up my phone and my ChapStick, and I can tell, even though I'm staring at the floor, that my new therapist is staring at me, waiting impatiently as if she's holding in a fart and cannot let it out until I get out of her office. I put my phone and ChapStick in my purse, zip it up like I should have in the first place, and swing my jacket around my arm. I hold my purse to my chest like a shield, and I quickly shuffle out of her office with my head bowed like a monk or an altar boy, and as I do this, I mutter I'm sorry excuse me excuse me sorry. And I mutter this with such a whispered urgency like we're in a movie theater and my cell phone just rang during the most intense scene, and to leave the theater and shut off my stupid iPhone, I have to scoot by this stranger with a bag of popcorn. And as I walk out of my new therapist's office and onto Central Park West, feeling the hot fall air hit my skin, I really don't know why I exited like that. And I really don't know why my head is still bowed down as if I'm praying or ashamed of something and that something is me and my ChapStick and my phone and my mind and my whole entire fucking existence.

Philosophy

Before meeting the infinite man, I was a freshman philosophy major at NYU. I was determined to explore the way an experience feels through the senses; the way one interprets life despite life's reality; the discrepancy, one could say, between truth and delusion. On a warm October night during my first semester, my roommate convinced me to go to a party with her in Alphabet City. She dressed me in a high-waisted leopard miniskirt that horribly contrasted with my olive skin and brought me to a rectangular loft that held bodies compactly together. Sweating amongst strangers, all I wanted was to be back in my dorm room or on the beach drinking with Tay.

I scanned the room for an exit, but that's when I saw him. His leather jacket. His pointy eyebrows like the tops of arrows. His concave cheeks bordered by feminine cheekbones that jutted out across his dark brown skin. He was tall, taller than everyone else there, and he towered over the crowd. As if by some supernatural force, the man began to scale past the crowd of people and migrate toward me, his eyes locked onto mine. The closer he came, the harder my heart beat against my spine and the ice in my Solo cup shook.

Then I heard a voice—round, smooth, dripping. Like clay in a master potter's hands:

Hey.

Together, he and I left the loft and went to Avenue B. Outside, I found a liquor store, and, using my fake ID, picked up a bottle of vodka. Wrapping the bottle in the brown paper bag, we found a bench at Tompkins Square Park and sat side by side. The way he looked at me, the way his eyes seemed to see past my material form and straight into my mind, no man had ever looked at me like that before. And so, when he said,

Tell me your story.

I wanted to, but I didn't know what he meant.

What story?

He spoke slowly and carefully, as if hiding something under his tongue:

Everyone has a story. What's yours?

I don't know.

Sure you do. Or I guess, you will. Eventually.

His cheek lifted toward his right eye. The brown of his iris contracting as a pursed-lip smirk ran diagonally across his face. His smirk made me think that he knew things that we, the rest of the world, did not. I wanted to know them. I wanted him to teach me. Better yet, I wanted to read him like one of my philosophy books.

As the sun broke through the crisp, thin air, we walked to his apartment: a studio on Twelfth Street whose entire square footage was covered with a purple oriental rug. Although his apartment was tiny, there was a large window on one of the walls. The enormity of the window compared to that little apartment was blinding. When my eyes finally adjusted, I looked around the room and found myself surrounded by drawings. No white walls. Only layers and layers of paper and pencil.

Slowly, I walked along the border of the apartment, looking from top to bottom, side to side. Each piece of paper was held up by either Scotch tape or silver thumbtacks. As the morning sun came in through his window, it illuminated the walls with a gliding contrast of light and shadow, guiding me picture to picture, story to story, like a flashlight giving me a tour inside this stranger's mind. There, in the pencil-scratched paper, were depictions of chaotic cityscapes, of trees that bore fruit that I couldn't decipher. Near the full-size bed, of a boy with blood dripping down his freckled forehead and a girl with a staff and a book in her hands. And then there was my all-time favorite: an anatomical heart that was intricately connected to a set of scattered shell-shocked faces. While I looked at his drawings, the infinite man stood quietly, leaning against the sink, staring at the rug. I realized then that he was letting me into a place where he had let no other.

———

In the earliest hours of that morning, a tiny white square sat in his mouth: a chemical-coated piece of paper. He said those squares are what had told him the truth about God.

God?

Mm-hmm.

So naturally I asked him for one. We sat side by side at his window, and despite not having slept, we were wide-awake with eager eyes. From behind the glass, we watched people speed-walking over the gum-stricken sidewalk to wherever they had so urgently to go. That's when I returned his question:

So what's your story?

With chemicals soaking into his bloodstream, he began by telling me what it was like to grow up Black in Texas, how he learned how to shoot a gun when he was ten, how it was a good thing that guns were legal for people like him where he lived. He spoke of his father, how he rode around that Texan lake on his bike every day to disintegrate the anger that seemed to appear in his hands; and of his teacher mother and how she was now alone in the house with her heavy-handed husband. Then he told me how he had spent his entire childhood singing onstage in his Christian megachurch, how churchgoers told him that his voice was a gift from God; how he believed this and came to New York to spread the word of Christ through his music. Then he told me about how one night, he put a white square on his tongue, and he realized God wasn't what they said God was. He stopped singing, dropped out of school, and was living off his savings from a Christian album he made when he was nine. Then he spoke of his anger with the world outside. He said that this place hurt so many people; that everyone was either hungry, getting killed, or going crazy. He was angry, but he said that he had a way to fix the pain. The white squares had told him how to. That's when he talked about the impossible possibilities for the world: systems falling and communities rising; large moneyless, sustainable villages; places where one lived by caring for the land in the day and making art in the evenings.

As the late-morning sun blinded me through the glass window, I said:

  I'm not sure that would ever happen, but I'd like to live in that world.

The infinite man smiled. I would learn later that he wasn't a boy who smiled like that very often. Still showing his teeth, he pulled up his sleeve to reveal the inside of his wrist. There, a tattoo was fresh and flaking. An infinity symbol outlined in bold black ink.

  What does that mean?

He answered:

> *I believe there are an infinite number of worlds to be created. Not by God but by us. The inhabitants of each world are the same as those here, like me or you, but not exactly the same: sometimes they are more beautiful and sometimes less. What I mean to say is that in some worlds, we are a fragment of ourselves, and in other worlds, more than ourselves.*

His voice shook, and I knew he had never said these words out loud before or perhaps he had but no one had listened:

> *Sometimes, we live in these worlds unwillingly. Sometimes even unknowingly. But once you realize the truth, you can create your own world.*

> *Oh.*

> *And I always knew I would start a new world with a girl who loved philosophy. I had a dream about it, a lucid dream.*

> *But do you actually think it's possible to create a new world? Like it sounds kind of crazy. Right?*

At that, he looked away from my eyes as if he remembered something and in this memory became scared of me. He stared at the gold necklace around my neck and said very seriously:

> *Do you?*

My stomach dropped. I could remember him asking me this before. I could remember how, as he asked it, my fingers were pulling at the hair tie around my wrist. Life, for a moment, felt like a memory.

The memory continued, unraveling itself into reality, until my hand moved to brush the hair from my eyes, and then I was back in the newness of existence. Was it the drugs? Or was this the beginning of creation?

Before I could answer, the infinite man said:

I think love is the key to making a new world.

Love. I thought of door frames, of footsteps, of being undressed in the kitchen, of china shaking in the curios, of the TV moaning downstairs, of the way, despite all of these things, we always had to say I love you to one another. I looked around the the studio apartment and noticed there was no TV. The infinite man could see the confusion on my face, so he tried:

I'm talking about love like in the Bible. Real love. First John 4:16: "God is love, and all who live in love live in God, and God lives in them." Funny enough that's my dad's favorite passage. Fucking hypocrite.

That's when it dawned on me:

Wait, you said acid told you the truth about God. What is it?

God isn't here anymore. He left us. But if we create a world like the one He intended for us: one without money, greed, dictators, and wars; one where everyone is safe and no one gets hurt. If we create a world like that, then maybe God will come back.

On the street below the windowsill, I saw a mother and daughter holding hands and skipping on the sidewalk. I watched them as I said:

I think God left too. All men do. One way or another.

The infinite man's face got very serious:

What if I promised to never leave?

I stared into his eyes, taking in the contrast between the white of his eyeballs and the dark brown of his skin. I felt my throat swallow the white square as I said:

Then I'd promise the same.

In the world we'll create, no one leaves. No one walks away. No matter how hard it gets.

Is it really that easy?

For sure.

I smiled. I smiled because I didn't feel so crazy when I was with him. I tilted my head sideways and asked:

What do you want our world to be like?

Well, I want to make a garden. For us. For everyone out there. It will be covered in flowers and greenery, and there'll be plenty of room for us to run around like kids. There'll be singing birds and hundreds of dragonflies. And fruit trees. Fruit trees that border the garden. And when we're hungry, we'll pick the fruits from the trees and eat them together in the grass. And at night, we'll make art and speak philosophy.

Like Eden?

He shook his head:

No. Like this. Right now. Look.

My eyes scanned the studio apartment, and I began to see a garden growing before me. There were ferns dripping from the corners of the room. A lake with fresh water in the sink. Patches of grass forming in the pattern of the rug. I could smell the soil. I could hear insect wings batting against the air. And his drawings had become a fence, a fortress of sorts, keeping the garden inside safe. As I saw this world form before my very eyes, I laughed, and he laughed, and we didn't stop laughing for a long time.

We spent that morning rolling in the grass and dancing amongst the insects. It was noon when, in the flowering of our garden, he returned from his closet, a cave in the garden, with a Polaroid camera. With his arm outstretched, he faced the camera toward us. I looked then not at the camera but at him, and he at me. Held sacredly in that room, in that garden, there was nothing in the outside world that could peel our eyes away from one another, not even the flash of his camera. He set the developing photo down on the bed of grass by the dandelions, and he moved toward me. My eyes closed and my vision catapulted into fractals. When our lips met for the first time, all I could feel was the tiny white square disintegrating in my stomach. Then I heard his voice:

Dear philosopher, will you transcribe our new theory here?

He handed me the Polaroid photo and motioned to the back of it.

I can't write theories yet. I'm supposed to just read books by other people. For like years.

We make the rules here.

I smiled, flowers blooming from my teeth. And so, that morning, in our growing garden, the birds sat perched amongst the furniture, and I wrote my first theory.

———

After that night and morning, I quickly gathered my things from my dorm room and moved in with him. In his apartment, we grew our own world together, and in our growing of place, we forgot about all responsibilities and duties to daily life. I spent my days drinking from a plastic cup and lying on the futon with my head in his lap, reading out loud the works of the philosophers I once so fervently loved. He listened to me page after page, never taking his eyes away from my face. Weeks into reading, he made me put the books away and think for myself. As he sat on the floor with a pencil in his hands and a square on his tongue, I would ask him questions upon questions until I could barely think anymore.

Why would Mary let them do that to Jesus? Why didn't she stop it? How could a mother allow people to hurt her own child?

When I finally arrived at a theory that could make sense in our world, he would tell me to write down the new theory on the back of the drawing he had just finished. Then we would hang our latest theory and drawing amongst the other pieces of paper on the walls. This is what we would do every day while most people our age were at parties, getting internships, or having sex. Throughout all our time together, I never had sex with the infinite man. He and I weren't interested in that. We only cared about each other's minds, and the philosophy that could come from them.

———

After weeks of philosophizing and drawing, emails from my professors suddenly flooded my inbox, notifying me of my absence and my ever-dwindling grade point average. My parents, hearing of my grades, cut me off from my trust and his savings were dwindling. Phone calls and text messages from our parents multiplied in bold lettering on our phones. When I eventually returned my mother's calls, she screamed at me from some pool in Greece, and when he FaceTimed his own mother, she had a black eye.

Because of all this, we were forced to leave our world every few days for life's apparent necessities: things like food, school, toilet paper, and jobs. Quickly, the realization settled within us that it was impossible to live only with theories and paper, to live solely within those four walls. We walked amongst the people of New York and listened to them speak loudly about the politicians running for president, the new skyrise construction downtown, and the bombings happening in other countries. That's when we learned of the recent shootings that were happening in our own country, men with skin like the infinite man being murdered for wearing hoodies or going to the bodega. When I asked him if he wanted to protest with the group in Union Square, he said:

> A protest is just like prayer, and we both know there's no one up there listening right now. No one out there protecting us. We're better off in the garden trying to get God back.

At first our optimistic days heavily outweighed our saddest, but with every month that passed, with every Black man or boy who was shot by the police or George Zimmerman, the worse it got. As the pessimism in the garden became more frequent, instead of sitting on the futon, speaking in existentialism, we lay there and kept asking each other what was wrong. Trying to remind myself of a time when life was enchanted, I would walk back and forth along the walls with a bottle in my hand, flipping over his sketches, looking for a theory that I could use. It was rare that I found anything except my black-ink words that now, on the page and in my brain, dissolved into an infant's gibberish: into an attempt to say something but mean nothing.

One Friday evening, there were hundreds of purple flowers covering the floor. An hour before, they had burst open the floorboards and grown between the weaves of the rug. A chipmunk scurried up the walls, the lake whispered, and the tree beside it hummed. I went into the trunk of the tree and placed my lips around a stream of liquid that burned my esophagus. It was cold next to the tree and suddenly it felt as if I had been there forever. How long was it? When had it kicked in? I turned to face the fence of the garden and saw a gray falcon floating toward and away from me.

I hear something.

A voice smooth like clay. My head turned toward the noise, and I saw the infinite man in the middle of the purple flowers. They had grown even taller than I remembered. How beautiful he looked there amongst them. He adjusted his legs, and I swore I saw a snake rustle near his feet and disappear into the sea of stems.

Is it God?

I moved away from the falcon, catching a glimpse of a faucet. A faucet? I walked toward the infinite man. He was cutting a long strip of LSD-coated paper that he kept wrapped in tinfoil. Another one? I sat beside him in the soil and rubbed the purple flowers between my fingertips. I had forgotten his question. I had forgotten that he'd asked anything at all. The flowers were so soft, so purple.

Do you hear that?

Like clay, like the flowers between my hands, now in my ears. An insect clicked. There was a scream outside beyond the fence. I turned to him. And that's when I saw a knife in his hand. I suddenly snapped back into reality: a studio apartment, a purple rug, a boy.

What are you doing?

I'm protecting you.

That night when the acid had loosened its grip, I sat in front of the window exhausted. The infinite man excitedly showed me what he had drawn, but they were just pages and pages of dark frantic lines that spilled over the edges of the page, leaving what looked like claw marks on the coffee table.

Do you see it?

I didn't have the heart to tell him that I thought the trip and drugs were getting to him. When he finally went to bed, I stayed awake. I kept thinking of him with the knife in his hand. Trying to erase the memory, I threw the new drawing in the trash. I grabbed my philosophy notebook and began to write. As the hours passed, my hand kept moving, and words poured out of me. The words came so fast I didn't know if I would ever stop writing, and my hands didn't even feel like my own as they scribbled across the page. I watched my body as a witness. I watched it write and write and write while I thought about bald planets spinning and spinning and spinning. When the words finally slowed, I laid my head on the futon and fell asleep. By the time morning came, I had forgotten all about the writing in my notebook.

———

Months later, it was summer, and the infinite man and I had turned into ever-emptying shells of ourselves, and our garden was overrun by fear. The optimism we had shared disintegrated into an overwhelming sadness, a misery rooted in our inability to fix the world and the struggle to even create our own. During every trip that summer, while he looked for God, I saw bullet wounds across his body like freckles. Blood pouring out of him and drenching the soil. I would pace around the apartment, muttering anxiously to myself. Sometimes I heard myself say:

I was supposed to save you. I was supposed to save you.

One time, I was hissing:

This is the devil's acid. This is the devil's acid.

When he heard me say this, he came over and slapped me. He told me I was scaring God away.

And then, just after July Fourth, it happened. A police officer shot and killed a Black child, twelve years old, who was simply playing on a playground. For six days, no matter how much sunlight pierced us through the studio window, neither of us could get out of bed. I couldn't read, he couldn't draw, and we couldn't even look at each other. We just lay there in bed with bodies that didn't work, and we waited for something to happen or for someone to speak. But for hours, there were only the sounds of sirens outside and the bad thoughts between our ears.

On the seventh day, I had a dream I was alone on the streets of Manhattan, wandering, walking aimlessly. I heard police sirens and a gunshot. Suddenly I realized the infinite man wasn't there. I began walking around the East Village calling out for him, shouting his name, screaming, but the more I called for him the more the boundaries of the dream world shook and began to collapse around me.

When I woke an eternity later, dripping with sweat, I opened my eyes to see the infinite man lying there next to me. I hadn't lost him. That world wasn't real. It was just a dream. My body relaxed into the bed. My breathing slowed. He was alive. Even if God had left, how could I be so sad when the infinite man was still here? With that, I woke into the seventh day of sadness with new purpose, and I began to clean the mess we had made.

The mess was an overgrown garden, untended, unloved, and abandoned for far too long. I started by cutting down the vines that grew out of the electrical socket, around the bed frame and up the drawing-scattered walls. I dusted the nightstands, lampshades, and the floor mirror's frame. My hands folded the clothes that had bloomed like wrinkled petals on our floor. I opened the window and lit a stick of lavender incense. Only after tending to the garden, I tried to wake him. With my words and hands, I whispered for him to get out of bed and come with me. Holding him by his frail arms, I guided him to the futon and knelt at his feet. There, I nursed his wounds and told him about my dream:

But I didn't really lose you. When I woke, you were right there next to me.

I hoped that this would make him smile. But all he said was:

And what about God?

He said these words so slowly as if he was half paralyzed from having been woken into a reality that he no longer wanted to be in. I said:

I don't know. I'm starting to think He's not coming.

Having to leave for a midday summer course to make up for last semester's D, I placed his sketchbook and pencil in front of him. As I went to leave, the infinite man looked up from the blank paper and asked me, weakly but quickly, as if running out of time, if I could call the dealer, that he would figure out a way to get the money. My body pivoted to face him, and I told him that the garden didn't need the drugs anymore. I motioned around the apartment:

Just look at the mess it's made.

Please— Please—

There in his voice, which once cradled me in its smooth embrace, it sounded as if he was carrying the weight of the world on his back. I sat down next to the infinite man. My hands reached for his, and I turned over his right wrist:

This is all we need. Remember? You and me. Infinity.

And with that, for the first time in a long time, he looked up and directly into my eyes, and I felt him believe me.

You and me. Infinity.

And I believed myself too.

—————

When I got to class, I sat down toward the back of the room and took out my notebook. My professor began by apologizing for canceling class last week, and I was relieved. I opened my notebook; *catharsis*, I was going to write, but as I flipped through the notebook for a blank page, I saw the words I had written the night of the knife, the night the infinite man said God appeared. I scanned through them. The words were also about God, at least somewhat about God. Perhaps I had written the theory I'd been looking for all along. To the sound of the professor's lecture, I read the pages I had written as if they were a completely foreign entity, an artifact from another world. When I got to the last sentence, I realized I hadn't written a theory at all. I had written a story. Its title was "American Love."

I quickly closed my notebook, and, muttering sorry, sorry, I squirmed past the sea of chairs and students and laptops, and ran out of class. I pushed open the door of the stairwell and ran down the stairs, blood rushing through me, the sentences I read replaying in my head. The world's chaos had nothing to do with God or a runaway God like the infinite man thought. It had to do with the Bible. Not just the Bible, but the Torah, the Quran, and all the books written by men who knew other men who, apparently, met God. I burst outside and ran toward Washington Square Park. Philosophy didn't matter. Proof was never needed. It was faulty stories that created this world. And if that was true, stories had the power to create *any* world. They were the only thing that ever made or could make a difference.

I reached the fountain at the center of the park and looked around, wondering if the entirety of New York had just had this epiphany with me. But everyone seemed normal, just skateboarding or lying out in a bikini or pushing a stroller on a summer day.

On my walk home from the park, I called my mother and told her that I was switching majors: I was going to study English and be a writer. She said that she would pray for me. I wanted to tell her that she didn't need to waste her words on prayers anymore because God didn't exist. And if God did somehow exist, He wasn't important anymore. But instead, I waited so that I could tell the infinite man first.

——

When I entered the apartment, the infinite man was sitting on the purple rug. Before I could speak, he said:

  I figured it out.

One part of me couldn't believe our revelation had come at the same time. The other part of me knew this was how our world worked, how we worked.

  It's Ecclesiastes.

I stopped short of the rug:

  Huh?

  The story in the Bible.

No, I know, but what do you mean?

That's what's happening. God is still here. He's just finished with us. He's destroying the world. He's the one responsible.

I shook my head and knelt next to him:

No, no. Don't worry. The Bible isn't real.

He looked at me with anger bursting from his eyes:

Yes it is.

And when he said this, I could see a white square on his tongue. I tried to explain:

No, listen to me, the Bible is just a story. There is no theory. There is no God. There are no multiple worlds. There are just stories. Ones we tell each other; ones we tell ourselves; ones the government tells us and the media. It's just a story that made this world. Trust me, we can fix—

He stood up from the rug and walked to the kitchen. I continued:

Listen. We can fix this if we just write the right story! We can even put your drawings in it. We can change what's happening out there with all the shootings and all the shit if we just tell the perfect story!

From the kitchen he said:

Oh yeah? You just need a story to save everyone from this hell. You wanna tell that to the Black kid who just died? Or the Black teenager before him or the Black father before that one?

Yes. I think we've just been living in the wrong narrative—

He slammed his hand against the refrigerator:

Shut up, Norma. Just shut up! You're fucking white. White and rich. And a drunk too. A fucking story.

He scoffed:

You're everything that's wrong with this world.

I didn't know which world he was talking about, ours or the one outside.

———

After our fight, the infinite man went to bed, and I sat on the futon unable to move. With the moonlight coming in through the window, I stared into our broken garden: at the dead ferns hanging from the corner of the room, at the dried lake, at the brown flaking grass.

Just after midnight, as the wind whipped against the window, I felt the garden calling me. I stood up from the futon and went to the closet. Kneeling on the ground, I found myself removing the infinite man's box of Polaroids. When I opened the lid, the first photo I saw was the one from the day we'd met, a time that existed over a year ago now. I looked at our faces. Neither of our eyes were focused on the lens, but instead they were fixated on each other.

Trying to understand why the garden had brought me here to our younger days, I removed the image from the box to stare closer at the happiness we once knew. The story I had told myself was that when we'd first met almost a year ago, we were both content, pure, that all was right in the world and in our minds. That we were just two adults falling in love. But what I saw in the photograph was nothing like the story in my head. In the meeting of our eyes was not love. Instead, our gaze was like a remedy, a fix for two young people who were in pain. I sat there on the floor and fished into my mind for an explanation. The infinite man said God was love, but I knew now that God probably didn't exist and so maybe love didn't either.

Unable to stand the sight, I turned the photograph over, and there, behind our heads, I saw the first theory I had ever written: a theory on the creation of worlds, on the return of God, on the power of love to change the world. I felt hopeful for a moment, but then I realized: this was never my theory, these weren't actually my words—they were the infinite man's. I knew then what I had to do.

Quietly so as not to wake him, I packed my belongings. I took my shirts and pants and folded them into my suitcase. Then my underwear, my beanies, and my socks. Lastly, I took my schoolbooks from under the futon and lined them around my clothes like a fence. With my bag packed, I stood there wondering if I should wake the infinite man. I could see it clearly: if he woke from dreams to find my body missing, his world would shatter and the garden would flood. Oceans would crash endlessly against his skin, forming lakes and ponds across his body. Continents would turn into hundreds of daggered masses, and I would no longer be there to pick the glass out from his skin, to tell him that the white world didn't mean to hurt him, not again, not ever. I wanted to wake him and explain, but I didn't have the words yet. I still didn't know why myself. All I knew was that I couldn't stay there anymore. Our world was collapsing. The garden crumbling into a home that we were too familiar with. Despite our world disintegrating, I know I could have searched for an entrance into a new one. I could have fought viciously for a new way of seeing, one that didn't begin with me leaving and end with the garden flooding. I could have fought to stay even just one more day, to try to heal the pain that had taken us over long before we met, to offer the infinite man just one more moment of philosophy, an endless moment suspended in a place beyond that gray city and that little apartment and the drugs we used to cover up our pain. He deserved more than a midnight exit. He deserved the entire exquisite garden and a girl beyond theory. But I was tired and worn, and sometimes we don't get to choose if we stay or if we go. Sometimes an idea or a story takes us away.

I placed my hand on the doorknob and looked at him lying asleep in bed. Despite what the infinite man might think, what I did next was the hardest thing I ever had to do: I turned away from the person who I'd promised I wouldn't abandon. No matter how hard it got. As I opened the front door, the air in the apartment went cold and the birds in the garden stopped singing. Everywhere went silent: no sirens, no fan spinning in circles, no pencil-scratching on paper. Simply nothingness. You see, this is the sound that ensues upon the destruction of a world. And in that non-sound, in that nothingness, I left.

————

But there's one part of the story that I left out; the part where the infinite man may have begun to think that I was the devil or a parasite in his garden. Perhaps he still thinks this, though I'm not sure. We haven't spoken in years. Before leaving, before I turned away from him, I placed our Polaroid photo inside my suitcase, and I took the one theory, the only theory, that ever mattered to him.

This was never my philosophy. This is my apology.

THE STUDY OF OBLIVION

twenty-two weeks since breakdown

You canceled on me last week. Did you not like "Philosophy"?

My new therapist says, I had a doctor's appointment.

Sometimes I forget my new therapist is a person with a body. I stare at her ballet flats to try and remember. Today they are leopard print. Oh là là.

Sometimes you forget you're a person with a body too, don't you?

I look away from her feet and at my new therapist's face, confused about whether she just said that or I did. She's looking down at her clipboard and seems unfazed, so maybe it was me. But speaking in the second person? When I was stuck in oblivion, my head used the second person a lot. As if the author was whispering secrets to the character, and the author and the character had the same voice so it was hard to distinguish one from the other. The voices of oblivion got much worse after the infinite man. Probably because of the drugs. Definitely because of the drugs. The past two weeks, the voices have started to creep in again. The Saran Wrap middleman between me and reality has begun to prevail, and everything is hazy like I'm floating through my life on a magic carpet with a monologue in my mind that won't shut the fuck up. Sometimes I have to open my eyes really big to see because my vision feels like a tiny telescope hole.

I decide in this very moment that oblivion has been deepening ever since the higher dose of Prozac and the Wellbutrin, and since I have a sex drive now, I'm going to stop taking the sex pill starting tomorrow and I should tell my new therapist this right now or at least during today's session, but I know that I won't because she scares me. My new therapist butts in:

Norma, how did you go from becoming an atheist to being spiritual and seeing god everywhere?

Oh, that comes later.

Later when?

Later in the story. I don't want to give it away. Unless you're getting bored.

I'm not bored.

(She has to say this, because it's her job to talk to me. Other people won't be so polite.)

The story goes chronologically.

Got it.

Did you know that my manuscript, despite it being a mess, has a higher likelihood of being published because I'm white? It would have an even higher likelihood of getting published if I wasn't gay. Should I lie and say I'm not gay?

My new therapist says, how is the writing coming?

Well, I've been looking through my old stories trying to find a through line. You know, like you suggested a while ago. But I can't find one. And so then I look at the news and I'm trying to find a through line there, but I can't find one either. And then I think about our sessions and I can't find one here either. I have concluded that there is no defining thread. That there's no end in sight. That there's no final story, in my manuscript or in my memory or in the news or in the Bible, that's going to bring this all together. So I have also concluded that I'll never be able to write The Last Story, and I'll never be able to figure out the genre of my goddamn book.

My new therapist says, I'm not sure I know what you mean by a through line.

Is she kidding? We talked about this three weeks ago! Before I can do anything about it, I feel it happen. My eyeballs arc like rainbows in their sockets and my eyelids slow-blink over them. I'm not sure how I started this bad habit of eye-rolling. I'm not sure when I began to think that sweeping an image around in my vision could make the image disappear or undo itself. Most times, I'm not even aware that I'm rolling my eyes. I only know I do it because my girlfriend tells me: *you just did it! Right there! You just did it again!* I've decided my eye rolls have gained their own consciousness and I am no longer in control of them. It's like they're permanently embedded in my millennial DNA. Like evolution led me to the eye roll for some Darwinian reason.

I say, sorry I have no control.

What?

I feel my eyes roll again.

SORRY!

Norma, are you okay?

Never mind. As I was saying, I thought the stories would come together eventually: plot points a, b, c, climax, the end. I thought the world was heading toward a utopia (just one more social justice cause to fight for and the history books will be finished, happily ever after). I thought the signs were edging me toward god's plan and that god's plan was benevolent and good. But now I'm not even sure about god. If god isn't the signs, then what is god? Nonexistent like I thought back then? Or is it a man like my mother says? Or like any of the holy books that exist in the universe say?

Let's talk this through:

If god is God with a capital G, then everyone on Dragon Island is going to hell, but that doesn't make any sense. You know, God, that God, promises all of us the promised land. But if that god is God and this is His world and He's all powerful, then why isn't the promised land delivered to us right now. Like right, right now. Why are we waiting to die for it? What if we wait our whole lives, letting the world pass us by, eyes focused on a post-death perfect existence, and then when we actually die, there is no such place? What if God is a shitty writer and the ending of His story isn't actually going to be that good? What if God is promising us some great fucking conclusion, but in reality, the middle of His book is the best part? If I've learned anything in this world, it's that promises aren't delivered on. And so we can't bank on a promise that some old-ass stories say a man is going to give us after we die. AFTER WE DIE. We can't trust any of this.

Can't trust what? I'm not following.

Joe Biden. When he removed the troops, he promised to get people in Afghanistan out of there before the Taliban took over, and hundreds who have the golden ticket can't even leave now. It's like promising a sequel and never actually getting one.

Does this bother you?

You know what bothers me? The justice system. It promises to deliver justice, and that clearly doesn't happen, like ever. And our government is built in such a way that we can't put the justice system on trial.

You seem very concerned by this?

I am concerned because our whole U.S. government is a failed promise. Life, liberty, and the pursuit of happiness? Please, please tell me which of the three you are experiencing right now. And if none of them apply please check the fourth box: Other.

Raise your hand if you were ever victimized by the United States government.

Norma, you seem very anxious today.

Well yes, because I've been thinking about the virtual world. How it promises to connect us. Find your old English teacher. Stay in touch with racist relatives. Check up on your adult children who moved to another state that you hate. But now the internet just tries to sell us things or ideas. What was supposed to garner connection is built to break us down.

Don't you think that's a little hyperbolic?

Think about those targeted ads I was getting when I kept breaking up with my girlfriend. The ads wanted to tear her and me apart. Those ads wanted to press into my current neurosis so deeply until I couldn't scream anymore and instead said PURCHASE, PURCHASE, PURCHASE, JUST GIVE ME SOMETHING TO MAKE THE PAIN GO AWAY, HERE'S MY APPLE PAY, YOU WANT MY SOCIAL SECURITY NUMBER TOO?

Now that you've stopped trying to break up with her, what are the ads trying to tell you?

They're trying to sell me online therapy sessions through accounts that specialize in *Living with Depression*. You see? The virtual world wants my money. It doesn't care about me or you. But you already knew this.

You watched *The Social Dilemma* documentary on Netflix, but you still kept all your accounts. You kept them all, and every time you clicked an ad, you screamed, I AM NOT THE PRODUCT. You did this to make yourself feel better. Oh wait, that wasn't you. That was me. That was me, clicking and shouting and buying whatever jewelry the ad was selling. Back then, I didn't have so many mental problems and social media only tried to sell me trendy jewelry.

Do you feel like the product?

Of course I do, because I *am* the product. I don't think that's up for discussion anymore. I am the product and the product is me and the product is:

A child born right before the turn of the millennium; an American girl born immigrant-white to parents who have achieved, and thereby believe in, the American Dream; a woman in the midst of the #MeToo movement where being a feminist is still considered filthy; an LGBTQ+ person who goes to therapy; a writer with no book deal. I am just a data point. A consumer. A social media profile transmuting through time to adapt to whatever app needs me.

Can you believe my mind, the most complex piece of technology on this earth, is being trained by uncensored, unregulated algorithms. Infant algorithms built by billionaires. Infant algorithms built with a mission to sell me something. Infinite algorithms built with the desire to push me toward the edge of some neurosis that it knows I am already inclined to: mathematical virtual equations that want to make choices for me. Mathematical virtual equations that are always listening.

But I'm not an anomalous product, I was shaped into *this*, this "me," by a society that would trade nature for the unnatural. That mutilates and then abandons the natural world, which gives it sustenance and oxygen for a digital, make-believe one, one that is created by and for the ones edging you toward it. What new mental disorders will we design in the metaverse? Perhaps one that will be the opposite of depersonalization: the thought that you are, in fact, real. Maybe NFT billionaires that run the metaverse will tell you that you're sick and maybe they'll call over Big Pharma to treat you for it, inject you with something, while your headset is still on. But no, this isn't *Black Mirror*, they'll say. And all I hear is noise. Nonstop noise. And all I want is for it to stop. For the noise to shut up, but I'm always yelling at the wrong person. We're always yelling at the wrong person. To shut our kids up, we give them an iPad so the algorithms will start working on them early. To shut our adults up, we give them a paycheck with just enough to survive and pay for a monthly streaming service that will numb their minds during the little free time they have left. To shut our elders up, we'll put them in a nursing home, and when one organ begins to fail because we haven't visited in weeks, we'll let the doctors let them die.

I realize I'm almost shouting now. I try to compose myself. But all my new therapist says to that is, mmm, which makes me completely lose my shit again.

Let me ask you a question, Doc: Why can't kids have alcohol? Because it's addicting? Because it alters brain chemistry? Because the underdeveloped brain shouldn't be exposed to an addicting and brain-altering substance? Or does alcohol have an age limit because it causes deaths if not used properly? Well, have you heard of all the teenagers and middle schoolers committing suicide because of what happens online? Have you heard about how technology alters our dopamine and serotonin? So shouldn't we ban it? BAN THE BOOKS! BURN THEM ALL! And don't even get me started on why alcohol is legal in general, despite it being, according to David Nutt, the most harmful drug overall even compared to heroin. You don't know who David Nutt is, do you?

She shakes her head.

Of course she doesn't.

David Nutt was the chairman of some drug advisory council in the UK. Keyword: *was.* When he still had his bigwig job, he was ordered to study and classify drugs based on harmfulness, in order to help policymakers make decisions. Bear with me here, I'm going somewhere. After his study, Nutt delivered his findings. His findings concluded (amongst many other things that you should look up) that alcohol was more harmful than any other substance he studied and that horse riding was as dangerous as taking ecstasy. Of course, the UK government didn't like these findings very much, so after his study was published, he was dismissed from his position. I mean, come on!, they weren't gonna ban alcohol and make psychedelics legal. Which I actually don't personally have an opinion on. Psychedelics only ever made oblivion deepen for me, if you didn't get that from the infinite man story.

I did. I hadn't realized you had any drug use in your past.

I've taken all the drugs except the really bad ones. I think that's pretty standard these days.

I want to say, grow up, lady, everyone's done cocaine. But I stop myself.

When asked to comment on Nutt's dismissal, the secretary of the ACMD said: *Nutt was asked to go because he cannot be both a government adviser and a campaigner against government policy.*

Which is very very very funny to me.

But because I know no one, Left or Right, is going to be happy with my above comments on how alcohol is just another ploy for the government to make you numb, let's return to the burning world.

You see, I like the earth. The earth doesn't promise us anything. Animals don't promise anything either. Not even our pets. Sometimes our cats, our dogs, our guinea pigs love us and then run away the same day. Nature doesn't promise us shit except for the fact that we're all going to die one day and nothing is permanent. Which means my girlfriend and I won't last.

I'm out of breath.

My new therapist looks up at me. Her face twists into what I think is supposed to be a smile but also looks almost like a grimace. I don't know what it's supposed to be exactly, but whatever it is, it looks painful.

I want her to say, *wow you're right. We live in a messed-up world and you're the least messed-up thing in it, and everyone is going to love your manuscript.*

But instead she says,

You say you haven't found a through line for the world, but it seems like you believe failed promises are the through line?

She looks at me, waiting for an answer, but I don't reply because I can't believe that's her response to all that I've said.

I stare at her pillows and bite the inside of my cheek.

She asks, why do you think it bothers you so much when people don't keep their promises?

I didn't say that.

You didn't?

Nope.

Well, how do you think this relates to your past sexual relationships with men.

Fine! You really want to know about all the guys I slept with?

She's so raunchy.

I'll send you a story about them this week.

Oh, and I forgot to tell you: last night I apologized to my girlfriend on behalf of both Joe Biden and Kim Kardashian's Met Gala outfit. She accepted my apology and then we had sex.

Keepsakes

In the bedroom of my East Village apartment, there was a large rug that covered the wooden floors. In the middle of the room, there was a table, and on that table sat a snakeskin box. The box's width was about the size of a novel. Its height: a martini glass.

Inside the box were relics of the men that I've left floating out in the world. Amongst the bones: a chopstick, a wooden cross, a potion in a bottle, two belts (one leather and one woven), a telescope, seven crystals, a copper bracelet, a dried-up air plant, and a Polaroid photo at the very bottom.

Back then, I had no apologies regarding the contents of the box or the box itself. I was trying to write a story and I was determined to find the perfect character. And if need be, I decided, I would create the character piece by piece, keepsake by keepsake. From these men, I collected only what was necessary.

———

I started with a man who was a self-proclaimed shaman. I was twenty, in my junior year of college. He was much older. This man's pale skin was decorated with kambo burns, and he had long curly hair that smelled of essential oils. I saw him at an art exhibition. I watched him, when a woman at the bar wasn't paying attention, pour something into her drink. I introduced myself and offered that we should go back to his hotel. With his silk kimono and sweaty skin, he looked like he had come from the jungle, but to my dismay I learned later that he lived in Los Angeles.

In his hotel bed in FiDi, he asked questions like he cared to know me, but he didn't listen to my answers. He used each of my answers to talk about himself and his new business: making "potions to catalyze people's ascension." He sold his potions in Venice Beach. He told me that he put gold in his potions, because gold decalcifies the pineal gland. Then he said he wanted to connect in a way that is spiritually impossible through words: to go down on me. I told him I had my period. He responded saying that he had acquired the taste. Then without another word from me, he slipped between my legs and tore down my underwear. He grabbed my tampon string and pulled it out of me slowly with his mouth open in awe. He showed the bloody cotton to me before flinging it backward over his shoulder onto the hotel room floor.

As I suspected, soon after, his acquired taste turned into wanting to have sex. He thrusted over me with my blood drying around his mouth and I wanted to laugh. When he was finished, he asked me to sleep over. I said maybe. Then I walked to the bathroom to find that I had no more tampons in my purse. I made a makeshift pad from toilet paper. By the time I was done, the lights were off and he was asleep. Quietly, I went into his suitcase and found his gold potions.

With my menstrual blood on his face and my tampon on the hotel floor, I left with one of his potions. I didn't take it because I believed it would make me ascend to some higher consciousness; I took it because I knew he loved it.

————

Then there was the man who didn't cry. He was a doctor at Mount Sinai whose Hinge profile said, "I don't date fat girls." When he came over, he told me that his patient had died earlier, and he added that he didn't even cry when it happened. He seemed proud of this. I told him that I liked to cry and that I did it a lot. I told him that I cried at movies about old people, at surprise parties that weren't my own, at zoos and animal parks even if they were conservation initiatives. These were all lies. I hadn't cried once since I moved to

New York. The last time he had cried, he told me, was twelve years ago when his dog died.

I'll make you cry one day.

I said this as if I were going to do him a favor. I said this because I knew, like I did with all the others, I wasn't going to fall in love with him, and if I couldn't fall in love with any man, I would at least teach them how to cry. Maybe then our world would be different, a better place more like what the infinite man wanted.

Sure enough, two weeks later, when I left him, he cried and cried like a little baby. And I collected his tears.

———

When Tay asked if she could come to the city and stay with me for the week, I said yes. It had been six years since we'd seen each other. When she arrived, she hugged me and I felt her breasts, now even fuller than when we were kids, press up against my bony body. We sat together on my couch, and she recounted all that I had missed in her life over the years: the boyfriends, the drama with her friends, her half sister from her dad's new wife, her mother, who also got remarried. I smiled at her and tried to keep myself from looking too obviously at her changed body. Her hips, rounder. Her waist, smaller. Her thighs, muscular. After she talked for hours, Tay fell asleep on the couch. I went into the TV console and pulled out a blanket. Gently, I placed it around her body.

———

And then there was the Kabbalah-studying older man who brought me an air plant as a commemorative gift for our first date and who also believed I could be his "bride." Then the single dad who owned a Tribeca strip club and liked introducing his four-year-old son to new potential moms. Then the editor who worked at Simon & Schuster who frequently published Republican autobiographies and anti-feminist self-help books on how to be a good wife. Then the guy with big lips who came inside of me even though I told him not to. Then my father's friend from college who had been trying to make it on Broadway for as long as I had been alive and who wanted to cum in my mouth. And all these men, I just kept stuffing in my box.

————

When I was twenty-four, my box was almost full, and I still didn't have a character for my story. One night, I met a man in a bar downtown. He was twenty-one, and I didn't typically go younger. But this man was beautiful (arguably the most beautiful man I've ever seen), and he wore a copper bracelet that looked identical to the bracelet my dad wore when I was growing up. The first night I met the beautiful man, I kissed his best friend. The second night in that same bar it was our turn. His hand cupped my face, and I felt the chill from his copper bracelet on my cheek.

An hour later, lying in my gray sheets, the beautiful man didn't want to take my clothes off. He wanted to talk. It was clear that he was lonely so I let him go on. He told me that he was a model signed to the best agency in the city. He told me about the older men who promised him a cover and thousands of dollars if only he would undress for them. At that moment I regretted bringing him home with me. There was something too familiar in his voice. I needed him to leave or I needed him to fuck me, but he wouldn't do either.

Then he told me of the older men who were more creative: inviting him over for a "career-changing shoot," only to find out it was a shoot where he wore leather in their apartment and the photographer was the old man himself. I sat there quietly as he spoke so that I could examine his beautiful face moving in the darkness. After he told me all of this, his body relaxed into the bed as if he had just finished cumming. When he left the next morning, I promised myself I wouldn't see him again. My box and I had nothing to gain from him, but then he texted me and I thought of his beauty and I wanted that type of beauty near me.

Every night after that night (and I only ever saw him during the night), the beautiful man looked at me the way a teenager looks at their first love. I told him to stop looking at me like that. He tried to hold me close. He wanted to show me what it felt like to be wanted, but all he did was leave me with bruises—usually on the outer edge of my thighs, on my neck, and on my stomach. He never meant to bruise me, but he was so strong and muscular. He would reach to hold me, I'd stare at his copper bracelet, and suddenly my skin would turn navy. Finally, outside of his beauty, he piqued my interest.

———

Like me, Tay woke early in the morning. The second day she was there, a man had stayed over. After the front door closed, she came into my bedroom and lay next to me. As she chatted about her escapades the night before, I could feel her density in my bed. The weight of her presence. The space she took up on my mattress that no man had ever inhabited.

On the third morning that she saw a man leave the apartment, she lay with me in bed and asked how I managed to live like this every day. I watched the ceiling fan spin in endless circles, and then told her the first thing that came to mind. I told her that it helped to focus on the beauty in life.

But what do you do when everything looks so ugly?

And as she asked this, I could sense exactly how many inches away her body was from mine.

I took a deep breath:

There is construction and destruction, and there is a fine line between remembering and dismembering. You must learn how to deconstruct and assemble a body, so that when a man lets you touch him, you can take what you need and piece the rest back

*together, enough so that he can walk out the door. Amongst the
keepsakes, you'll start to remember a time when both you and the
world were beautiful.*

She laughed and turned on her side, one of her breasts falling on
top of the other in her white camisole:

Girl, you're crazy.

Then she asked if I wanted to get brunch in SoHo.

––––––

One night, I asked the beautiful man about his copper bracelet. The
beautiful man told me that he had bought the bracelet at a holiday
market in Queens two years ago. I don't think I ever believed a word
he said after that. But this is beside the point. I didn't care that I
couldn't trust him. I cared only about his careless strength and the
way he never noticed how I winced every time he touched me.

There was a man years before the beautiful one who also colored my
skin in navy hues, but unlike the beautiful man, he was purposeful.
He was a graffiti artist who lived in Brooklyn. He liked mythology
and space documentaries, and in his spare time he visited the plan-
etarium. This man and his man bun would perfectly plan each mark
on my body from the action and impact to the shape and shade
of blue. The bruises he gave to me scattered across my skin like
constellations, telling ancient stories of gods and monsters. One
time, this man crunched his teeth into the back of my arm. The next
morning a circular bruise had formed around the bite mark like an
eclipse. That man turned me into a galaxy. In the end what I took
from him was a half-empty spray can.

But the beautiful man was different. When he would leave my bed in
the morning, I would connect the bruises he left with my fingertips,
looking for pictures or hidden messages, but there were none—only
olive skin and careless black and blue. It felt like such a waste.

———

Tay brought us to a restaurant in SoHo that served bottomless mimosas. When we finished our fourth glass, I said:

I have a confession. I steal from them.

From who?

The guys.

No fucking way! Good for you!

She flipped her hair over her shoulder.

The funny thing is none of them have ever called asking for their shit back.

She motioned for the waiter to pour us another glass:

They probably don't even know it's missing. Or maybe they don't suspect you took it. You don't look like the crazy type. Me, on the other hand.

She brushed nonexistent dust off her shoulder and I laughed. The waitress filled our glasses. Tay asked:

Is there any guy you haven't stolen from?

My friend Felix. But we haven't slept together so maybe that's why.

Do you feel guilty? For the guys?

Not a single one—

I never got to finish my sentence, because a call came in on Tay's phone. A new guy she was dating. A day later, Tay left with nothing less than what she came with. Three weeks later, the beautiful man was in my bed for the first time.

———

A month after our first meeting, the beautiful man was desperate for me to fall in love with him. So he stopped kissing me and started speaking words like "only" and "really," "now," and "in a year from now." The sounds coming from his mouth were tied together with a childish smile, a smile that stayed on his face as he waited for me to say something, to return enamor with enamor. He assumed that this was how love worked. I looked at his copper bracelet.

For a moment I listened to the heater whisper hot air into the room. Then I said:

I had a dream the other day. You were lying on my rug with your mouth wide open. One by one your teeth fell out of their sockets and into the back of your throat. I couldn't move, and so from my bed I watched the blood slide over the corners of your mouth and travel diagonally down your face. It slithered down past your jawbone toward the back of your neck. By the time you had no teeth left, I think I felt myself love you.

Immediately after I said it, I felt sick to my stomach.

The next morning, I told the beautiful man that we couldn't see each other anymore. Then I asked for his copper bracelet.

Why?

I'm trying to write a story. I've been collecting stuff. And I think I need this bracelet to finish it.

And then the beautiful man just gave it to me.

When he left, I put his copper bracelet in my box, thought of the space Tay took up in my bed, and tried to fall asleep.

———

The day Tay asked me about the men and my life and the box, there were things that I left out. Like the fact that my mother had bought me the snakeskin box as an eighteenth-birthday present. Like the fact that despite my box of keepsakes, I haven't written anything in months. At the time, I didn't think that she needed to know, but the more nights that I spend alone in this East Village room, the more infectious the things unsaid become.

That morning what I should have told Tay is that the scariest nights are the ones when a man doesn't sleep next to me. It's on these nights when I lie beneath the sheets that I can still feel him, each and every him in my bed and on my skin. Every night when I lie alone in bed, they keep me up with their laughter and tears. They ooze onto my table and drip memories onto the rug. They crawl between my thighs, scratch at my neck and sternum, and hiss my name. In the dark I lie still with eyelids fastened and try to make the world go numb.

I should have told Tay all of this. I should have warned her about the keepsakes that I keep locked away. But now there is nothing left to say to her. Like the men, she went away one morning and never came back.

OCTOBER

If modern thought is difficult and runs counter to common sense, this is because it is concerned with truth; experience no longer allows it to settle for the clear and straightforward notions which common sense cherishes because they bring peace of mind.

Maurice Merleau-Ponty

THE STUDY OF OBLIVION

twenty-three weeks since breakdown

I have a confession to make.

I say to my new therapist's navy blue ballet flats that have a pointed toe. She's getting more and more bold with her shoe choices lately.

I stopped taking the Wellbutrin and I'm back to taking ten milligrams of Prozac, and I'm sorry for not telling you, but I feel so much better now.

Oh really? She seems genuinely surprised.

I know you said ten milligrams wouldn't work for depression, but also look at me. I'm one hundred pounds. I can finally feel my feet on the floor.

Okay, good.

That's all?

No punishment?

No yells?

Silence.

Silence.

Silence.

My new therapist kind of smiles at me and tilts her head to the side as if to say, continue, go ahead and rant. But I don't have a rant today.

I applied to some jobs this week, five to be exact. Other nonprofit admin stuff. Even one copy editor job. I haven't heard back yet.

That's great.

And I'm still going to that writers' workshop. The facilitator keeps saying that my stories are too long and I need to edit them down, but I don't know how to edit a life down. Everything seems important. The facilitator said, *you have to pick and choose, that's the work of a writer.* And when she said this, she seemed annoyed with me like I'm acting too human to be a real writer.

What is a real writer anyways? What is a real anything? Not like oblivion-real, but like legitimate-real. Maybe to be a legitimate real writer you've got to be valuable to the literary community. How can you be valuable to a literary community while not ever leaving your apartment?

My new therapist says, was she talking about the story you sent me this week?

Yeah. She said it wasn't clear what the narrator actually wanted and why she was with all the men, those particular men. She said I need to do work *outside of the story* to figure out her unconscious motive. Then everything in the story needs to point to that motive. But the narrator doesn't know why she did what she did. She was just doing what came naturally to her.

Didn't you say she was looking for something?

Did I?

What was she looking for?

Umm, maybe I think she just wanted their ears.

What? My new therapist says as if I have four heads or four ears or a stash of ears in my purse.

Like she just wanted the guys to hear her, you know, maybe.

My new therapist looks out the window. I guess she's not happy with my answer. Still, I continue:

I think the character probably gave them her body in exchange for their ears, and if she still couldn't get their ears, then she'd have to take something else.

My new therapist is still looking out the window. I wonder if I should turn and look out the window too. Maybe there's something interesting out there.

Since she refuses to participate in our conversation, I go back to complaining:

So then the facilitator looked at me in front of the whole group and said, *Tell me, Norma, what's the copper bracelet about?* I said, I don't know. It just came out when I was writing. *After he tells her where he got the bracelet, the narrator says she doesn't believe a word the beautiful man says. But she actually does believe him, doesn't she?* I don't know. It just came out like that. *Her distrust has something to do with her father wearing an identical bracelet, but the beautiful man isn't like her father. In fact, he's more like the narrator. So what's going on with all of that?* I DON'T KNOW. *That's the work you have to do as a writer. Figure out what the story is trying to say.*

So basically, the facilitator made me feel like the story knows something I don't, and I really don't like that idea.

Why?

Because who's in control then? Me or the story?

Silence.

Who's the conscious or unconscious one? Me or the narrator?

I'm losing you now.

WHY MUST I EXPLAIN EVERYTHING TO HER.

Okay, so if you think of a book:

There's the author who's truly driving the story.

The characters who think they're running the show.

And the manuscript itself that holds all the author's and characters' desires, memories, and contradictions alike.

If you think of a person:

There's the unconscious mind truly driving the person.

The person's conscious mind who thinks it's running the show.

And there's the person's body that holds all the conscious and unconscious desires, memories, and contradictions alike (in its fascia).

My new therapist says, I can see the metaphor you're trying to make.

So when I said who is the conscious and unconscious one, I thought I, as the author, was the one running the show. But now it seems like the story knows more than I do.

But you wrote the story?

That's what I thought.

Silence.

Silence.

Silence.

I say, do you want to know the missing piece of the metaphor?

My new therapist says, sure.

It's God, obviously, that God with a capital *G*. So for a person, God is the judge who's going to deem the person saint or sinner, good or bad, great or terrible, worth it or not worth it. For a book, God is the reader. The critics get to decide if the book is good or bad, great or terrible, worth it or not worth it. They get to decide if you'll make it.

I guess I did have a rant somewhere in me today. Who knew? Probably my unconscious, the real author of my life.

But there's another part to the metaphor. As the author, you can always edit the story later, right? I think that's therapy for a person.

Wow, the metaphor just keeps going.

I could do this all day. I should have a job where I get to make metaphors from nine to five. I'd be really good at it.

But to be honest, right now all this heady talk is making the room hazy. I can't feel my feet anymore.

You're dissociating?

A little bit.

It's great progress that you can identify it when it happens now.

I guess. I used to really like oblivion. Now, I really don't.

My new therapist says, it's because you realize you don't have to dissociate now. Part Of You Now Recognizes That It's Safe To Be Here.

I want to say, don't be flattered. It's not because of you. It's because of her.

But instead I say,

You know, all my life, maybe since my own umbilical cord tried to kill me or maybe since my second memory, I was nostalgic for something and in a constant state of longing. The thing is I didn't know what I was missing. I longed for a time or place or feeling that I'd never experienced before. Maybe a time or place that existed before the planets in the solar system went bald. Maybe a feeling or person from another lifetime (that's what my old therapist said). I wasn't sure what it was that I was missing, but I could feel it in my bones. They were aching. But when I met my girlfriend, the nostalgia drifted away. The missing feeling wasn't missing anymore. It was right there in front of me. In her eyes. On her skin. In the space between our bodies.

What do you mean?

My 1,008th memory is when her and I first began texting. She asked me about which nondairy cheese I liked. To a normal person, I would have responded, well Daiya isn't my favorite but it's okay. But to her, I said, *fuck Daiya.* From the moment we began speaking about nondairy cheese, I could be myself, a self that I barely knew but recognized immediately. My weird, messed-up, uncensored self. I don't know how but I just could. It came naturally with her. She responded, *I know, right. Fuck Daiya. They suck. Most people don't know that.* And as we spoke about how awful most vegan cheese brands are, it's like this veil I had placed over myself just fell off in her presence. And guess what? I actually liked what was underneath the veil. I actually liked myself. It seemed so foreign, and I assumed it was just a fluke, a result of texting before ever seeing the person. But then I met her in person, and even more layers that I had built around myself dropped to the floor. I hadn't even known they were removable. I hadn't even known they were there.

So, my 1,008th through 1,977th memories all involve her and me, and a life without nostalgia grabbing at my hair. A life where we were just living, laughing, having great sex, and being ourselves together. Then Memorial Day. Then I began losing her to oblivion and the signs. And there's no feeling more terrible than that. Not even the feeling of missing something that you've never known before.

But what exactly is this terrible feeling that have you've been experiencing?

I've been feeling the grief of losing a life that I had in my hands, a life that I now know truly exists, and not knowing how to get it back.

I notice you never use the word *love.*

What do you mean?

It seems like you meant to say: what I've been feeling is the grief of losing a Love that I had in my hands, a Love that I now know truly exists, and not knowing how to get it back.

I'm very impressed at my new therapist's ability to repeat exactly what I just said. She must have gone to a really good psychology school.

When I don't say anything, my new therapist says, that word scares you, doesn't it?

Instead of using the word *love*, I call her my one.

Your one?

My new therapist seems concerned.

Yes. I always believed that there was *the one* out there for me and that they were going to take away the nostalgia. Then she came and it really happened. So I call her my one.

I thought you liked the number seven?

eye roll

She continues: Maybe it's more correct to say that your girlfriend didn't take away the nostalgia. Instead, she helped the *real* you emerge, which self-cured the nostalgia?

I don't get it.

You felt nostalgic because you missed yourself, your true self.

I still don't get it.

My new therapist opens her mouth to speak again, but I cut her off:

But anyways my mental breakdown is evidence of my girlfriend not being the one anymore, because if she was the one, this wouldn't have happened.

Maybe she's not the one, because "the one" doesn't exist.

My new therapist puts air quotes around the phrase to diminish its existence. Kind of like when my father says, *oh now you're a "feminist."*

I look at my new therapist and say, my girlfriend doesn't think the one exists either. She says there's just a person across from you and you make it work or you don't. But obviously, she's biased.

I actually agree with her.

I think, of course you do.

But instead I say, if she's not my one, are you saying we should break up?

My new therapist sighs and says, I'm not saying that at all.

But aren't you?

No, I'm saying: "The One" Is A Fairytale Notion. But In Reality, Love (Or Life As You Call It) Is Much More Complex Than It's Portrayed In Books Or Movies. The Complexity Of Real Relationships Is Hard For You, Because Ambivalence Is Concerning To You.

I forgot what ambivalence means and now I'll have to google it again.

Ambivalence: the state of having mixed feelings or contradictory ideas about something or someone.

My new therapist continues, But Ambivalence Is Part Of Every Relationship, Romantic Or Otherwise. Sometimes you'll be enamored with the person, other times they'll annoy you. Sometimes you'll want to be around them, other times you'll want your time alone, maybe so you can write. That's normal. That's healthy.

BUT THAT'S NOT WHAT THEY SAY IN THE BOOKS!

The haze is hazier now.

And all that I'm saying about ambivalence and "the one" not existing . . . these things don't diminish the fact that your girlfriend brings out the best in you, and it is not a sign that you should break up.

She repeats:

It Is Not A Sign.

Then what is it? I want to ask. Instead, I stare at the rug and wonder when the haze will stop hazing so much.

Silence.

Silence.

Silence.

My new therapist says, do you want to tell me how you guys met?

Well then I have to tell you how I came out.

I think that would be very useful to us.

Fertile Ashes

Cinnamon I

Since she announced her pregnancy in December, I have asked my older sister to name her second and upcoming child Phoenix. I have asked her this more than once, though each time she refuses. Over the phone, she asks:

Where'd you come up with that name anyway?

Frankincense I

After my freshman year of college, after the infinite man, I remember thinking that love was like a bird. I was young and willing, back then, to fall in love. I think my willingness came from a belief that I too, like a bird, had wings. Or maybe, that love is what would give me the wings. To be honest, I can't remember exactly what I believed, but what I do remember is that every day I wore a necklace: a long gold chain with a singular bird charm at the end of it. The bird sat directly over my breastbone, perfectly positioned like armor over my heart. I'm not sure where I bought the necklace. Likewise, I'm not sure where the necklace went or flew off to. It left me sometime in college. Perhaps, back then, I thought that love was a bird, because it always flew home. Even without a map. It simply felt where home was and traveled toward it, soaring on and against all elements to get there.

Cassia I

Two months ago, I changed my settings on Hinge.

Frankincense II

These days, I don't often think of love as a bird. Truthfully, I haven't thought of love this way in years. I had even forgotten that I once believed these things until today.

Ginger I

This morning, over hot water and honey, an old friend from high school who had the tendency to turn all the straight guys curious tells me on the phone that fear is the weakest of all the emotions. Truth, he goes on to say, *es la gran cosa.*

Cedar I

In high school, Emily Kavanaugh didn't tell her friends about Rachel from Massachusetts. Emily never told them that Rachel's favorite snacks were, and would always be, Oreos, or that if you asked Rachel to make a baby dinosaur sound, she would perform a tiny squall that could make anyone in the room laugh, even those put off by her buzzed haircut. Emily didn't tell her friends about Rachel, and so she certainly never told them:

Hey Rachel, I'm falling in love with you.

I had spoken to Emily only once before, but of course, I knew her name. Everyone knew her name. She was popular and beautiful like women in the magazines. When we were both sophomores, I was standing in front of her in the cafeteria line, and she asked me if I could hold her spot. She ran over to her boyfriend, who was the star of the water polo team, and kissed him. I watched as he grabbed her butt, as other girls in the dining hall who were also watching wished to be her. I quickly turned away as Emily came running back into the line, out of breath, and thanked me.

Senior year Emily was still dating the water polo star, and I was on the library computer working on my college applications. When I opened Safari, Emily's Facebook popped up, still logged in. I knew what the right thing to do was, but still I went to her messages. That's where I found out about Rachel, the girl she had met on her summer vacation to the Caribbean. I saw their messages and the photos they sent to one another: of the two of them kissing in bikinis on a white sand beach.

Emily, That was a close call yesterday with your boyfriend. This sucks. But one day I know we'll be together.

Ginger II

To my old friend over the phone:

Doesn't our fear come from our past tragedies?

And what is the greatest tragedy?

When I don't answer, he asks:

Who is he?

Cinnamon II

One night, I walked over to my sister's room and told her what I had found on the library computer. Maybe she could help me understand. But after I told her, my sister only said:

If Emily's parents find out, they'll burn her alive. They didn't bring her to America to be gay.

I wanted to tell my sister that Emily was white, and I was pretty sure her great-grandparents had owned slaves. But I didn't say these things. Instead, I nodded and took note.

A couple of mintues later, my sister said,

Good night. I love you.

Cedar II

After that day in the library, I would sit in the dining hall with the few friends I had made from honors English class, but I wouldn't talk very much. Instead, I'd watch Emily from across the room. The way she lunged over the table to whisper a secret into her boyfriend's ear. The way her friends and his friends would cheer and *coo* when they kissed. It had been this way for two years, but now, knowing what I did, I couldn't stop seeing Emily's secret woven into every one of her movements. One day during Spanish class, Emily sat beside me. Our teacher was running late, so kids sat on each other's desks and gossiped, or texted on their Sidekick phones. Out of the blue, Emily turned to me and asked:

Can I count the beauty marks on your arm?

I nodded. She began:

One—two—three—

As she counted, she touched each beauty mark. Beauty marks that I always called freckles. As she touched my skin for the thirty-sixth time, our teacher walked into the room and class began.

Myrrh I

Every day before sitting at my desk to write, I light a stick of palo santo. Some mornings I light the palo santo and, for a long time, I sit there and watch the flames engulf it. The fire circling, twisting, rising. The orange flame, for the briefest of moments, becoming still and revealing the purest red in its center. Sometimes, I feel the urge to touch the blazing stick to the furniture, to the bookshelf, to the walls, to the bed frame. I imagine sitting back and watching the room combust, witnessing the fire grow. To not have to contain it. To not have to be afraid of what it is, what it can do, and what it will do to me. This morning is no exception. The fire is burning. I can smell it in the air.

Myrrh II

Before this week, if someone asked me what, if not a bird, was love to me, I would have said fire.

Cassia II

Two weeks ago, I swiped right.

Cinnamon III

When my sister was pregnant with her first child, I took the train and visited her and her husband's home in Connecticut. I didn't tell my parents that I was in town. I decided it was easier not to. The first night I was there, my sister and I sat on her couch. She took out her at-home ultrasound device and pressed the wand against her stomach, looking for the baby's heartbeat. She searched patiently until she found the sound waves emanating from her womb.

My sister said:

It sounds like a girl's heartbeat, doesn't it?

I didn't know what she meant, so I asked:

Is it? A girl?

We're waiting until the birth.

I responded, saying:

Well it doesn't really matter anyways, right? They could grow up to be transgender or gay or be a girl who likes sports. You never know.

My sister's face suddenly shape-shifted, and she stood up from the couch, glaring at me with her naked belly a foot away from my face.

Why would you say that? My child isn't going to be gay.

And then she stormed off into the other room.

Cedar, Cinnamon, and Myrrh I

Today, when I think of fire, I think of Emily's parents burning her alive and the terror in my sister's face when I told her that her own child could be gay.

Cinnamon IV

When my first niece was born, my sister named her after my mother. I drove in from New York City to meet her. At the hospital, I cried when I first saw the baby. As I held her that day, I remember hoping for this tiny little human's sake, this little baby who could barely open her eyes yet, that she would be exactly what my sister and brother-in-law hoped for her to be. I kissed my niece's forehead and then I whispered in her ear:

But no matter what, Auntie will always love you. Can you hear me? No matter what.

Cedar III

Later that day, I drove to Starbucks to get coffees for the whole family. As I walked toward the entrance, I saw a blond woman holding a man's face, kissing him on the sidewalk of this picturesque little town that I grew up in. The diamond wedding band on the woman's finger glistened in the light. When their kissing faces parted, I realized it was Emily and her water polo boyfriend. I quickly ran into the Starbucks. I'm not sure why I did this. It wasn't as if they would remember me, the shy girl who spent a lot of time in the library. When the couple left in their own car, I walked back to mine with a trayful of Starbucks cups, wondering if Emily still talked to Rachel. If she ever saw her again. If she missed Rachel or herself more. But maybe this was presumptuous of me. Maybe Emily was happy and missed no one.

Ginger III

An hour ago, when my friend on the phone asked what I believed the truest tragedy was, I wish I had said: the truest tragedy is our inability to admit what we're feeling; the way we hide, even from ourselves. Perhaps, without even saying it, this *is* what I said.

Ginger IV

To this day, I have never admitted to my friends that I have never cum with a man.

Until today, I have never admitted to myself that I have never cum with a man.

Cassia III

Two months ago, I changed my settings on Hinge. Two weeks ago, I swiped right. Yesterday, I met her for the first time.

Cassia IV

Her skin was brown and tattooed. Her hair, bleached blond. Her eyes, amber and piercing with an intensity I hadn't known from her pictures. The spring sun was shining on us, but I was shivering. An hour in, She turned and straddled the park bench we were sitting on. Her body faced mine. She asked me if I've ever told someone I was falling in love with them first. I said:

I haven't. The guy has always said it first. And the longest a guy has waited is four weeks.

We both laughed.

You can't know someone in four weeks! Never mind love them!

I agreed with her. Truly, at that moment, I agreed. Then I said:

Truth is, I don't know if I've ever actually loved a man.

How about a woman?

My shivers suddenly turned to heat. The heat rose into my cheeks. In my silence, She looked at me, and I looked at her. At the very edge of her left iris, at the spot closest to her nose, there was a trapezoid-shaped cutout of light, light brown, almost yellow. In her eyes, a crack of sunlight amidst the darkness. Her and I both stayed there staring at one another for just a moment too long; a second too poignant for either of us to conceal. In my chest, where that golden bird used to hang like armor, I felt that missing something, that thing I once felt but couldn't admit to, rise and give birth to itself.

Cassia V

Last night, after we left one another, we spent four hours on Face-Time, and I watched her smile under the purple lights of her bedroom.

Cinnamon V

A month after my niece was born, I was feeling guilty, so I called my sister to apologize for what I had said when we were listening to the heartbeat. I told her that she was right, that it *was* a girl. My sister said:

I don't know what you're talking about.

Deciding to let her erased memory live in peace, I changed the subject to a new animated movie that had just come out. It was a kids' movie, but I told her she'd like it. Then she said:

Remember when we were kids and you said you had a crush on Jasmine. Good thing you grew out of that.

And then she laughed.

Myrrh, Cinnamon, and Cassia I

Today, I awaken, and She is the first thing I think of. To keep from texting her, I wash my face and sit down at my desk. Though I cannot, my writing this morning says it all. My hands, here on the keyboard, have hesitated to give her a name, but She has appeared between every disjointed metaphor. My mind cannot think of anything to write of except of love, and as I write of love, I think of her. To the scent of burning wood and the sunrise of Manhattan, I realize that I'm doing what I've never done so soon. I'm doing, perhaps, what I have never done at all. Still, I can't tell her how I feel. How can I after all we said yesterday? How can I when Emily is married to a man?

Ginger V

Another tragedy, in the midst of many tragedies, is finding yourself falling in love with someone while speaking of the impossibility of such a thing. Another tragedy is letting someone go because you're scared of how they make you feel.

Frankincense and Myrrh I

Most people know that a phoenix dies by bursting into flames and finds new life by rising from its pyre. But what I learn today at my desk is that when a phoenix rises from its ashes, it returns to itself only to live another cycle of life, another five hundred years. It is said that only one phoenix exists on earth at a time. And so it is said that only once in five hundred years, a fire, unlike any other, can be witnessed. I wonder what it looks like when the phoenix sets fire to itself. When its desire for rebirth finally overcomes its fear of death. Fear: the weakest emotion. The cause of the truest tragedy, like not being able to say what I really feel. *You're a woman, I just met you, and I think I could, like none of the others, love you.* I wonder if the bursting of oneself into flames hurts just as much as being burned by someone else's fire.

Myrrh III

Every day I light the palo santo at my desk, and I sit there watching the elements, like a person, dance around the wood. For a moment, I get lost among them. I would like for this moment to last forever. But eventually, I blow the fire out. Most likely, I blow it out before it's necessary, because I don't want to get burned. I'm cautious. I always have been. I have been taught to be since I was too young to know what a crush really meant. Though I didn't know what was happening, I remember my skin aflame. My organs, my heart, in ashes. The ashes blowing away in the wind like a bird but with no wings. Today, I wonder where my ashes settled. I wonder if they somehow silently found their way back to me.

I never gave my heart a map, but maybe, like a bird, it could just feel its way back home.

Pyre I

Today, if someone asked me what, if not a bird, if not fire, is love to me, I would most likely say, surrender.

Pyre II

When I finish writing about love this morning, I go on Facebook. Back in high school, this is where everything happened. Now it's just a scrapbook for wedding, baby, and funeral announcements. I click to begin a new message. I type in my sister's name. Her profile picture pops up with her, her husband, her daughter, and her new belly. This time around, my sister wanted to know the gender. Another girl. In the message box, I write: *I like girls. I always have. I'm telling Mom and Dad tonight.*

Then I go to type *I'm sorry*, but I delete it.

Instead, I write *I hope you'll still let me see your daughters.*

And as I type this, I feel tears on my cheeks.

Pyre III

Before the phoenix surrenders itself to its own fire, it creates a nest it will burn itself atop of. It collects items to make this deathbed, which will then become its own womb. It dresses the nest with wood and spices like myrrh, cinnamon, cassia, ginger, and frankincense. Once the nest is made, the phoenix bursts into flames. When its bone and marrow are completely burned, only ash remains. Legend says, from the ash, a worm grows and from that worm, another phoenix "miraculously" rises. There is no prescribed time before one rises again. There is no warning sign or incubation date. Perhaps the process of rebirth is ignited in the simplest of moments: the adjusting of a dating app setting, the vision of a particular woman's smile, a singular swipe right, and the courage to type *hey.* Or perhaps it begins when two pairs of eyes meet for just a moment too long, revealing a crack of sunlight that can no longer be denied or forgotten. Perhaps there is an art we must learn from the phoenix. The art to fearlessly choose for ourselves. To choose when we finally let go of the past and allow ourselves to be reborn from the fertile ashes of who we once were.

Ashes I

To the scent of burning wood, I click Send and close my laptop. I pick up my phone and go to her name. I write, *I can't stop thinking about that moment yesterday.* I see three dots appear on the screen. And then, *I can't either. Maybe four weeks isn't that long.*

THE STUDY OF OBLIVION

twenty-four weeks since breakdown

You see, to look into a mirror is not always enjoyable—

Next stop Twenty-third Street.

Ugh. I roll my eyes. This conductor keeps interrupting me. I try to ignore the sounds and continue:

—Often when we look at the mirror, we don't see the face before us. We see only the mirror itself. Frequently, this is the case because we are in a rush. Other times, we choose not to look, because we have been taught that our faces will have something wrong with them and they will be ugly. So we'd rather turn away.

Her response: I would have to argue with you, though, because I look in the mirror every day to do my hair or my makeup or just to brush my teeth.

Right. You look in the mirror—

Twenty-third Street. Do not hold the doors open. I repeat, do not hold the doors open.

I start again:

You look in the mirror *to do* something to yourself; to make yourself better or presentable or clean. But have you ever looked in the mirror just to look?

Sometimes.

And when you look in the mirror, do you ever get closer just to stare into your own eyes?

No. Unless I have a piece of lint or an eyelash in there.

Of course. Unless something is bothering you.

She asks: Do *you* look into your own eyes?

Not every day. But sometimes when I'm brave enough, yes. Or sometimes it is not bravery, but curiosity that takes over, and then, before I know it, my nose is leaning against the glass and I am staring into my eyes. I see my eyes looking back at me and me looking back at my eyes, and they are so close. It's unsettling. My eyes should be familiar, but they are the most unfamiliar thing in the world. And I hear myself say to myself in the mirror: *There I am.* It's terrifying. Soon after, I have to walk away from the mirror, because—

Does anyone have any spare change? Can you help me? Just a quarter.

Sorry, all card.

As I was saying, if you haven't done this before, I encourage you to try it.

Have you said anything else to your own eyes as you look into them through the mirror?

I have, though I'd like to get back to the topic of my manuscript.

Why would you want to share this type of work with the public? It's pretty depressing and insane. What benefit exists in sharing this if, like you say, the world is dying?

Benefit?

Yes, benefit.

The benefit is the mirror it creates. The moment where someone looks into it and hears themselves saying: *There I am.* And then one can walk away from the story. From there, whatever the person does with what they saw of themselves may seem beneficial to someone and exactly the opposite to another. Stories themselves are not beneficial (unless we're speaking of dollars in publishing houses' pockets). It is what people *do* after they read them—

Norma, there are some packages for you in the mail room. Lots of Chewy boxes.

I'll get them tomorrow. Thanks!

Can you see how your writing can be difficult to read and comprehend sometimes, almost nonsensical? Why is that?

Because sometimes nonsense is the only sense that can be made from what presents itself. For example, reality. It is utterly nonsensical. To make sense of it would be to completely unwrite its essence. The writing reflects the concept of which it tries to conceptualize.

And the targeted concept of this current…conversation?

Understanding—

What floor?

Twenty-fourth. Thanks.

And the form reflects itself how?

Through dialogue. A back-and-forth. The said and the unsaid. The boundaries and non-boundaries between the two. The attempt to answer questions that have not yet been asked. The attempt to ask questions that do not, up to this point, have answers. To find the answers through imagination, which, like language, is a mechanism for trying to understand.

To be honest, this book seems like too ambitious of a project.

When you use the phrase "too ambitious," I get the sense that you believe it will fail. What if it doesn't—

Hi, honey!

Hi!

None of this conversation actually happens between me and my new therapist. She canceled on me again this week, so this conversation only happens in my head when I'm on the subway coming back from an eye doctor appointment where the doctor said I definitely have a lot of mucus in my eyes but she's not sure where it's coming from and can't help me.

In my head, there is a woman interviewing me about my manuscript-turned-book. She is sitting on a purple velvet chair, and she tells me, before they start filming, that the interview will be released on their highly popular YouTube channel and it will do wonders for my book.

I like to call this exercise positive visualization, but maybe the imaginary conversation went on too long and will be diagnosed as Maladaptive Daydreaming. I'm sure my new therapist would diagnose it like that. Anyways, when I get home, I have to cut the interview short because the cats greet me at the door and my girlfriend, who is sitting on the couch, has loudly said, *hi, honey*, which means she's in the mood to chitchat. She opens her arms for me to come lie with her, but I tell her I have to wash my armpits first, because I forgot deodorant today and I stink. When I come back from the bathroom, I tell her I sent my new therapist the story I wrote about meeting her. My girlfriend gets excited, because she loves that story.

When I first showed the story to my girlfriend, she said it was a little confusing and that she had a hard time understanding the spices. So I explained it to her, and when she read it again, she said it was her favorite story in the whole world. I told you she loves a love story. Plus, she's a Libra, so she likes to be written about.

THE STUDY OF OBLIVION

twenty-five weeks since breakdown

You know, you're the one who said I need therapy twice a week, and now you're the one canceling my sessions, leaving me floating around without supervision for two weeks at a time. Your time management sucks and it's very unprofessional especially in your line of work and it makes me feel abandoned and awful and you've really gotta stop this shit.

That's what I want to say to my new therapist, but instead I say,

You canceled again, is everything okay?

My new therapist says, everything is good, and then she smiles as if she just returned from vacation and is feeling so rejuvenated.

I want to scream, but instead I just adjust my bangs over my forehead, and say,

Did you read "Fertile Ashes"?

I sound little when I say this. Like miniature. Like a Polly Pocket. Like I'm begging for something. I really need to work on my vocal tone.

I did read it. I was wondering: how *did* your parents take your coming out?

Well they certainly didn't burn me alive.

What was their response?

My mom called me disgusting, threatened to cut me off, said that she was going to kill herself, and then didn't talk to me for a while. Two months later, she called me: said her hair was thinning and that she would accept me because it was, surely, just a phase. Almost a year after coming out, I made my parents meet my girlfriend. Actually they met her for the first time the Wednesday after Memorial Day.

Really? My new therapist says while vigorously scribbling something down on her clipboard. Yesterday I asked my girlfriend if one day she would break into my new therapist's office with me and steal my file. She said, of course, without hesitation. This is why we work.

But yeah, my mom still calls every once in a while and says she still wants to kill herself but doesn't exactly say why. I'm guessing it's my fault.

That's a terrible thing to say to your child.

Is it?

Yes.

Huh. I shrug. Seems normal to me.

And your father's response to your coming out?

He seemed ... I know it's weird to say ... but happy. Or maybe proud. Or maybe just like he understood. Like yeah, duh, women are fucking hot. Then immediately after I told him he asked what my girlfriend looked like.

I laugh when I finish my sentence, like ha ha isn't my dad so cool? But then my new therapist goes, that's kind of odd that he wanted to know her physical appearance before asking any other questions about her.

My new therapist insists on ruining everything.

My new therapist continues, and that was a Big Risk, you telling your parents after just having met her and not knowing what was going to happen between you two?

Yeah.

My new therapist keeps going: your girlfriend Meant That Much To You that you wanted to live a truthful life. That's really beautiful.

I guess.

It reminds me of what we talked about two weeks ago with her bringing out this side of you that inspires you to be yourself.

I feel the room start to magnify in my eyes, my therapist's feet inching closer and closer to my face while getting, simultaneously, blurrier. I try to speak it away:

To be honest, I think I was just ready to tell my parents. I had known I was gay for a whole year before I met her, starting back when I scraped all the men out.

My new therapist cocks her head to the side, confused.

I remember when I used to think she looked like a dog when she did this. Now I see a dog cock its head and I think of her.

She says, scraped . . . all . . . the . . . men . . . out . . . ? . . . ? . . . ?

Yeah, like got them out of my body.

Got them out of your body?

Ugh. I need a translator.

Yeah. It was the shittiest time in my life.

Well, actually, *this* shitty time has topped *that* shitty time. I wonder what shittier thing will come next.

Oh? Why haven't we spoken about it before?

I'd rather forget it.

I mean, I'm forgetful, remember?

Right.

Why was it such a bad time?

A lot changed.

Change is hard for you.

You can say that again.

Change is hard for you.

So what had happened was...

I got HPV and that's when I realized all the men I'd let into my body had made me sick, and this appearance of these nasty abnormal cells that were almost cervical cancer were god's way of saying, halt, wrong direction, assess. So then I had to halt, look around, and assess, and it sucked.

I wish my new therapist would assess her pillow placement. God could send her an interior decorator as a patient, and the interior decorator could say, *ma'am, I'm paying you, but you should be paying me. Let's do an exchange and I'll turn this office into a paradise.* My new therapist would, at first, be offended, but then after her office was all white and beige with no wooden robot and no textile pillows, she'd be really happy.

Norma?

Yeah.

You stopped talking mid-sentence.

Oh. Where did I leave off?

You said, what had happened was . . . And then you trailed off.

I want to laugh out loud when my new therapist says, what had happened was, but instead I wonder what else I can make her repeat.

Boogie-woogie.

Huh?

Never mind.

My new therapist says, I'm very curious as to why we haven't spoken about this time before, and I'd like to speak about it when you're ready.

So I say, oh don't worry. I'll send you a story about it this week. But remember the story comes *before* "Fertile Ashes."

I thought the stories were in chronological order?

They're in whatever order is necessary for the story to make sense. Remember, there's supposed to be an arc.

An arc as dramatic as my eye rolls.

But like my eye rolls, I don't think I have control over the story anymore.

I say, you'll finally get to see the character's "inner reckoning"!

I want her to say, *ooh I'm excited. Sounds juicy*, but instead she says:

I was thinking… you never explained why you call the infinite man the infinite man.

Oh god, she's still caught up on *that* story. I think the drugs really threw her off.

I say, because he gave me my writing.

What does that have to do with infinity?

Well, because my words, read or not, aren't mortal like me. They'll exist on earth long after I'm gone. And maybe even, when the next meteor crashes into earth, the pages of my work, stuck in a landfill somewhere, will be propelled into space from the impact. Pieces of my manuscript will be floating in the darkness, pages and pages of words floating around the spinning bald planets for centuries, or maybe even long after the sun burns out, long after time becomes immeasurable. My writing dancing around meaningless, spinning. Evidence of existence spiraling, again and again, around nothingness. You know?

Really, I say: I don't know.

I see. Well, I was just wondering, because he's got a lot of real estate in your manuscript.

Don't remind me. I think my girlfriend will be jealous. But he was important.

How?

I think in a weird way, even though we isolated ourselves from it, the infinite man made me aware of the world. It's paradoxical, I know. But he opened my eyes to things beyond myself. For example, I didn't care about politics before him.

I realize how stupid that sounds: this person was important because they made me care about politics.

Yuck.

Anyways, can we stop talking about him, because the narrative has moved on, and he hated New York City and this next story is my love letter to the city?

Okay.

Thank god.

I go to stand up and pick up my purse, but my new therapist says,

Where are you going? We still have ten minutes left.

UGHHHHH.

The F Train

Since the moment I was born, I have been dying. Always perpetually dying. When I was twenty-five, the world *finally* acknowledged this truth after years of persisting that I was very much alive and more alive with each day. They had no choice but to agree with me that summer; my body was decaying before their very eyes. I understood people's hesitation to admit that my dying wasn't new. For if they admitted to *my* ever-approaching demise, they would've had to admit to their own. Death scares people.

When we reached the antiques mall, Felix and I went straight to the fourth floor, the mecca of glass curios filled with miniature delicacies of history, otherwise known by my mother as "garbage." It was the last standing antiques mall in Manhattan, which unfortunately would soon be closing its first and second floors, leaving only the fourth floor with the gems of its collection. The owners planned to rent out the main floors to some chain restaurant in order to make Flatiron rent. Those days, survival, it seemed, depended on the emptying and scraping of the old—with its memories made to rust and tarnish in a way that only a few, like Felix, could appreciate—to make way for some false promise of pleasure or permanence.

Felix and I walked through each aisle of antiques, turning back and forth, kneeling and standing, maneuvering our bodies in such a way as to not miss a thing in the crowded cabinets. As we did this, I told Felix about my belief: that we were *all*, *always* dying, that it had been this way since our first breaths and snips of our umbilical cords, perhaps even before that, when we, not yet we but two halves of "we," met and formed as one. Felix listened to me with his eyebrows thickly stacked over his brown, almost black, eyes.

From behind his circular gold-framed glasses, Felix said:

*In your proposed paradigm, life seems to be equivalent to dying.
So if we die in life do you think we live in death?*

Greenwich Village

During the first week of sophomore year at NYU, I arrived for my
first creative writing workshop fifteen minutes early. A boy arrived a
minute later, sat down beside me, and placed a vintage film camera
in front of him in the place of a notebook. He introduced himself:

Felix. Felix Yang.

He held out his hand for me to shake. It was odd: this guy my age
being so genuinely formal. When I shook his hand, he didn't collapse his wrist or loosen his grip for me. Likewise, he didn't squeeze
harder to overcompensate nor did he caress my skin with his
thumb. I decided then that I wouldn't steal from him. As we talked
about our prospective dorms, Felix and I overheard the couple next
to us talking about Coney Island. One of them mentioned that to get
there, they could take the F. Felix whispered:

The F to Coney Island!!

We both laughed, thinking the overheard conversation was a sexual
innuendo, a joke about lovers entering a metaphorical funhouse.
Transportation to paradise? F for fucking. Neither of us knew that
this was truly how one arrived at Coney Island, with its boardwalk
of fried food and the Cyclone: by taking the F train. We learned this
a couple of days later at the dining hall. Together we laughed again.
This time at our naivety. In our defense, we had just moved to New
York City only a year ago (he from Hong Kong, I from Connecticut),
and for a whole year neither of us had taken the subway.

Two weeks after our first meeting, Felix and I took a trip out to Coney Island. When we got there, I smiled at the vision of the ocean, and Felix smiled at me. As nineteen-year-olds, we tried our fake IDs at the bars and when that didn't work, like children, we played carnival games and rode the Tilt-A-Whirl. Sweat blanketed our skin as we ate Nathan's hot dogs and talked about our dreams: he wanted to be a gallery curator and I wanted to be a writer. Our artistic dreams could only, we decided, be accomplished in a city as grand as this one. We pinkie promised then, as the sun penetrated our pores, that we, side by side, wouldn't leave New York City until we both made our dreams come true.

Flatiron

I was considering Felix's question as I looked into the curio before me. There were sniffing bottles from China and gold-plated jewelry from the thirties. I finally responded:

> *Yeah, I'd like to think that life begins in death. This "living in life" thing has been kind of a drag.*

Felix tilted his head slightly to the right, and I could tell that my pessimism had become an art piece for him. His eyes scanned my face: the middle of my forehead then down my nose, circling around my eyes and cheekbones, my pointy chin. He looked at me as if I were a framed photograph that he must hang on the walls of the gallery that he worked for downtown. He had, by that time, already made his dream of being a curator come true. I, on the other hand, was still struggling to write my first book.

Felix's mouth curled downward, as if asking himself where would he put me: what wall could hold me and what wall could *I* hold? But then an old wallet-sized photograph caught his eye and Felix exclaimed, almost shouting:

That child had to have been sitting like that for at least four min-
utes in order for the photographer to get that picture! Look at how
clear it is! Gorgeous!

I looked into the photograph of the child. A light from behind our
heads reflected off the glass cabinet, making me shift my body to
the right in order to get a clear look at the curly-haired forever-still
adolescent. The girl had on a white dress with frilly, fancy socks.
They were almost identical to the ones my mother used to dress me
in when I was the model's age. I remembered wearing those socks
on the summer day that my parents dropped me and my sister off
at Harry's house, leaving us with an old family friend for their first
solo vacation "since the kids." My mother always said that I was the
best-dressed kid in our town.

Felix kept maneuvering around the curio to look at the little girl from
all angles. Only a photograph could puncture Felix's composure like
that. I always thought Felix's self-containment was a result of his
being Chinese and raised Buddhist. To him, life was not a pleasure
palace, but instead it was a place where you worked hard, performed
your duty, appreciated the benefits (not too much), and took death
when it came with a sense of gratitude and relief: your work, finally,
completed. To sum it up Western-style: *it is what it is.* For Felix, art
existed in the slow unraveling of *life's processes*, the *becoming* of
something. Because of this, Felix was the only person I had ever told
about the memory that returned in my early twenties, the memory
that I once, sincerely, believed was a dream. I knew that Felix would
respond to it with neutrality and an air of disinterest, and because
of this, I would feel unbroken.

I, on the other hand, saw life as more hopelessly romantic; anach-
ronic events dancing along a climactic arc. Even as a child with my
Barbies, I had the ability to connect seemingly minuscule and dis-
parate events into a dramatic story. There was a reason for every-

thing: every drop of an eyelash or flick of a cigarette, and I could find it. Unlike Felix, I found art in the *drama* of life, the *narrative* one imposes on events. And my life proved to present itself in this plot-like way; the climax most probably when I first heard about my diagnosis on a Wednesday at two p.m.

Chelsea

To the sensation of spontaneous combustion, I thanked the doctor, hung up the phone, and began to weep, loudly. Then I placed my forehead to the floor, which I had already been kneeling on since I first heard the C word a minute before. This time double C. With my forehead on the floor, boogers defeated gravity and came up and out of my nose. My cat, Fiero, watched this happen from his cream-colored perch by the sofa. Mid-sobbing, I thought, suddenly outside of myself, what a terribly tragic vision: a young girl in desperate agony and genuinely overtaken by emotions. A wondrous portrayal! A thickening, surprising plot! *Brava!* I applauded quietly within myself like a true patron of the art world. Then, to my dismay, I was shoved back into my body to face reality: that my cervix was consuming itself, that my own cells had turned against me.

I was one of the unlucky ones, the smallest percentage, the defeater of the stats. Even before the whole ordeal, I had refuted the concept of statistics or likelihoods as a coping mechanism or a crystal ball. Probability didn't account for individual actuality, and one person could fit anywhere, even in the 1 percent. In the beginning of it all, I wasn't so anomalous (or like Felix described my predicament: "unique"). At first, I was just one of the many: young woman, abnormal cells, HPV. Then I was one of the unlucky: high-risk abnormality, CIN III, severe dysplasia, which meant spreading. Then I turned into one of the even unluckier few: precancerous, still spreading, aggressive. Then I was the very smallest percentage, the very unfortunate, unlucky elite: cancerous. That's when I fell to my knees and cried, the plot unraveling.

Me to C was a progression that happened over two years. After I went in for the initial cell removal procedure, back when I only had HPV and was still sleeping with (and stealing from) a different man every week, I would sometimes fantasize about getting C. I fantasized about this because I believed that words held more weight coming from someone who was dying as if, because the person was closer to leaving this world, they became a prophet, a medium between here and the other side. They gained respect. That would be useful, I thought, as it related to my dreams of being a famous writer. Maybe I would finally publish the book I'd been working on for years, and because of the diagnosis, people would read it. I also thought that I would like to, if I got C, tell Tay what I actually thought about her marrying a guy from Cape Cod. I thought: if I'm dying, I won't need a filter, won't have enough time for a filter.

In case you were wondering, dying doesn't gain you respect. Your words don't turn to scripture. Your monologues aren't recorded or rehearsed. It's more like you're just constantly trying not to cry, and you spend most of your time telling the people who love you that you're okay and going to be okay (a lie), and while you're trying to convince yourself that a miracle is possible and heaven is real, your family and friends will need convincing of this too. This is your job. After all, you're the one who's dying.

Also, if you decide to *not* do what the doctors tell you will keep you alive (only alive for a bit longer . . . remember we all die at some point), you should prepare to be verbally assaulted by those closest to you. My sister had a lot to say about my not getting chemo and radiation:

   You're acting like a fucking idiot!

And then there was my mother, who couldn't fathom why I had chosen to forgo the invasive treatments and rely solely on naturopathic and herbal medicine. She called me on the phone almost every day cursing at me. And when she was, instead, standing in the living room of my apartment, she would grab me by my shoulders and shake me, as if her force could somehow rattle some sense into me.

After I had just spent the whole day trying to edit a short story only to, in the end, find the new draft even worse than the last, my mother called me for a fourth time:

> *Don't be stupid, Norma. This isn't a joke. I told you not to have sex before you were married. This is what happens. Men are disgusting. Men are pigs! How could you let this happen?*

My mother thought that there was something seriously wrong with me, even worse than the C word, because I wasn't crying with her on the phone, but a few days earlier, with a wad of California roll in my mouth, I had already promised myself: *no more!* no more tears, no more spilling anything out of myself except for words. This was a necessary promise after having spent every day post-finding-out-about-C sobbing, watching Netflix, and ordering shitty sushi delivery. Enough was enough, I decided. I didn't need to get parasites and mercury poisoning on top of everything. No more two-star sushi delivery and no more crying.

To my relief, after I told Felix about C, he remained utterly himself, entertaining me with the same old topics at our same old lunch dates. I expected nothing less or more from Felix. He displayed the perfect amount of neutrality on the topic of mortality in order to make me feel like I wasn't, even for an afternoon, dying, or at least if I was dying (which we all are) that it didn't matter.

Greenwich Village

We were twenty-three. Felix and I were at Dante's, celebrating his promotion. He was now in a position to curate a handful of shows at the Terchin Gallery downtown. We had just touched our champagne glasses in a toast when he looked at me, right hand still holding his glass, his left moving to the music of his words, and said:

Life is an exhibit, and you are the curator. You decide which pieces of art stand alone and which should be seen as a whole.

I decided, at that moment, to give Felix his own pedestal in the gallery of my ever-dying life.

You see, Norma, you adjust the lighting and angle the frames. And you and only you mark the opening and closing of the show.

He paused for effect.

But, of course, you already know what I mean. Your collection of poetry.

Despite telling Felix for years that I wrote works of fiction, not poetry, he always referred to my work as such. It confused me each time he did this, making me feel that he was not a forgetful friend but rather that he was trying to send me a message. He was always subtle with his offering of opinions in relation to everything except visual art. Some may have said that his lack of opinions was evidence of his lack of care, but I thought he was this way because he allowed people to be whoever they needed to be.

Like, for example, Felix detested cigarettes, but when I smoked in front of him, he would always say:

It just fits you so well! And the writer in you. It just works.

That was back then when I smoked half a pack a day. Now it had been a year, two months, and seven days since I'd stopped smoking. With every ounce of desire, my lungs craved to have American Spirits fill them again. In fact, to have any cigarettes fill them; give me Camel Crush for all I cared! It was a terrible, symptomatic "lifestyle change" (the words of my naturopath), which had the potential to, perhaps, stop the cell growth from getting worse: cancer-izing as I liked to call it. It could, she said, even reverse the whole process. But quitting smoking didn't live up to its potential. I still got C, and now I had no cigarettes, which made me wish more than ever before that there was a heaven, so that when I got there I could chain-smoke my days away. I'd be there in the sky, sitting with my grandmother Rose, ashing our cigarettes into the clouds, her telling me how lovely it was to have me there and exactly why she jumped when she got to America. God, I hoped heaven existed and that it was like that. But since I unbaptized myself in college, I was running low on faith.

East Village

A few months after the failed cell removal procedure, Felix and I met for breakfast at Veselka. By the time our food arrived, we had already sunk deep into the rhythmic ranting of two artists. I said:

> I think there are unseen forgotten forces which drive us. The concept of free will is more like the will of a Pavlovian past or multiple pasts if someone believes in reincarnation, like you.

Felix placed his elbows on the table and clasped his hands in front of his chin:

> And what have you concluded from your consideration?

> Oh, that I have no free will. The unseen forces of others were once thrust upon me, and now I carry their burden. Choice isn't real, but instead my choices are built from others' "choices," which are built from others and so on and so forth.

Like Harry.

A shock ran through my body as I remembered that someone out-side of myself knew of Harry and what he did, and that *I* had told them. Harry's face flooded my mind's eye. I tried to hold down the pancakes. Felix continued:

I've been meaning to ask you something. Have you considered—

Felix sipped from the edge of his coffee cup as if killing time. I had never seen him stall before.

—therapy?

For what?

I looked Felix directly in his eyes as if warning him not to go any further. It was a look my mother used to give me and my sister when we giggled in Mass on Sunday morning: a silent warning, which we surrendered to immediately. Felix, however, did not surrender:

For what happened.

I placed my fork down on the table, the nausea rising:

No. I'm perfectly fine.

What happened to you—And you just remembering after all these years. It's hard to process alone—

No, Felix. I'm good, really. It's not like I didn't remember at all. It's more like I wasn't conscious that I knew it.

Yeah, but you wouldn't be the first artist in therapy.

Felix.

It's quite common actual—

Stop! Just stop it!

The words spewed from my lips like a dog's bark. Felix sulked against his chair as if he was a sculptor who had just accidentally, with a slip of his tool, made a chip in his masterpiece. Silence echoed across the table, and I bargained with my brain to, once again, store away Harry's name and face to the outer edges of my mind. I bargained with my brain by offering it a dopamine hit, chocolate, immediately after breakfast. It didn't take.

Finally, after what felt like an hour (it was probably more like three to five minutes), Felix found a way to restore the fractured artwork. By completely ignoring the chip's existence. As if the prior conversation had never happened, Felix said:

I forgot to ask, how's your mother doing?

I nodded. Once and small enough so that only he could see it. It was an act of forgiveness and forgetting.

Same old. She wants me to move back.

I mocked:

"Die with us, Norma. Die with us."

My mother couldn't understand, like really couldn't even begin to understand, why I wanted to die alone in New York rather than in Connecticut around family. To be honest, no one but Felix understood it. For ten years, following my move to the city, I'd held the innate belief that there was no place other than New York City worth living in, and similarly, I felt in the end, worth dying in. I couldn't move away from the city that taught me about art and fueled my writing, the city that brought me to Felix and summer days in Coney Island. Besides, I still hadn't made my dreams come true. I couldn't leave until I did. I had made a promise to Felix.

And what do you want?

Flatiron

I watched as Felix called over an employee and asked them questions about the photograph of the little girl. He was wearing his brown army jacket, vintage of course, and his camera hanging across his chest. I remember the day he bought that jacket from a shop in the Village. He showed up to lunch at Frida's wearing it, and, when he saw me, he did a little pirouette. Whenever I pictured Felix in my mind, I always saw him in that army jacket. It was as if he existed inseparably from that article of clothing: shearling collar, light brown distress marks etched into soft brown leather, his hands peeking out of the sleeves with one ring on his index finger, a silver band wrapped around his skin. Forever when I thought of Felix I was sure that I would think of him in that jacket. Perhaps, I would—I could only hope—think of him like this too in death. Felix's camera bobbed against his rib cage as he shook the employee's hand.

From the handshake, I'm guessing you bought it.

He smiled proudly:

Yes, I did.

Now let's find something for you, my poet.

What Felix didn't know was that after getting C, my dreams of being a famous writer drained out of me along with the vaginal suppositories of Fem-Dophilus and Curamin, which stained my underwear yellow. Instead, writing simply became a coping mechanism for my condition. My naturopath told me that this would happen, not the writing stuff, but the stained underwear. Though she didn't tell me that it wouldn't be an egg-yolk yellow that slithered out of me, but instead a blazing yellow that was closer to a neon orange, the color of the sun as it set over Jersey. Before I started the treatment, my naturopath recommended that I wear underwear I didn't care about during that time—that time being once daily for six months, and then when the abnormal cells kept spreading, once daily for a year, and then when the C came, twice daily for a year and eight months. So really just to switch over to ugly granny panties all the time, for the rest of my life.

Upon her initial recommendation, I then had to go to Marshalls to buy underwear that I didn't "care about." I wore them both in the day and in the night, since the liquid that was supposed to heal me liked to ooze out of me at the most inconvenient times. After weeks of the orange that was supposed to be yellow, I realized that I would most likely die in cheap cotton underwear from Marshalls that had orange stains in the crotch. I decided that I would make an amendment to my will, which did not yet exist: *Bury me in a Victoria's Secret thong* alongside *NO BRA*. The latter I thought should be obvious. I hadn't worn a bra since senior year of high school, when I realized that I was blessed with breasts and nipples that were petite enough to be set free, my rib cage and shoulders unburdened by the pressure of being squeezed and hoisted by a contraption that society had somehow made women believe was beautiful, necessary, and comfortable. Bras were, I thought, similar to a mental hospital: a wire-bordered cage with padding on the walls to make it bearable. Bras were either similar to a mental hospital or similar to life altogether. To be honest, it doesn't matter. They're the same thing.

Coney Island

One summer day in Coney Island with Felix when we were twenty-three, my small, unhinged breasts flipped upside down as we looped around the orange tracks of the Thunderbolt while Felix screamed. It was undeniably the most emotion I had ever seen come out of Felix's body. I laughed endlessly at his foreign sounds as we zigzagged through the remainder of the ride. When the lap bar went up, Felix was nauseous and spent from all the emotion. We cured the nausea with two cheap tequila sunrises from Tom's. We sat outside under an umbrella, and as we got drunk, we imagined intricate life stories for the people who passed by us on the boardwalk. We would alternate sentence after sentence, adding on to the narrative that the other had created. An hour and a half and three tequila sunrises later, we had exhausted our imaginations and decided to make our way to the F train. Manhattan was calling, reminding us that we had work tomorrow: Felix at the gallery, me at my desk with my new short story. The alcohol buzzed in our brains as we waited for the F train.

This was back when I could drink alcohol like a normal person. During the initial HPV consult with my naturopath, she said:

> I'm glad you're forgoing the Western treatment. I can work with you and treat it holistically. But I have rules. No cigs. No alcohol. A special diet. Lots of herbs. Oh, and no dating.

By "dating" she meant "having sex," which I found interesting. To my naturopath's surprise, I was relieved by this news. It was nice to have been given a reason why I couldn't sleep with men. I enjoyed their company, but sex . . . I would never really say I enjoyed it. I would do it because, well, what else is there to do. When I was drunk I could tolerate sex. But when I was sober I thought of Harry, and I never knew why. It was odd. With a guy's dick inside of me, I thought of Harry's face, my sister and I playing *Spyro* in his living room (her, obviously, winning and traveling into portals while I watched her in awe). It was the summer my parents went on their first trip without the kids. Harry telling six-year-old me that I needed to take a shower. No, my sister could stay there. She was nine. For years, I could only remember my sister on the couch playing *Spyro* and Harry's awful '90s tracksuit leading me upstairs.

The F Train

I first told Felix about C over an hour-long train ride to Coney Island. My hands were shaking.

> *I'm sorry, Norma. But hey, it's not a lost cause. You know there's chemo and radiation.*

I interrupted Felix by shaking my head definitively. The train lurched to a stop and one person got off.

> *No?*

I shook my head again. Remembering that day at Veselka when I almost bit his head off about therapy, his speech slowed:

> *Okay . . . well . . . now what?*

Staring out the train window at the blur of Brooklyn, I said:

> *We spend today just like we would any other. Riding roller coasters, wasting our money at the games, and going back to Manhattan hoping we don't have sunburns.*

Felix was silent, and I thought that his mind must have wandered to whether he had applied sunscreen or not, or, perhaps, to some facet of the art world to ponder over. I peeled my vision away from the window and turned to look at him. His eyes were fixed on his lap, and there was one tear rolling down his cheek. It was the first time in eight years that I had ever seen him cry. I hated that somehow C had managed to crack stoic, measured Felix down to a human like me. I tried then, as the dying do, to make him feel better.

Felix, you of all people know that there is an art to dying. It is, after all, the final step of the artistic process. Are you jealous that I get to do it before you?

Felix raised his eyes to meet mine, his singular tear bobbing at his chin. He said, almost whispering:

Are you scared?

One stop later and six stops away from Coney Island, I finally managed to respond.

Yes, I'm scared—

Tears began to form in my eyes, but I held them back. It was just an artistic rant. It was just philosophy.

I'm scared of ceasing to exist. Of dying only to find that this was the only show, the only gallery. That there are no others, and the exhibition has been permanently taken down. Then being outside on the street in the dark, and there's not even a street, and there's not even me, and no one else is there. And if that's true, then I'm scared of never having written what I needed to write—

I took a deep breath and continued:

—I'm scared of dying with my dreams stuck inside of me and the vision of his face in my head.

Finally, I had said out loud what I could never say to my mother, sister, or naturopath.

Felix turned his body toward mine, sliding his vintage jeans on the slippery blue of the subway seats. He stared directly into my eyes, into a place that could only be properly described as the soul, and just as quickly as his stoic strength broke, it resurrected. He grabbed my hand:

Norma, of course . . . of course, you will be able to write in heaven.

I looked at him in shock and through my tears burst out laughing.

But you're Buddhist?!

To this, Felix laughed his perfect laugh and shrugged his shoulders. We spent the rest of that day as if we were eighteen again, and I felt as if I would live forever.

Lower East Side

Before C, before my naturopath, before Veselka, and before the yellow-staining suppositories, back when I first started beating the statistics, my gynecologist mentioned an invasive treatment where she could open me up, carve into my cervix, and scrape the bad cells away. I refused at first, telling her that Pap smears were already a nightmare. Still, she said it could save my life.

It's only twenty minutes. A simple standard procedure. We do dozens of these a day.

She said this with a tone that insinuated that I and my drama were bothering her.

After months of her insisting, I decided to try it. After all, I didn't want to get C. My mother came in from Connecticut to accompany me to the procedure, saying hopefully it was quick with no complications because she had a plane to catch the next day. My mother sat beside me as the gynecologist lubricated the speculum between my naked, spread-apart legs. A shiver ran up my body from the AC, and the gynecologist said:

You're gonna feel a little pressure.

Then she placed the large, slimy metal contraption inside of me. At the feeling of the unwanted object sliding into me, I winced and my body contracted.

We're gonna open you up now to get a clear look at the cervix. Then we can start.

The doctor pressed the speculum open, and the metal pushed violently against the walls of my vagina, spreading them away from each other, the diameter of my cylindrical insides multiplying by twenty. The act created unbearable pressure in my lower stomach and jolted my system into a panic. Flashing before my eyes, I saw my sister playing *Spyro*. My feet in white frilly socks walking up the slippery stairs. Harry walking ahead of me. Then Harry's hands and hairy knuckles. My mother's voice on the phone. Me begging her to come home. Her confusion and my silence. The doctor adjusted the speculum again, and my pelvis ached with a more precise pressure. I groaned in pain.

My mother grabbed my hand:

It's okay. Just breathe.

The doctor sat there between my legs, looking into me with another tool in her hands now. She worked her way in, hovering the tool inside of me, passing through the meat-bound cylinder soundless, like Operation. But then going against the rules, the alarm sounding, the doctor pressed the metal against my cervix and dug. The pain and discomfort amplified. It expanded into my legs and stomach, climbing up my spine, crashing against the underside of my diaphragm. The doctor pressed harder. Harry's face again. "You need to shower. You're dirty." The feeling of his body taking up every inch of that shower as he stepped inside with me. I tried to breathe, but the pain burst from my heart out into the room. Metal scraping against my cervix, the discomfort spread even wider than my body. The tiled walls. The silver showerhead. The pain seeping into every crevice of the moment. The pressure deepening as my vagina worked harder against the contraption to close itself. The water too cold and then too hot. His privates, how they were all I could see, and then couldn't see. My insides pleading with every ounce of survival to be closed, to please, please, take it out.

Instead, the doctor dug deeper, this time breaking skin. The pain permeated and replaced the oxygen in the room, suffocating me. My mother squeezed my hands tighter. Blood oozed down the tunnel of me, coating the speculum in red. Bleeding out of me and onto the white paper that covered the table: Harry's face, the pain consuming me, every ounce of my existence, every memory of art and Coney Island, literature and love, crumbling down and replaced with the feeling of being ripped apart from the inside out. The blood below me, like the first time, was evidence for my brokenness. And as the blood spilled out of my body, the memory I had tucked away when I was six showed itself fully in my mind.

That day, the doctor peeled open a suppressed memory, a raw, aching wound within me, into the LED lighting of a white-walled room, and I yelled for her to stop. My mother tried to placate me, but I demanded that I was done: to get it out of me, all of it, and away from me. The gynecologist rolled her eyes, and my mother shook her head in defeat. That was the last time I went to my gynecologist and the last time I would try any Western medical treatment to rid myself of the virus spreading within me.

Yellow Cab

In a taxi on the way back to my apartment, my insides still throbbing, my mother looked at me, anger forming on her face between brown curls of her hair. And when she asked me:

Why for heaven's sake are you doing this to me?

I, as if I was six again, couldn't give her a reason. She continued:

You realize if you don't do this procedure, you're going to get cancer and die.

Her words traveled through the thickness of pain-permeated air that still surrounded me. I turned from the window where I was watching the pelvis of each skyrise building on the infamous Fifth Avenue zoom past my eyes. I looked at my mother. To the sound of a honking SUV trying to merge into our lane, I tried to tell her what I could now remember, but the words trapped themselves in my esophagus. I tried again, but still nothing.

I knew if I didn't say the words that my mother would be right: I would get C one day and it *would* eventually attack enough of my body that I would have to travel back to Connecticut, that I would have to die in my hometown. I pictured myself shriveling away in my childhood bedroom and being buried beside my grandmother in the family's five-body lot that was just down the road from Harry's house. His name made me shudder. The thought of his house made me cringe. The realization that, by then, he had two kids made me nauseous. I thought that this terrifying scenario of dying in Connecticut seemed highly unlikely, as if my heart would automatically stop itself before my body got to that point.

With my mother staring at me as if she would kill me before anything else did, I tried to speak again, but nothing. No, I would find a way to die in New York City. I would. Maybe Felix would take care of me. But then the questions started to flood my mind: Would a taxi carry my body to the gravesite? And where would I be buried? And on the way there, where would they process my lifeless body? By the infinite man's old studio near Tompkins Square Park? By my old East Village apartment where Tay came to visit? Perhaps in front of the building by Washington Square Park where Felix and I met?

I reached over and grabbed my mother's hand:

Will you do me a favor?

What, Norma?

When I die—

I cleared my throat.

—don't say that I died of cancer, okay? Don't say that I died of some infectious disease, or of a mental disorder gone awry, or even, if it comes to get me first, of a car, plane, or train accident. Say, instead, that I died of what we all do, of what we all will—

I paused for a moment, my eyes as certain and stoic as Felix's.

—say I died of life.

Silence sat between us for a moment. My poetic words filled the old taxi, and I was pleased with myself. But then without warning, my mother broke free of my hand and slapped me across the face.

Do you know what I went through with your father? And look at me, I'm living!

She was yelling, spit leaking out the sides of her mouth:

I could have killed myself too, but I didn't. You selfish bitch!

And then she reached over and slapped me again. This time harder. But upon both impacts, I didn't cry a single tear. I had learned a long time ago that tears were a worthless currency in our home.

The taxi driver looked in the rearview mirror with an air of disinterest that only a NYC taxi driver can have. To this day, I don't blame my mother for her reaction. I had forgotten that I wasn't talking to Felix. I was talking to an immigrant woman from a faraway land, a woman with a father who disappointed her, a woman with a husband who did the same.

Flatiron

In the second aisle of the fourth floor of the antique mall with FOR SALE chandeliers hanging from the ceiling, I was on my knees staring at a small, brown snakeskin box with a lever lock opening. It reminded me of the box I had given up when I moved out of the Village and into my new Chelsea apartment. Felix was staring into the top shelf of the same cabinet.

Suddenly:

Norma! Look how beautiful!

I lifted myself off the floor and placed my eyes in the direction of Felix's pointer finger that was pressing against the glass cabinet. Between a gold snake bracelet with green gemstone eyes and a decorative hair clip, there was a black leatherbound journal with an etched phoenix on the cover. The binding was still tight. The pages, one could tell from the way they peeked out from its edges, hadn't yet yellowed in the sun. They were perfectly cream colored, perfectly bound within the leather, perfectly fastened and held by a black braided string.

Felix began to fall into a linguistic trance:

> *Imagine . . . you on the train to Coney Island. It's empty. The train leaves the tunnel and enters the open air. You're writing in this incredible journal. Poetry flowing. It's the next great masterpiece, like Frost or Dickinson, and as you write the final line, the roller coasters suddenly appear in the windows behind you. And then, in that exact moment, I take a photograph of you there. And that first poem in this new journal. What would the title be?*

I tried to picture Felix taking a photograph of me while I sat with the vintage journal on the F train. I tried to imagine myself writing a short story or perhaps, like he always wanted, a poem to the bumps of the subway track. I tried to imagine myself scribbling down words, ones that were more than just C coping mechanisms, ones that meant something to someone other than me. I tried to imagine my life the way Felix and I had once imagined the lives of many while drinking at Tom's that August day, but for the first time in my life, I couldn't imagine anything. It was only dark in my mind. Dark and blank. The plot, transparent. The elements, transient.

I looked away from the journal and down at the zipper of my jeans, at the cells that had betrayed me.

I'm not sure, Felix. I'm not sure what I would call it.

And suddenly, hearing myself speak these words into the air, I heard the hopelessness that accidently slipped between the letters. I had not meant to sound so sad. I did not know that I was. Suddenly, it hit me. I was dying and that terrified me.

For the first time since sushi, tears started to swell into and out of my eyes. My dreams of becoming a writer had long since drained out of me. My insides had given up hope of one day being romanced rather than ripped apart. My mother still cried every day, and her slap still stung. The C was spreading faster now, and Harry's face haunted me in the night. Soon, I would be too sick to ride the Cyclone at Coney Island, and despite how fervently I denied it, I knew that soon I would have to leave New York and go back to Connecticut where it all began. All of this, and what bothered me the most was that I still didn't know if heaven was real or if, perhaps, I was truly living in the exhibition's closing days, the final, epilogue-less chapter.

As I wept inconsolably for the first time in over a year in the second aisle of the antiques mall, Felix rubbed my back with careful, curated care while his camera pressed gently against my hip.

You know, Norma, maybe there is a reason for all of this. Remember what you told me about Tay? And about the freckle girl in high school? How you felt, like actually felt, something? Maybe this is your opportunity to start over. Maybe you can even write about all of this in one of your poems. All the best artists use their pain for art.

Feeling the warmth of his palm on my spine and the feeling of tears cascading down my cheeks, I thought maybe Felix was right: maybe pain could be channeled, maybe the weight of Tay on my bed meant something.

Chelsea

When I got home that afternoon, I called the gynecologist and asked her what my options were. After making three different appointments with three different C specialists in the city, I lay down in bed and tried to fall asleep, but my mind rumbled beneath my skull:

If there truly was a heaven, how would I get there? When my heart stopped, would my soul automatically float up from my body into the sky? Or would an angel, perhaps my grandmother, come to fetch me and bring me there? Or maybe—I heard Felix's voice in my head—I would have to take the subway.

The F train to heaven.

THE STUDY OF OBLIVION

twenty-six weeks since breakdown

This last story...

No, no, no, no nooooo. That's not "The Last Story." It's "The F Train."

Yes, "The F Train." It's very...

She keeps stumbling on her words, losing her composure, and I think:

She loves it. I'm going to be a big writing star!

And then she pivots:

I noticed that the character's father isn't in it. It seems weird that he doesn't have an opinion on his daughter dying.

Not every character is in every story.

Right. Well, what do you think "The F Train" is about?

Wait a second. Did she even read it?

I say, I think it's fiction. Sure, I got HPV and saw a naturopath. Who doesn't? But early on I actually removed the abnormal cells so I never got cancer. After that, I turned around, opened my arms wide, and fell backward into the warm embrace of new-age spirituality. There was something about the metaphor of scraping out the old and starting fresh. Yeah, the metaphor was so good it made me believe in god. Has that ever happened to you? A metaphor changing your life?

She shakes her head no.

What about a simile?

She shakes her head again and goes, the man who raped her—

Oh, *I* was never raped.

But the fictional Harry stands in for someone in your own life, doesn't he? And that man may not have raped you, but whatever he did to you, it felt like he raped you?

My mouth goes dry and words start scurrying out like a pack of scorpions in the Sahara Desert:

You know, this week I was thinking about my character. You know, her grandmother's self-portraits from the beginning? Well, I still don't know what genre my manuscript is, but I do know that it's made up of many self-portraits of one girl. They are her story from her eyes. And there's no through line to it. And that's okay. Just like different paintings by the same artist and how they can all be hung in the same gallery with no questions. The paintings don't have to have a through line. Each painting is real and true in its own right. Each of my stories is just canvas and paint.

You never mentioned why your grandmother committed suicide?

Something with her father.

As in?

I think something sexual.

Oh, really? How do you know that?

I don't know. I'm just guessing.

My new therapist looks at me like I'm a treasure chest she's about to open or as if a light just went off in her cartoon head.

Why do you think you need to see your grandmother's paintings so badly?

Oh, my grandmother never painted. Well at least not that I know of. That's fiction.

Well, We Know That Most Of Your Manuscript Is Nonfiction, So Why Do You Think You Wrote That Part Into The Story?

I don't know.

Maybe your unconscious wrote it in for a reason.

Like the story knows more than I do? I already told you that I don't like that idea.

Okay.

Silence.

Silence.

Silence.

Norma, who is your grandmother?

What does that even mean?

She's your father's mother, right? Why do you think it's so important that you come to understand the woman who bore your father?

You're interrupting my train of thought. You see, in my manuscript there's no through line and I've realized that life is the same. There's no connecting thread. There's no god guiding us to a utopia. There's no government leading us toward one either. In fact, there's no utopia to reach at all. It's all in our heads. Instead, we're heading toward the meta-verse and making the real world unreal. Which is exactly the opposite of what you've been trying to do with me. So what's the point? You know, I've been thinking about writing lately, trying to build a meta-phor for it. And I think I've finally got one:

Norma, stay with me.

The first draft of a manuscript is you building a puzzle from scratch, but at first, you don't know what image you're trying to make. So you just keep writing and writing and sitting patiently, creating your puzzle pieces and trying to figure out what picture is emerging from them as you place them next to each other. Eventually the picture starts to show. You keep writing and at some point, maybe eight years later, the pieces are all there and the picture is obvious, but it's a total mess, and there's superfluous extras that you need to omit or soften out.

Norma? Your grandmother?

Anyways, no one talks about what happened with my grandmother. And they don't talk about it because there's no reason for what happened.

The second/third/fourth draft of a manuscript is you sitting in front of your puzzle with just the border put together, so at least you've got the boundaries, which means at least you've got direction. You've taken all your puzzle pieces out and laid them all over the table (and you hope your cat didn't smack one and hide it under the couch). Now you've got to make the picture look clear. A puzzle could be a Thomas Kinkade "masterpiece" or an abstract color clusterfuck, but always, even if the picture depicts chaos, the picture must be clear. So you start putting your puzzle pieces back inside one by one. You let the border guide you.

My new therapist says, you used to think there was a reason for everything.

Yeah. A spiritual reason for everything. Every flick of a dragonfly's wings. Every trip on the sidewalk. Every pimple and broken toe. Always a reason. If you had a heart attack, then you weren't spiritually aligned and god, through your heart attack, was leading you to alignment. But then you put me on these meds and I started to look at little kids with cancer and their bald heads, and the blind people on my block and I just thought...Fuck. There's no reason for anything. Not even me getting HPV. There's no cause and effect. Especially not one like being spiritually fucking aligned.

The next stage of your manuscript is you showing your finished puzzle to someone and saying, do you like it, do you get it, will you buy it, is it worth anything?

My new therapist says, what I'm hearing is that you've come to realize that there's no reason for what happened to you. It was your father, wasn't it?

Like fuck! Life is meaningless, and if something is meaningless, how does it have any value? We prescribe every piece of meaning to life. And every piece of value is reliant on what we give meaning to. It's all subjective. And god isn't here anymore.

And if someone does sort of like your puzzle, your manuscript reaches its next stage and now you've got puzzle editors and puzzle agents and puzzle publishers who are trying to get your puzzle into Target. But each stage of your manuscript is its own world, and each world has its own rules that you, the puzzlemaker, don't fully understand.

My new therapist says, and god didn't stop it from happening to you.

Or at least god isn't everywhere like I thought. Maybe god just exists in little glimpses. Maybe god doesn't exist at all. I don't know.

And all you've got are questions about each world that your manuscript will enter into:

My new therapist says, and you're angry with god for not protecting you.

You know what the hardest thing about all of this has been? Realizing oblivion isn't some special power.

Like does the narrative have enough of an arc for this century?

My new therapist says, and your narcissistic mother didn't protect you from your father either.

Oblivion isn't some miraculous place or some fucking higher consciousness.

Like will my manuscript ever become a book?

My new therapist says, and neither did your old therapist.

Oblivion is just trauma and life and aren't those two the same at this point? We're all traumatized by our families, by our god or lack thereof, even by our own mortality.

Like how many rejection letters will I get in the meantime?

My new therapist says, and neither did your grandmother.

You see, we all walk around petrified to die. Petrified to live. Holding the constant fear of which direction should I go and what's the right answer. But there is no right answer.

And will the author ever show herself and tell the real truth?

My new therapist says, what happened to you wasn't your fault.

Ha. There is no right answer. There's just life. There's just the earth spinning and spinning and spinning in a dark galaxy.

And will the narrator ever say exactly what she means?

My new therapist says, you can Get Better.

Just the earth with a perfect mixture of elements to create existence.

And will the manuscript when it becomes a book, like a body, be able to see into its own fascia and finally make sense of it all?

Norma, awareness is the first step, and I know it can be disturbing initially.

Earth like a stage for us to dance upon.

And will the font and binding accurately depict the contents?

But from there we can integrate.

Earth like the ruins of an ancient theater.

And will anyone even be able to understand what I'm trying to say?

It takes courage to see all of this.

Earth like a dollhouse.

And will the prose be too self-conscious to be called art and who will write the prologue?

But we don't have to rush anything. It's a process.

Earth and earth and earth and us.

And how will I ever find a publisher patient enough to sit through this?

We'll take it slow.

And each of us teeters in and out of oblivion and attempts, with all our might, to avoid such an existential dungeon, or if you are as sad and scared as I was, then you too may attempt, with all your might, to stay in such a place like a black hole, because there, you are safe; there you can deny that anything ever happened to you; there you can pretend that those meant to protect you actually did their job; there, at the very least, you can pretend that when you were four, five, six, seven, eight, your father did in fact have to get naked and shower with you, that it was imperative to your getting clean; there, at the very least, you can pretend like your dad didn't try to see you naked when you were fifteen and sleeping; there, at the very least, you can forget about hearing the word *fuck* from your parents' bedroom or the TV moaning downstairs or your mother always leaving or yelling or, later, threatening to kill herself; and there you can numb the memory and emotion into a deafening static noise that has the exquisite ability to tune out the beating of your own heart, and you like this because your heart is a reminder of your body, and your body is a reminder of your parents, and they are a reminder that love is not what they say love is and family is not what they say family is and no one can be trusted, not even the woman who holds you as you're going insane, as the medicine kicks in, as you're remembering and kicking and screaming, and who won't let go no matter how many times you push her away, no matter how many times she wakes up to your cold sweats, no matter how many times you tell her you can't have sex again tonight, no matter how many times you tell her love doesn't exist and, in fact, nothing exists anymore, but if nothing exists anymore then perhaps you're brave for staying with her even when you are utterly terrified, perhaps you're brave for returning each week to this office that seems to hold all of your worst memories and all of the silence in the fucking world, perhaps you're brave for trying everything you can to not just survive anymore, but, instead, to actually live, and now you can see it there, a seed is sprouting on a gray bald planet in your vision and you can see the spinning green amongst the grayscale galaxy, and now you feel that you might, you just might, make it out of this.

Today was a big step.

I'll tell you a secret: it doesn't matter if it never gets published.

THE STUDY OF OBLIVION

twenty six and a half weeks since breakdown

Sorry I smell like cigarettes today; they stopped selling flavored vapes in the city, so I'm back to the OGs. I start laughing but it sounds less like a laugh when it comes out and more like a forced cackle.

My new therapist does her smile-grimace and says, Norma, I'm glad you called for an emergency session. Should we start where we left off last time?

I hear myself say, and isn't it JUST hilarious that the one—THE ONE—regulation the government wants to make has to directly fuck with me? I mean did you see Facebook's new branding announcement? It wasn't so much a branding announcement but a press conference led by Zuckerberg's NFT with no platform for questions or rebuttals such as: *Are new agreements to terms and conditions automatically signing us up for the virtual world?* Following the new branding announcement, I did a deep YouTube dive on the metaverse and found that its initial investor is the government (surprise, surprise), and following my research I walked to the bathtub and filled it up six inches with steaming-hot water. Then I turned off the water and lay in the tub like a dying fish. My girlfriend came home to see me, barely submerged, lying on my side and staring at the corner of the tub. She said, *what's going on.* And I said, I've given up on life.

If the metaverse is coming, then writing is just a record of pre-metaverse times, of the real-life-non-virtual era. Maybe we'll start a new calendar:

BC, AD, and M. Meta. In this period, we won't need Elon's microchips anymore. We won't need interstellar travel. We'll just need a headset and some sensors and a roof over our heads, and, hey, maybe it'll be good for the environment. That's the only plus I see. We'll all be willfully at home and nature can emerge.

When my girlfriend left me in the tub and went to cook dinner, I found myself not only paralyzed by fear of the virtual world but also very disappointed. Why? Because they're creating an artificial universe, but in this non-real universe, they're still including and utilizing the concept of money. That's lame. Lame as fuck. But also expected. So now that I've given up on life, maybe I'm ready for the metaverse. Or maybe I'm being dramatic and the world within a manuscript is its own type of metaverse and my thinking is catastrophic like always.

How's that for some self-awareness?

Norma, how are you feeling today?

I feel awful.

Really?

My anxiety has never been worse. I haven't left the house since our last session. It's not supposed to be like this.

Like what?

You told me I would Get Better if I admitted to my past. And I have. I told you the big secret. And I get it: it's not oblivion. I am chronically depressed. I have depersonalization/derealization disorder and immense anxiety from significant trauma, starting with my father. And obviously, my mother's volatility didn't help. See, I can admit to it now. But the anxiety isn't going away. Or maybe I'm not totally better because I can only remember the bedroom thing with my dad in my teens, and I can't remember exactly what happened in the shower with him and to Get Better I have to.

This isn't like the movies where confessing to a memory heals everything.

Maybe you can hypnotize me.

That's not how it works.

But I can't Get Better if I don't know.

That's not true. We can't remember everything that's happened in our life. It's impossible.

But the anxiety is still here! I need to remember! It needs to go away! I'm losing my mind!

It's not that easy. It's a process.

The process is done.

My new therapist says, The Process Is Just Beginning.

THE FUCK?!

Norma, it is becoming clearer now that your worries about love have roots in your mother and father's tumultuous relationship. And it's also becoming apparent that you're afraid of your own desire for women, because the only other person you were close to who was attracted to women had a desire that was so unhinged and dangerous. A desire that hurt you. You're afraid that you'll be like him.

As she speaks, I can feel the green neon laser beam start to scan over me again.

You're afraid you could hurt someone like he hurt you. And you think you are capable of this, because he is the parent you identify with more. Since you are not like your screaming, homophobic mother who loved you in such an unpredictable, violent way.

My body goes ice-cold as if this woman in ballet flats just shoved me in a freezer like a kidnapping victim on a *Law & Order: SVU* episode.

So your anxiety, depression, and derealization come from your parents' relationship, but also from the fear that you will hurt your girlfriend. Either with your desire, like your father hurt you. Or by cheating on her, like your father did to your mother.

I'm shivering now.

And you so badly don't want to hurt your girlfriend because you love her. So now your anxiety is you being hypervigilant to your every thought and move because you're looking for proof that you do or don't love her, or that you will or won't hurt her. And you need to know exactly what will happen in the future because you don't want to lose or hurt her, but the future isn't possible to predict.

My new therapist isn't real. This room isn't real.

In addition to that, when a person is exposed to repeated trauma, their system becomes hardwired for trauma. Trauma with a capital *T*, like the memory with your father. And trauma with a lowercase *t*, like your mother's repeated behavior. These traumas make it hard for you to tolerate happiness as if something terrible can and will happen if you experience joy or comfort or any positive emotion.

I can't even appreciate my new therapist's attention to capitalization, because I can barely see her through the Saran Wrap.

Just like this breakdown is your own form of self-punishment for your happiness with your girlfriend. So now we're going to have to work on your ability to tolerate happiness.

From under my Saran Wrap I say, you promised I would Get Better.

I never promised that.

Yes, you did.

No, I said if we worked together, you would certainly feel better than you had been feeling when I first met you. Maybe you misheard me.

YOU FUCKING LIED JUST LIKE JOE BIDEN!

Spit comes out of my mouth when I say this and it reminds me of the way my mother yells. Maybe I'm more like her than I thought.

My new therapist doesn't even flinch.

Instead, she just places her pen down on her clipboard and says, you talked about reading Maggie Nelson's *On Freedom*, right?

I can't nod because I can't move because the room is getting blurrier and blurrier.

My new therapist continues, Well, Getting Better Isn't Like Utter Liberation. It Is Patient Labor. Your Freedom From The Effects Of Trauma, Your Getting Better, Will Be A Process Of Continuously And Patiently Laboring Through The Minutes, The Days, The Months, The Years. It Will Be An Ongoing Process. Like Traversing A Spiral Upward: Ascending The Ache And Then Returning To It With Self-Awareness And More Precise Tools To Face It.

This time, *I* blink at her. Once. Then twice. Then many times. As if I can understand her better if I can see and then unsee her lounging feet.

Wait.

Are you saying that it will never end?

The Saran Wrap tightens around my skin and the room starts to spin.

Like, literally spin.

Getting Better is a Constant Practice.

It's spinning faster now, and I feel like I'm going to throw up.

I shut my eyes tight trying to stabilize the room.

In the spinning darkness, I say, so living will always be hard work?

I hear her on a loudspeaker in my head, as if her voice is my own:

Life Becomes More Tolerable When You Know Your Pain And What Ignites Your Pain. That's What We've Been Doing. There's No Magic Or Mantra To Make It All Go Away. You Can't Erase The Memories Or Edit What Happened. You Just Learn How To Move Forward With Resilience And Persistence.

Spinning in silence.

Spinning in silence.

Spinning in silence.

Getting Better Isn't A Cure Or A Destination.

I open my eyes and think, you know what? Fuck this shit.

But really I shout, YOU KNOW WHAT? FUCK THIS SHIT.

I abruptly stand up, trying to rip the Saran Wrap off me. In the middle of the spinning, I storm over to her couch. I grab each of her stray textile pillows and shove them behind the pillow in the middle. Two behind the one. Perfectly symmetrical.

HOW FUCKING HARD WAS THAT?

I'm towering over her now. I'm so dizzy. I may pass out. I point at her ballet flats.

AND YOU'RE RUDE FOR NEVER GREETING ME AT THE DOOR AND ALWAYS HAVING YOUR FEET UP LIKE YOU'RE WATCHING A FUCKING MOVIE. I'M NOT A MOVIE. I'M A PERSON. THAT IS, OF COURSE—UNLESS, UNLESS—

My voice gets quieter now:

Unless you can't actually walk and in that case, I'm very sorry. But if you can walk,

I'm pointing at her face now.

FUCK YOU.

And then I grab my purse and run out of her office, slamming the door behind me with a bang.

During the whole ordeal, my new therapist never stands up. She barely even blinks.

By leaving early, I wasted $134.10. This kills me.

However, the fact that I did not drop my ChapStick or phone during my dramatic exit makes me very happy.

Who said I couldn't tolerate happiness?

NOVEMBER

There's no place like oblivion.

Dorothy, *The Wizard of Oz*

THE STUDY OF OBLIVION

twenty-eight weeks since breakdown

I don't want to write tonight, but I have to because the agent emailed me asking where my manuscript is. I guess I sold the manuscript really well when I told the agent about my vision for it. My girlfriend and I were at a bar eating nuts and drinking mocktails when the woman beside my girlfriend struck up a conversation with her. When my girlfriend learned the woman was a literary agent, she said, *honey, you've got to meet this lady.* So I sat with the woman and told her what I've been working on. She gave me her business card and said to email her when I was finished. So I'm trying. The thing is: trying isn't cutting it. Tonight, I am a ball of mush, a groggy mashed potato. The lighting in Felix's apartment doesn't help. I've been here for five days, and I haven't gone outside once. I've been living off soft-boiled eggs and raw broccoli. And mostly sitting on Felix's blue velvet couch and trying to write. Except writing is hard when oblivion has its talons in my neck. Then again, maybe I should be grateful because I wanted to study oblivion and now it's back full-fucking-force.

It's raining outside tonight. If this was six months ago, I'd think the rain was god crying, because I broke up with my girlfriend, but today I know it's just rain. I came home from therapy last week and told her to move out. I really did it this time. It's the first thing I've succeeded at in a while. I told her I'd leave until she was gone. She told me it was just another bad day. She reminded me that I promised to stop doing this. I said this was the last and final time. I didn't tell her why this time was different from all the others. I didn't tell her that I loved her and wished it wasn't this way. I didn't tell her that I was leaving because I didn't want to hurt her anymore. I didn't tell her that I was never going to get better, that it wasn't possible for someone like me, that our life together would forever be tainted by derealization, depression, anxiety, and significant trauma. It would forever be a psychological thriller and that's not what I wanted the genre of the manuscript to be. Or her life to be. Or mine.

You see, I didn't tell her any of this, because I knew if I did, she would stay and say it was okay. But living like this forever doesn't feel okay. After she cried and cried, she made me promise to call her when I'm better. I promised, knowing that better isn't on the menu for me. When I left, I blocked her number and went to Felix's apartment.

In Felix's overcrowded Lower East Side neighborhood, it's quiet tonight. At Felix's painting station, there's a new canvas on the easel, and, beside it, tubes of oil paints and an unused disposable palette. I should mention Felix is not a photographer or a gallery curator as I've written him to be. He is a painter. A painter gaining traction. Shown at Art Basel. Already, at twenty-eight years old. Sometimes when I look into his paintings, I feel like I don't even know Felix. I wonder if that's how she felt when she read my writing.

Earlier, when I was looking for a spatula in the kitchen so I could make fried eggs instead of boiled eggs (it was the most exciting part of my week), I opened a kitchen drawer and found a bottle of Xanax. They weren't prescribed to Felix, but to a girl. I wonder if he has a girlfriend. I wonder why he never told me about her. I wonder what she looks like and why she needs Xanax and why my ex–new therapist didn't prescribe me any. I took a Xanax and then ended up here at my laptop writing. I don't think the words make sense, but that's all I'm trying to do lately: make sense of what's happened the past couple of months. The past twenty-seven years of my existence.

The hardest part is I can barely remember who I was before all of this. For instance, on the first day of May, I can't remember what thoughts I woke up with. Or what dreams I had for the summer. It's all blank before Memorial Day. Rereading my old stories, apparently I used to like philosophy books and riff eloquently and obnoxiously about works of art with Felix. I could try to do this with Felix again, try to recall the woman I once was, but Felix isn't here anymore. He moved to Chicago two months ago. I guess he got tired of waiting for me to finish my manuscript. Or perhaps, in his newfound fame, he forgot that we ever made this New York City promise.

If I could go back in time and begin my manuscript again, I would not have named him and I would not have lied to you about his profession. I'm tired of hiding, tired of lying. But once an unreliable narrator, always an unreliable narrator. In other words: I've made my bed and I will lie in it. Well, really I've made Felix's bed and I will lie in it as soon as the sun comes up, sleeping for twelve or more hours. But now, in the middle of the night when all is quiet in the Lower East Side, I'm sitting here in Felix's apartment with all his expensive art hanging on the walls and loads of art books on the coffee table. And as I sit here, I realize that I hate art books and coffee table books, and I truly believe they are a waste of paper. I wonder how many trees it took to make Yayoi Kusama's polka dot book. I wonder how many trees it will take to make my book. If I really care about the environment, I would release it only as an eBook, but I won't do this, because I can't stand not being able to write in the margins. And so, as always, I am a hypocrite.

I've come to realize I am full of opinions and no action. I am full of theories and no solutions. I am. I am. I am. Just the same as the world I hate. The infinite man knew this. The infinite man proved this. I made a promise to him, and I broke it on a selfish whim. And then, when I had my whole present and future in my hands, I did the same to her. I broke every promise I made to her. I broke every wish and dream I had for us.

I am no better or worse than anyone I have mentioned here. Not Joe Biden. Not Bezos. Not Donald Trump. Well, maybe a little better than Trump. But on average, I am no more and no less human than every other person on this planet. I forget to recycle sometimes. I travel on airplanes. I pee in the pool. I consume nicotine. I'm on antidepressants. I buy too many clothes that I don't need, and I don't always buy from sustainable places because I'm cheap and they're too expensive. I don't thrift-shop.

And God definitely isn't going to help us fix any of my shit or our shit. At least not that God. That God with a capital G that supposedly cares about what I'm wearing or if I go confess my sins to a rapey priest; the same God who created dogs to sniff each other's butts but who also, apparently, cares if I lick a pussy versus a penis or if I have sex before I have a paper from town hall. So, no, I'm not banking on that God helping, but maybe god will. Some god. And right now I think the closest thing to god is the earth, animals, and babies. Things that just *be* and don't try to *be* anything except what they are. And when it comes to the devil, well, if what my ex–new therapist said is true—that my mind projects my worse fears onto reality—then in this metaphor, in this life, I think the real devil is the human mind.

But now I'm going down another rabbit hole. To stop myself, I walk over to Felix's painting station and sit in front of the new canvas. I decide that if I can't write a self-portrait of a girl tonight, then I'll paint instead. As long as my hand is moving, I can track time. I think of the Union Square clock. I think of my girlfriend's eyes. I think of all the nights I wanted to leave her because I thought oblivion would stop strangling me if I did, and yet here I am alone and oblivion has only tightened its grip. It even broke through the Prozac to get me.

Tonight, I'm going to paint until all of Felix's untouched canvases are riddled with my fingerprints. I'm sure he has plenty of other canvases in Chicago. I'm sure he won't even miss these New York City ones.

Philosophy Part 2

It is Wednesday, November 17, just after sunrise in New York City, and there is oil paint on my nose. With the sun beaming in through Felix's windows, I lie down on the couch, finally tired enough to sleep.

Soon after my eyes close, I awake on a couch in an apartment that is supposed to be mine, but the furniture is all wrong. It is night-time, and the city sky looks almost purple, and the purple is coming in through the floor-to-ceiling windows that border the room. I remember that shade of purple, the color of a Manhattan sky turning to dawn. *This is a dream.* Suddenly, I am lucid, awake in the dream world. I lift my body from the couch and stand. In the apartment that is supposed to be mine but is not mine, a density begins to take shape before me, a figure forming in the purple darkness. The density transforms into a man. Then the infinite man is standing across the room wearing his leather jacket. It is the first time I've seen him, either in the real world or the dream world, since that winter night.

Lit by the purple sky, the infinite man looks at me and says nothing. Then slowly, carefully, he smirks, and it's as if we are eighteen again, as if he still knows something that I do not. I can't help but smile as my heart beats against my spine. As if by some supernatural force, my body begins to move toward him, and then I am directly in front of him, looking into his brown skin and the firework hue of infinity's glowing eyes. We stare at one another, and our smiles do not fade.

Together, we walk the streets of New York City—which aren't exactly New York. There are trees growing out from the sides of skyscrapers and ferns dripping from the traffic lights. Some city streets replaced by rivers. As we walk together, we speak without speaking. What is there to say? Every so often I lose the infinite man, only to, in a moment, without panicking, without shouting his name into the void, find him around the corner surrounded by dragonflies.

After what feels like eons, I awake from the dream. I'm in Felix's apartment. It takes me a second to remember this life, this reality. I rub my eyes, and then my hands reach for my phone on the coffee table. I scroll through my contacts to a name I haven't looked at— have tried not to look at—in years. My finger presses the name, and the phone begins to ring.

And then a voice, smooth like clay in a master potter's hands:

Norma?

Immediately, just in the way the infinite man says my name, I hear that the unbearable gravity that once braided his voice together is gone. Just in the way that he says my name, I can hear that he is happy, and for the first time ever, I can hear what happiness sounds like on him. I remember what he said about those people at his old megachurch in Texas: they used to say his voice was a gift from God.

Yeah. It's me.

I thought it was your number, but I didn't believe it.

I don't know what to say. I didn't think of what I was going to say.

Well—

He says.

—hey.

And then he laughs and I laugh, and for a minute or so we can't stop laughing.

The infinite man lives in Hawai'i now on a farm where his sleeping quarters are surrounded by dragonfruit trees, which grow and wrap themselves around twenty or so mango trees. For several years, he was a cook for a vegan restaurant and then work-traded on a farm, taking care of the land to live there for free, and now on another farm, the one with the mangoes, again tending to the land and drawing in the evening. When he tells me all of this, I picture him on the farm with enough space for him to run around like a child, surrounded by fruit that he can pick and eat. As he takes a bite of a freshly picked mango, the bright yellow juice of the fruit falls over his hands and down his right wrist over his infinity tattoo. I think of our first night together and the possibilities he saw for the world, the ones that I thought were impossible.

Suddenly, I am weeping on the phone. To my tears, he quickly says that he has a girlfriend.

Don't worry. I'm not calling because of anything like that. I just . . . I had a dre—

I stop myself. I don't finish the sentence. I don't even apologize like I want to, because I can't burden him with the weight of who we once were. And my philosophy is no longer his to hold. The tears stream heavier down my face now, but I am not crying because I am not the woman he lives amongst the mangoes with. I'm crying because, suddenly, in hearing *his* happiness, I feel like I am finally allowed to find my own.

———

Before the dream ended, before I woke into this world and called the infinite man, I said to him:

Can I ask you a question about love?

We were standing on the sidewalk. Vines were growing against the brick wall behind him. As I waited for his response, the vines forked and grew exponentially up the building.

He smiled bigger than I'd ever seen before and shook his head:

Do you have to?

I have always been so full of questions. I had always looked for the infinite man or some man or some therapist or Her to answer them. But when we were there in the dream and the infinite man smiled like that, I didn't ask him what I wanted to. Instead, I hugged the infinite man, and he hugged me back, and in this embrace in this place where we were together as whole people, I was happy. And he was happy. And happiness was something we were both able to feel.

After seven minutes on the phone, I hear a woman's voice in the background and the infinite man says that he's sorry, that he has to go now. I feel reality stop, destroy itself, and begin again. We say goodbye at reality's moment of conception. Then we hang up to return to our separate worlds.

When we first met, the infinite man and I were both so young. There we were alone in the middle of New York City: just two kids trying to change a broken world without realizing that we were just as broken. Now with the infinite man's happiness ringing in my ears like the music he gave up, I finally realize something: brokenness is not a permanent fate.

I walk to my laptop, wiping my tears away and knowing I have been wrong for all these years, all this time that I've spent writing an apology for faulty philosophy.

I feel my fingers moving on the keyboard:

Perhaps it was never that making a new world filled with love was impossible. Perhaps it's just about finding a person who is willing to help you excavate the ruins of the old world, to clear away the rubble of an ancient, flawed kingdom, and build a new home alongside you, piece by piece. And, perhaps, it's not about waiting for the *right* or perfect person. Instead, it is choosing to be with the person who doesn't walk away when things get hard. And deciding, against all odds, to have faith in the one who keeps their promises.

But I should stop here, because I don't write philosophical theories anymore. I only write stories.

DECEMBER

*My time is running out. My words are thinning to frail
thread. My soul is eclipsing into another. I step aside to let
what remains say what it yearns to say before I go. Before I
go. I would like to apologize to my body but still I can't find
the words to say that I love you without including a lie. My
heart is a dried well. My limbs: stone carving tools. My eyes:
fogged and narrow. Forget what came and went. Forget me
too and forget me not; the flowers we shared the smell of, the
touch of them in our hands—*

Alana Saab

THE STUDY OF OBLIVION

thirty-one weeks since breakdown

I start by saying, I think you need to up my dose. I'm not doing well.

Well you are on—

I know. Such a low dose.

My new therapist says, well we can certainly raise it to twenty milligrams, but why don't we wait and see how today's session goes?

I can't believe this certified drug dealer doesn't want to give me more drugs.

I say, okay.

Silence.

Silence.

Silence.

So, you came back?

You know the infinite man from "Philosophy"? He lives in Hawai'i now.

Oh, really?

Yeah. I spoke to him, and after the call, I realized that if I hate this world so much, I could run off to an island too. I could get paid under the table and never have to do taxes again. I could pick fresh fruit from the garden and drink coconut water from an actual coconut. But for whatever reason, I'm here and asking you to give me more anti-depressants.

And why is that?

I'd like to think it's because I can't turn away from this world. That I have to stay and help. Somehow, I have to fix it. And meanwhile I'll do my best to live in it, which apparently right now means more pills. But of course, that would make me a martyr and I'm not a martyr. Maybe I'm too scared. Or maybe I'm a masochist. Or maybe there are things here that I don't want to lose.

Silence.

Like her.

Didn't you say in your email that you broke up with her?

I'm really not doing well. Did I say that already? Now that I've said it I can't stop saying it. I'm really not doing well. Oblivion used to be an anesthetic, but now it's a weighted blanket while I'm trying to run a marathon. I thought when I broke up with her it would go away, but oblivion is worse than before.

My new therapist clicks her pen. I continue:

Last night, I left Felix's apartment and went to mine for the first time since we broke up. When I got there, I looked into every corner of the apartment as if I were a landlord coming to inspect my latest tenants' move-out process; checking to make sure that all the holes in the walls were patched, that the scratches on the floors were the same ones that were there before, wondering if I should point out something of substance so I could keep the security deposit. But there was no trace of her. Her closet was empty. The La Croix cans that she used to leave around the house like breadcrumbs were gone. She had even emptied her array of hot sauces in the refrigerator or perhaps she took them with her wherever she went. (I don't know where she went; I blocked her on every social media channel.) The trash can was empty, no bag, no nothing. The recycling too. I felt myself, somewhere outside of my Saran Wrap, be sad. Too sad.

So I ran a bath until it was a quarter of the way filled. Then I shut off the water, lay in the barely filled tub, and closed my eyes. There, the thoughts got darker than they have in months. This time it wasn't about the metaverse or pre-meta times, and this time I didn't think about the empty galaxies. I didn't think about walking into lava. I thought about doing it her old way: a razor to my arms. When I opened my eyes, there was blood floating in the bathtub. I thought my body had carried out the fantasies in my mind without me knowing it. But then I realized I had just gotten my period. The blood was still seeping out of my vagina. I've always heard that you don't bleed in the tub. In fact, women rarely bleed in any body of water. But there I was bleeding against all odds.

Using my two fingers like a widening peace sign, I opened my labia to help the blood escape. It came and it just kept coming.

Now, you may think this is gross but after that, I stayed in the tub. I watched my blood dance around my body, twirling and twirling, spinning and spinning. Spinning as if there is anything in the world to spin for. And as the blood spun, its edges drifted away from the whole and then danced itself into dissolve, disappearing into the clear water. After a while all the blood had mixed into the bathwater, and there was nothing left to see. But I needed to see it.

I got onto my knees in the tub and began to push for more blood. But nothing came. I pushed harder and harder. Then the cramps started. They came on so fast and strong that I thought I would pass out. Not death by lava, but death by drowning in a one-quarter-filled bathtub. Pathetic, really. My cramps were so bad that my first instinct was to stay on my knees and push as if I were giving birth. So I did just that. I took a deep breath and pushed as hard as I could to get the blood out.

Instead, I farted.

I kept pushing. Still no blood. Still only pain. I closed my eyes tight and pushed even harder, this time bringing in some birth breathing I have only ever seen on television. The sound of air propelling from my lungs and into the bathroom, like arctic wind coming into the house through a barely open window. And then my girlfriend appeared beside me. She was kneeling against the bathtub. She was breathing with me, cheering me on. She was very serious but also smiling. I stared at the whites of her teeth then the sliver of light in her eye. She whispered, *you can do this, our baby is almost here.*

Of course, I just imagined all of this. Of course, she was never there. Of course, I will never have children because I'm scared to be like my mother. And perhaps last night was not so much a birth but something more like a funeral. It was silent in the apartment except for my breathing and the water splashing against the tub every time I moved to reposition my slipping knees. In the silence that I so often crave, I missed her voice. I missed her snores. I missed the way she always sounded so alive.

As the pain grew with each minute, I pushed and pushed for more blood, for relief, but my body refused. So eventually, I lay back down, grabbed my phone, opened a Note document, and began to write.

What did you write?

I'll tell you in a second. I'm not done.

God, my new therapist is impatient.

After I finished writing, my cramps had subsided and I got out of the tub. I went to the toilet to pee before bed and then a huge plop of blood came out of me. A gush the size of a pancake. I wanted the blood in the bathtub, dancing around my limbs, but it waited until the moment I got out. After that, I felt so much better. Like oblivion had let go a little bit.

Hmm.

What?

You felt better after you started bleeding?

Yeah. After the birth.

You know, she says, looking at her clipboard, maybe it *is* PMDD and the hormone fluctuations are causing the heightened anxiety.

So maybe it's not depression or DPDR or sexual trauma. Now you think it's PMDD too? Which side are you on?

It could *also* be PMDD. We won't know until you track your cycles and your mood fluctuations.

How long will that take?

We'll need about three months of data.

Are you fucking kidding?

No, I'm not.

Okay. Well, I'm done with my story. Can I read you what I wrote now?

Yes.

I warn you. You're not going to like it.

Why?

Because it's about oblivion.

I take my phone out of my jacket pocket, open to Notes, and begin to read:

> Oblivion was never just what happened with my dad or any
> of the other men. It wasn't conjured from one moment but
> many moments, not one gender but this whole entire species.
> And for this, oblivion is not just mine. I am not special. I was
> and am just like everyone. A few details morphed here and
> there but ultimately: I am the same as all of you. I am simply
> skin stuffed full of characteristics and dreams and stories that
> someone else or something else gave to me. Like Philippe
> Parreno's Ann Lee. *I am no ghost. Just a shell.*

> Oblivion, the way I experience it, is the sum of every hand
> and eye on my body, every movie on my big, flat-screen TV,
> every book on my bookshelf, every sermon at the pulpit. It is
> the sum of the floorplan of my childhood home, the distance
> between the city and the suburbs, the mixture of bile and
> alcohol, the fucked-up translated holy books that horrify and
> haunt us with a fantasy of hell.

> To exist in this world, we need oblivion. We need it because
> oblivion numbs us so we can survive. I bet I would've
> never known oblivion if I lived as a cavewoman. I bet
> then I wouldn't need Prozac or Wellbutrin or vitamin D
> supplements. But then again, maybe oblivion is just the next

logical step in our degenerating evolution. Medicated to get by. Godlessness to dodge a judgy, omniscient male gaze. NFT to escape reality. America, land of the cowardly and caged. Derealization or death.

You see, oblivion is the only natural response to this world, because it would be mad not to be depressed in this world; not to have anxiety when our grandchildren will have only half of this world; not to dissociate into a state that turns this entire crumbling place unreal. Because for the most part, wouldn't it be lovely if it wasn't real?

And wouldn't we be utterly insane *not* to be insane when we can get any answer we want on Google in less than a second? And we can get the opposite answer of that one in another millisecond? And guns are more accessible than health care? And we have a better chance at being a victim of a school shooting than seeing a shooting star? And abortions are being banned? And genocides are not historical anomalistic atrocities but current and permanent tools for power? And presidents of the land of the free are overt white supremacists? And people can't use the bathroom they feel safest in? And suicide is the number one killer in the world: not terrorists, not serial killers, not natural disasters, not mass murderers? And children (children!) would rather be dead than alive? And parents can't even sue the tech companies that enact this psychological, neurological warfare on their kids.

If you're not deemed "mentally ill" by this fucked-up society, I worry for you. I think of you. I pray for you.

I look up from my phone and she's smiling.

I don't know what that means so I say:

I bet you think that's my depression talking. Don't you, Dr. Raya?

Did you just call me by my name?

Silence.

Silence.

Silence.

My new therapist asks, so do you really think that's the next logical step in our evolution? Derealization or death?

I sigh and look down at my hands.

Honestly, I think the next logical step is that we choose to collectively dismantle the structures that have made us want to disappear into oblivion, to want to kill ourselves, to want to kill others, to want to leave the ones who cherish us because being cherished is too painful for a body and mind that has been mutated to accept pain and only pain.

I look directly into my new therapist's eyes.

This, of course, would be the next logical step if only we could liberate ourselves. But, Dr. Raya, you told me once that liberation for people like me is a practice of patient labor. Well, this right now, this written now, is my labor patiently laboring itself in the attempt to free myself from the confines of this depressing, anxious, dissociative existence.

But I know that I will never be totally free. Never utterly liberated.

And honestly, I'm probably going to forget everything I just said by lunchtime. All the clarity will disappear soon. It will be replaced with a new follow on Instagram. Or my anxiety over another celebrity couple breaking up. Or my outrage at another news story of foreign war or a Black man shot in the back. And this knowing makes it all seem so worthless.

But still, look at me, I'm here.

Silence.

Silence.

Silence.

I'm not giving up, but I just need to say this is really fucking hard.

THE STUDY OF OBLIVION

thirty-two weeks since breakdown

I stare at my laptop screen waiting for her to appear. I think about switching screens to my manuscript and editing, but then she's there and I'm being asked to connect my audio. I oblige, and then I'm greeted by her voice:

Hi, Norma.

I can't see my new therapist's feet for once. Just her face up close, closer than ever before. I can see the wrinkles around her hazel eyes. They're kind of endearing. Almost kind. She makes her crooked smile and says,

I'm sorry about this, but the new Omicron outbreak makes it too risky to meet in person, especially before the holidays.

That's okay.

And it *is* honestly okay, because it's really cold today and I didn't want to go outside anyways.

How are you doing?

I'm good.

But I can hear in my voice that I sound tired, very tired, despite having slept ten hours last night.

I'm going home for the holidays.

My new therapist says, aren't you home?

That's not what I meant. I meant—

I look out the window onto Sixth Avenue, where two cabdrivers are standing outside their cars arguing with each other.

Actually, yes, you're right. I *am* home.

This is why she's my new therapist.

I meant to say I'm going to my parents' house in Connecticut for Christmas.

Mmm.

It'll be the first time I've seen them since my breakdown. My girlfriend was supposed to come with me. Obviously she's not now.

And how are you handling the breakup?

I miss her.

Silence.

Silence.

Silence.

And I'm frustrated.

Why?

Because I know how her and I end now, but I *still* can't write The Last Story.

Mmm.

And now, I'm going back to Connecticut and I definitely won't be able to write there.

Why is that?

Because of the little girl on the ladder from my story.

You mean you.

I want to say in a *Gossip Girl* voice: an artist never tells. But instead I say,

It's hard to tell any other story except that one when I'm there. You know, the story of a girl secretly placing her books on a bookshelf, because she needs someone, anyone, to know she exists. Even if confirmation of her existence depends on the next owners to find her. Probably after she's dead. How depressing.

Well you *are* chronically depressed.

So you keep telling me.

My new therapist looks at something off-screen as she says:

How do you feel about going to your parents' house?

I'm scared.

Mmm.

You know, the day after my first date with my girlfriend... well ex-girlfriend, I guess... I wrote a flash fiction piece about the relationship between the words *scared* and *sacred*. In it, I talked about religion. How I was raised to think all humans were sinners. How she was raised to believe Allah hated her because she was gay. Anyways, after I wrote it, I asked my girl—*ex*-girlfriend: don't you think it's funny how if someone was reading too quickly, they could mistake the word *scared* for *sacred*? I didn't know if she would get it. She looked up at the ceiling, thinking. And then she said, *scarred too*. I said, what? And she said, *scarred, scared and sacred*. I remember smiling. Smiling really big. Then I gave her the flash fiction piece. It was the first story I ever let her read.

Mmm.

That's all my new therapist does today. She just moans at me.

But anyways, this isn't about my ex-girlfriend. None of oblivion has been about her. If anything, it's been the opposite of her. So, can we talk about the fact that I'm going to visit my parents for the holidays and I'm scared?

And sacred, my new therapist adds. Then she kind of chuckles at herself.

And then I chuckle too.

And at that, I like my new therapist for a moment.

Maybe it's because I can't see her feet.

Home Part 2

I step into my mother's Mercedes, recline the passenger seat and close my eyes. I sleep the whole car ride from the train station. I wake up to my mother saying:

We're home.

I grab my duffel bag from the trunk, and my mother waves to the couple next door, who are outside shoveling snow.

Those are our new neighbors. They have a little girl too. About your age.

A girl who looks about ten years old comes running out the neighbors' front door and crashes into her father. My mother starts again:

Come on. Let's go say hi.

I'll meet you inside.

My mother hands me the keys and says:

You're being a bad girl. Do you want a time-out?

When I walk through the front door, the house smells the same, though it looks slightly different, as if it is a "find the differences" game in a children's magazine. Maybe a new rug or piece of china in the curios, but I can't tell. With my duffel bag on my shoulder, I pass the library and go straight upstairs to avoid my mother's inevitable prying about what happened between me and my girlfriend; in the end, I know she'll say that God always has a plan while pretending to be sad for me. Pretending, because truly she's hoping this means I'm straight again. As I walk up the staircase to the second floor, I want to caress the carved wooden banister like I did when I was a child, but a garland is smothering it like a boa constrictor. When we were kids, my sister used to swing her legs around the banister when my parents weren't looking and slide down. From the bottom of the staircase, she'd look up at me, waiting for me to join her, but I never managed to follow her, not even once. I was always more cautious than she was.

I walk into my old bedroom and place my duffel bag on the comforter to find that it's the same bedding I had as a girl. In fact, nothing has changed in the room. Only certain items have been moved slightly, like my one-eyed teddy bear has shifted from the middle of the queen-size bed to the left side. I imagine the maid in here throughout the past decade, examining the remnants from my childhood. I wonder who she thinks I am. I wonder if she thinks that I did that to my own stuffed animal.

I walk down the foyer. Under my feet the wood in the hallway creaks. The sound is so foreign, I jump when it first happens, but by the end of the hallway, I'm already used to it. It's just part of the house's symphony now. In my sister's old bedroom, the furniture is different and the walls have been painted a dark maroon. I look into the guest bedroom next. A new comforter and a new lamp. I walk back down the foyer to the bathroom, the one with the shower. The bathroom is so much smaller than I remember. I feel like a giant inside it. I stare into the mirror, and trying to avoid the two new crater-like lines connecting my nose to my mouth, I fix my hair, which is tied into a messy ponytail. I adjust my bangs on my forehead before looking into the tiled shower. To my surprise, I feel nothing when I do this. I leave the bathroom and walk back to my room. Under the chandelier that used to comfort me, I feel unsettled. Unlike the other rooms, my room has been retained as if it's a shrine. Or as if one day I will change back into a little girl and inhabit this room again. My mother shouts from downstairs:

Want to help Mommy set the table?

Back downstairs, I am greeted by the old yellow couch and a Christmas tree decorated in blue and silver. I can't believe my mom hasn't bought a new couch or my father hasn't fixed this one. The TV is on, though no one is watching it. I look at the large 4K flat screen mounted to the wall. Suddenly I miss VHS tapes and the way my sister and I would always struggle to find the second tape to *Titanic*. I can't even count the number of times we watched only the first half of that movie. My mother walks into the living room from the kitchen and asks me if I will be moving home since my girlfriend and I broke up. I excuse myself, saying I have to go to the bathroom.

Oh, you must have a really bad bellyache, sweetie.

I go up one flight of stairs and then up another to where my mother will never think to look for me. When I open the attic door, I'm greeted by a great wall of cardboard boxes; squares and rectangles of family keepsakes. There are so many boxes that I can barely see the attic floors. I look around at the place that once terrified me, but in the afternoon light, the attic isn't as scary as I remember. A flapping crashes above me, and I look up at the unfinished ceiling, knowing there's either a bird or a bat, or a family of either, and I am intruding on their home.

Since I'll be hiding up here for a while, I begin rummaging around in search of my late grandmother's paintings, her self-portraits that I caught a glimpse of only once. I still don't know why my grandmother Rose jumped to her death when she came to this country, and no one will tell me. Or maybe the truth is no one actually knows her story. Maybe she never wrote it down. One by one, I open the cardbard boxes. Old school papers, report cards, terrible drawings. Christmas decorations, my past Halloween costumes, my father's med school diploma. Barbies, Barbie accessories, Barbie houses and cars. The wall slowly comes down.

At sunset, after going through every box, I still haven't found my grandmother's paintings. So I sit in a heap on the floor and look at the underside of the roof with its wooden beams like a cage, a fence, that closes me into the house. I can almost feel the sky beyond them. I can almost taste the fresh air. Almost. I lie down on the dusty floor and stare above me at *the almost*, willing the sky to show itself. As the room begins to darken, I lie there watching the darkness replace the light. Through the old walls, I hear my father's voice downstairs. He must have just gotten home. My eyes close and my ears listen to the muffled sounds of my parents arguing with each other. Their voices getting louder and louder. Their voices pulsing through the walls of the house. If I hold my breath, I can hear the house's heart beating in sync with them, or perhaps their voices *are* the house's heartbeat, I don't know. When we were kids, my sister would sit across from me at dinner, and when my parents weren't looking, she would hold her breath for as long as she could until her face turned purple, until she started shaking, almost convulsing. Then she would surrender and we would laugh for ages. After my second niece was born, my sister told me that she is more okay than me because she learned to block out the bad memories and keep only the good ones, like sliding down that staircase and holding her breath until she almost passed out. She doesn't remember any of the yelling in the house. She doesn't remember the floors that creaked. I should probably go back downstairs now.

I lift my body and open my eyes, but when I do, I gasp and my body jolts back down, paralyzed, pressing into the floorboards. Hanging from the wooden planks above me is a long, red, pulsating piece of flesh. It is thick like a giant gooey snake, dangling right above my body. I rub my eyes, knowing that I must be imagining it. My eyes have been so bad lately, so itchy. But as I rub my eyes, a force drops, like a bomb, into my stomach. The wind knocked out of me. I can't breathe. I grab my belly, but the giant cord of pulsating flesh is now one with my belly button, the cord filling with my blood, sucking my blood upward, into the roof. I want to scream for help, I almost do, but then I remember no one here can help me. I squirm, but the flesh only pulls tighter. I sit up and try to yank the slimy cord connecting me to the roof, but it pulls even stronger this time, almost lifting my body from the floor. Then in a struggle between me and it, the cord wraps itself around my neck twice. I feel my face fill with pressure. My airway collapses. Like my sister at family dinners, I begin to shake, my face turning purple, my cells fighting against one another for just the smallest sip of oxygen.

I struggle to look behind me to find something, anything, to help. Trying not to wiggle my body too much, I stretch backward with my right hand, straining my neck, and just barely grasp onto a loose piece of crown molding. I pull it toward me with all my might. The movement makes the blood in my abdomen rush upward into the dangling piece of meat, siphoning out of me. I hold the crown molding up to the flesh. My hands are trembling, the nails from the broken crown molding are digging into my palms. The umbilical cord pulls tighter around my neck. I remember being a little girl sitting at the bottom of the staircase, crying, begging my mother not to make me go upstairs to my bedroom. I kept repeating that there were ghosts, beings, creatures hiding in the halls, under the furniture, laughing in the attic, moaning in the living room. I told her they were going to get me one day. My mother rolled her eyes and said nothing was there. Her suitcase was packed and standing next to the front door. She was leaving the next day. She was happy; it was foreign. But nothing, I said to her, doesn't make the floorboards creak or my bedroom door open or the shower run too hot. Nothing, I said to her, doesn't feel like this place does. Still, good little girls go upstairs when they're told to, they do everything they're told to do. As I lay in bed that night, I counted how many times I heard their footsteps, seven, felt their breath under the bed, seven, smelled their rotting bodies seeping from the foundation, seven.

Holding the wood in my right hand, I whack the crown molding against the dangling flesh. The nails dig into the side. Blood spurts out from the puncture wound. I hear wings above flap in fear. I peel my hand back, feeling splinters seep into my skin, and, this time with more force, I swing again. Another puncture, another spurt of blood that splashes against the walls. I keep swinging and banging, my face growing more and more dense. Then I remember the same bed but I was older and I was sleeping naked like my Barbies. Exiting dreams, my eyes closed, I counted the door creaks and the footsteps as they came closer, as the seven footsteps pulled down the sheet to expose my body. I counted the seconds it took me to turn as if I was just having a bad dream to scare away the footsteps, seven. I remember never opening my eyes because I felt bad for him. The number of footsteps it took for him to walk back to the door and close it again slowly? Seven, it was always seven.

Finally, in one final breathless bang, I ram the crown molding against the cord. The flesh splits in two. The cord retracts toward the roof with a violent *swoosh*, and my body falls back onto the floor. My lungs fill with air again and the air feels like knives cutting into my chest. As my blood drains from the flesh above and out onto the attic floor, soaking the bottom of the cardboard boxes, I cry out from the sharpness in my lungs. My cries echo against the walls and escape through the chimney. With my hands, I quickly unwrap the flesh from around my neck and throw it away from me. I press my hand against my stomach to stop the bleeding. I barely have strength to keep pressure on the wound, but I know if I don't press hard enough, I will die in this house where I could scream for help but wouldn't be heard. I will die to the vision of the underside of the roof where I can almost see the sky, but can't. I lie there and press down as forcefully as I can. I remember being two and a half. I remember my second memory of the world emptying. I remember my third and fourth and hundredth and thousandth memory. I remember my mother. I remember my father. No, I remember Her. The light in her eye. The vitality in her voice. I feel the blood begin to work with me and settle back into my body. Her. My breathing begins to slow. Her. The stabbing feeling in my lungs dissipates. I lie there soaked in goo and blood, and I realize that I can't hear my parents' voices through the walls anymore. I can't hear the house's heartbeat either.

As I press against my stomach, I can hear only one thing: the beating of my own heart. And to the sound of being alive, I fall asleep naked on the floor.

———

I wake up sometime later to my mother calling my name. When I open my eyes, I am fully clothed again, the cord hanging from the ceiling is gone, and the blood around me has dried into the wooden floorboards. I walk downstairs to the first floor. My mother, father, and sister are sitting around the dining room table eating pork chops.

Before I can speak, my mother looks up at me and spitefully says:

Where have you been?

In the attic.

We're about to eat.

You know I don't eat meat anymore.

Sure you do. You love it.

I turn to my sister:

Where are the girls?

What girls? We are the girls.

My sister looks genuinely confused. My mother closes her eyes and clasps her hands in prayer. My father takes a big bite of meat. My sister stares at me and takes a deep breath in. She holds the air in her mouth and puffs out her cheeks.

As her face turns purple, as her body begins to shake, I remember one room in the house that I haven't checked:

I'll be right back.

My father is still looking at his plate. With her eyes closed, my mother says:

Okay, honey.

When I turn to leave, my sister still hasn't exhaled.

I walk out of the kitchen, into the front hallway, and turn in to the library. The library, like my own room, looks untouched, identical to how it was twenty years ago. I stand in front of the bookshelf. I place my foot on the ladder. I see *Bridge to Terabithia* perfectly smushed between the old faded books, exactly where I placed it years ago. I take two steps up the ladder with no hands, without even looking: like riding a bike, like muscle memory, like my body has been waiting to do this my whole life. And in a matter of seconds, I am staring directly into the highest shelf of the library, the one shelf I could never reach.

My eyes scan the contents of this mystery shelf, but to my dismay there is no glass teddy bear eye and no grandmother's paintings. There are just many copies of the same book side by side, over and over again. So many copies of this one book that it fills the entire row. The binding reads *Please Stop Trying to Leave Me*. I've never heard of the book before, so I reach for one of the copies and fan through it, but before I can gather what the story is about, tucked into the binding is an old photograph: a black-and-white image of a middle-aged woman. She's standing in a kitchen I don't recognize, wearing a house dress and looking directly at the camera. She doesn't look happy. She doesn't look sad or angry either. More confused than anything. Or maybe exhausted. Or lost. I flip over the photograph and see handwriting on the back: *Rose, 1972*. My grandmother.

Holding the book in one hand and the photo in the other, I descend the ladder. To get a closer look at my grandmother, I place the novel face down on the library desk. But then the back of the book catches my attention: a summary, a price, an author photo—a young woman smiling with bright white teeth on a boardwalk. She has subtle wrinkles around her eyes, eyes that are glistening, drawing me in. There is a ferry behind the woman. A small store, almost like a bodega, in the far background. A bay reflecting the afternoon sun. I recognize the place: Dragon Island. I see a name printed next to the author photo. My name.

I look back at Rose. And then at the book. I place them side by side and stare into the two faces: one of a lady who once looked so familiar and one *not* of a little girl, but of a woman, me but a different me, a happier me on Dragon Island. With my eyes shifting back and forth between the two images, I realize two things simultaneously.

The first: my grandmother and I look nothing alike.

JANUARY

It increasingly seems to me that the goal of [writers'] patient labor is not our own liberation per se, but a deepened capacity to give it away, with an ever-diminishing attachment to outcome.

Maggie Nelson

THE STUDY OF OBLIVION

thirty-five weeks since breakdown

Today I read an article that said the world is facing a growing food supply crisis and we may need to start eating insects and not only eating them but farming them. I didn't make this up. Well, I haven't made anything up thus far, but I feel like I need to be very clear that I read this particular article in *The Economist* online. Also, this morning, I walked to Starbucks in this freezing weather to get a chai, and I saw a police officer helping an old blind man walk up Sixth Avenue. At that moment, I felt hopeful. Hopeful like when I see people reading on the subway. Of course, the police officer was a Black woman, which makes sense. You know, I've been praying lately. I know. I know. But it's not what you think. I've been kneeling on the ground with my forehead on the floor (the way my girlfriend used to), and I've been praying to Stardust and Dirt. The winds of the North, East, South, and West. To the elements of Water, Earth, Air, and Fire. Yes, I have been praying to a dying thing: to the earth. More like, sitting with her and speaking to her as if I'm her daughter and she's my mother in hospice care. I kneel at her bedside with my forehead in her abdomen and ask her about her fondest memories. Then I tell her about my regrets and I say that I'm sorry a million times.

That's great, Norma.

You know what I figured out last night?

No, I don't know.

That was rhetorical.

I know.

Then why'd you respond?

My new therapist shrugs.

I give her the side-eye but I end up just looking at her wooden robot.

Hold on. Her robot has three feet, not two. How have I never noticed this before?

She says, are you going to tell me what happened last night?

Nothing happened. I was just cutting my toenails, but then it hit me: the answer to why we'd prefer to stay blind to our own oblivion.

My new therapist's eyes glaze over at my mention of oblivion.

Yes, I know. I'm going to talk about oblivion one more time. After all, this is The Study of Oblivion and I have to finish it.

She sighs and says, okay. Why do you think people prefer to stay blind to their oblivion?

She actually says the word.

I don't think it's our fault. I don't even think it's our parents' fault or their parents' or even their parents'. Oblivion is just easier. Simple as that.

In what way?

Well first of all, it's scary to not be in oblivion, terrifying to admit that you've been living a scripted life.

Mmm.

Second of all, if people woke up from oblivion, if people became aware of *everything* happening out there—

I point to her window.

And in here—

I point to my head.

Not only what's happening but what *has* happened, they would feel hopeless. Because like you said, Getting Better is an infinite, fucking awful process.

My new therapist butts in: I don't think I said those exact words.

You didn't, but I am, because it's the truth and you like to sugarcoat things.

Oh.

I continue:

So if escaping oblivion is a grueling, long-ass process... Well, I don't think that anyone feels like they have the stamina or time to do it. They have bills to pay. Jobs to keep. Kids to take care of.

My new therapist scribbles on her clipboard. What was so interesting about that? I try to ignore her:

And that's all fine. I get it. But you know, when I was in my parents' library, I remembered the golden rule to writing a story.

And that is?

Never ever have a passive protagonist.

What do you mean by that?

No one wants to read a story where life just happens to your main character. They have to be active. Your character has to want something and go for it, say something and mean it. They have to make choices. Hard choices, preferably. Those are the most interesting to witness.

Hmm.

Yeah. Hmm.

I realized I've just mocked her, so quickly I continue,

I don't think writing a story is that different from living a life. And I'm starting to see that I've been a passive protagonist in *my* life. I kept thinking I was making my own decisions, but in reality, I was letting someone else write my own goddamn story.

Who wrote it, then?

Dr. Raya, you're not listening. It doesn't matter who wrote my story or our story, what ancestor or divine algorithm made it this way. What matters is that now *we're* the main characters, and if we want a good story, we can't be passive anymore. We have to do something different than we've ever done. We have to go after what we want. We have to make choices. Hard ones. And if we do this, I believe we *can* all wake up from oblivion. We can make ourselves better *and* the world better.

I scratch an itch on my nose:

I don't know, maybe that's too optimistic. Maybe *that's* fiction. But even if it is fiction, I have to believe it. I have to.

I look toward my new therapist's pillows, which are back in their original haphazard spots (I guess she really does like them that way), and say:

And in the end, if we can't build a global utopia, if that's truly impossible, then, at the very least, we can build a safe house for one another.

I scratch my nose again, but this time the itch is near my nostril.

I'm not picking my nose, I say defensively.

My new therapist says, I didn't say that you were.

When I finish scratching my poorly placed itch, I say:

I used to think I was being active in my life by writing, but now I don't know. I kind of just let oblivion fuck me up in the meantime. Don't you think?

Silence.

Silence and direct eye contact.

Silence and she hasn't blinked once.

I place my hands over my eyes in disappointment. I let my ice-cold fingertips run down my face like water:

Why don't you ever answer my questions?

Because I don't know the answer to that.

I say, sure you do.

My new therapist sighs. She places her clipboard and pen down on her lap. She looks around the room. She's about to give in. I'm about to win therapy.

She says, weren't you, with your writing, trying to study oblivion?

The crowd goes *booooooooooo*.

I say, that's another question.

She says, just trust me.

JUST!?!? Like trust isn't the hardest thing in the world.

But what else am I going to do?

Yeah.

But were you *actually* studying oblivion?

Um... I don't know. Sometimes.

And other times?

Other times... Other times I think I was trying to study love. But now I'm not sure if you can know what love is from a story.

I think, my new therapist says, you still don't trust that love exists outside of a story. When we first met, real love was too big of a concept for your mind to understand, because it didn't look like your parents' love and it didn't look like the fairy tales either. What love *really* is terrifies you. And we both know it terrifies you, because you ran from a good person who was offering it.

She picks up her pen again and clicks it once. Then she says,

I think you know what love is. At least you're starting to.

But if I actually know what love is, then why do I feel the need to write? What are the words for?

My opinion?

Your expert opinion.

I almost wink at her, but then I remember the last time I did this and how creepy it was. I stabilize my eye.

My new therapist says, I think writing helps you to create meaning.

I don't get it.

You're obsessed with your manuscript having meaning, with it all connecting and having a through line, because you don't want life to be purposeless. You want what happens, not only to you, but to Black people, to the earth, to the Native Americans, to those in Afghanistan, to have a reason, a good, logical or spiritual reason, for having happened. Even if, to find the reason, you have to change the setting or the details. And in having a good reason for having happened, you think you can find a solution to stop these things from occurring in the future.

So I write because I'm a control freak?

She ignores me: and without finding meaning in every good and bad event, every thought and feeling, the world feels very scary to you.

My brain thinks: my new therapist is on a roll today. Did she take an Adderall this morning?

Simultaneously, my mouth says:

Maybe you're right. Maybe I wrote to create meaning. And maybe, in reality, there is no reason for this whole crumbling world, and therefore no solution. Maybe I just have to accept that life isn't a book where every object, thought, and event that's mentioned is going to come together by the last chapter, wrapped in a tight binding. Maybe life doesn't have a *hallelujah* moment followed by *the end*.

But if my life *was* a manuscript, I would make it make sense. I would be obsessed with the number seven, because I heard seven footsteps coming toward my bed that day. I would have dated men for so long, because I unconsciously wanted to relive the trauma over and over again. Eventually, the trauma would have consumed me. I would have unlocked a repressed memory and gotten cancer. Thanks to Felix, I would've eventually gone for treatment. When I was better, I would have met my girlfriend, come out to my parents, and had my breakdown after a perfect few days on Dragon Island, because unconsciously I struggle to believe in love when 1) I like girls (and therefore, I am a creep and adulterer like men) and 2) my parents' marriage failed so horribly. And after apologizing to the infinite man, I would have gone back to my childhood home and cut myself away from the trauma: freed myself from it once and for all. The end.

See, it would make perfect sense. And because it made sense, it would give people hope. It would have them believe that our minds and our trauma and our futures are so easily dissectible and, therefore, curable.

But this isn't a manuscript.

The truth is: I don't know how many footsteps came toward my bed. I don't even know anymore if that's the crux of my issue. I don't know why I dated men for years when I knew I was gay, or why, after my gynecologist scraped out the HPV cells, I felt like I could finally come out of the closet. I don't know why I broke down on a completely normal day after taking a nap with her. I don't know why months and months later I'm still not better and feel like I'll *never* be normal again. And to be honest, you haven't really helped me figure any of this shit out. I don't know if you ever will.

Because of this, I'm not sure what hope I have to give to the world. I'm not sure what story I can tell that will make someone, anyone, feel better about this life, this world. And I'm not sure how to say that it's all going to be okay, because I don't know if it will be.

Maybe, my new therapist says, not everything has to make sense in order to give people hope.

Eh. I grunt out loud.

But, Norma, from what you're saying, it seems like You Write Not Only To Create Meaning, But Also To Build One Of Those Safe Houses You Mentioned, Which, Actually, Doesn't Sound Like You're Being A Passive Character At All. Maybe The Protagonist In Your Short Stories Is, But You're Not.

I sigh and adjust my bangs:

I don't know about that. All I know is that I still have one story left to write. What does The Last Story need to be in order to complete the manuscript?

She shrugs: *That* I don't know. I'm not a writer. I'm just a therapist.

Please.

This time she sighs and looks toward her pillows.

Then she says,

Well, maybe, oblivion has to die in order for your character to live.

I think about it for a moment.

   How to kill oblivion: 27,600,000 results (0.52 seconds)

      VIDEO: *Elder Scrolls Oblivion:* How to Kill Anyone
      VIDEO: *Oblivion* How To: Kill Umbra at level 1.

Well, that was useless. Google fails for once.

But maybe my new therapist is right. Oblivion has to die.

So then, just to see if she'll react, I say:

If oblivion has to die, so do I.

My new therapist slowly takes her feet off her footrest.

Oh. My. God.

I see her ballet flats on the ground for the first time in my life.

I don't think I will ever forget this moment.

My new therapist leans forward and says that she'll have to call someone.

My old therapist would never have said such a thing. He would have invited me over for dinner. Back then, I probably would have said yes.

I say, no, no, no, noooo. I is a character in my book. All people are characters.

She says, it's the law.

Shit. Now I have to plead my case. I sigh and say slowly:

I know you probably don't believe me. Because of the lava. Because of my rants. Because of everything, to be honest. But after all these months of me trying to "get better"—

Yes, I put it in quotes and lowercase.

—you should know the truth: that every session, every story, every pill—after all, you didn't shove them down my throat—is proof that I don't actually want to wither away and disappear. Unlike my character, I want to live.

She purses her lips and scans my face.

She looks semi-suspicious of me when she says, okay, and sits back in her chair.

Thank you, I say, because for a second, I really didn't know if she was going to lock me up in a mental hospital and that would have been a shame, because we're finally getting somewhere.

Then she says, you're welcome.

Which is annoying because *she's* the one who misunderstood me. But anyways, I continue:

Now that we've cleared that up. Like I was saying, the main character has to die.

Why is that the only narrative option?

Because it's too late for my character.

It's never too late.

That's such a therapist thing to say. I'm the author, remember?

She sighs as if she's upset that I kicked her out of the creative process. This isn't a writers' room, lady. I continue:

Anyways, if the main character dies, the manuscript will have to end.

Then you'll finally finish it and figure out the genre.

Right. So how should she die, I ask.

Silence.

Should she kill herself? No, that's awful.

Silence.

Should there be an accident just as she's Getting Better?

Silence.

Should I buy a whiteboard and brainstorm all the ways in which she could die and find the most plausible ones and then choose from there?

Silence.

Or should that list itself be the ending?

Silence.

Or should I ask my ex-girlfriend?

My new therapist perks up.

She puts her feet back on her footrest:

Well, what makes you want to ask her?

Because I don't know how to end the story and I value her opinion.

Weren't you concerned about value before?

Yeah.

So her presence in your life is valuable to you?

Check.

Anyone who reads a lot is valuable to someone who is trying to write a book.

Uncheck.

But she's not just anyone, is she?

I look at the three-footed robot on the bookshelf.

My new therapist says,

You're afraid to answer, because if you do, then you'll have to admit that she means a lot to you. And then you'll have to admit that, because she means a lot to you, you are terrified of losing her and that, in fact, you actually *do* want to be with her. You Want That More Than Anything In The World. Even More Than Finishing Your Manuscript. But to be with her, you have to face your worst fear.

Which fear? I have a lot of them.

In real life, if you choose to be with her, you will never know how your story with her ends. And for this, you'll have to be okay living with uncertainty. You see, Norma:

Uncertainty Is The Price We Pay For Love.

Silence.

Silence.

Silence.

In the silence, I adjust the gold rings on my hands. The same hands that have flipped and fanned through hundreds of books. The same hands that *click* across the keyboard in the middle of the night like an incoming thunderstorm. I imagine a wedding ring on these hands one day. I feel myself smile. I look at the wooden robot on the bookshelf. I decide that it's not so much creepy as it is quirky. And I guess my new therapist's textile pillows aren't as much awful as they are, also, quirky. And I guess my new therapist isn't so new and she's just my therapist now. I guess. I am still smiling.

When I turn to look at my therapist, she is also smiling.

Then, as if the question headbutts me, I say, wait, Dr. Raya, are you married?

She shifts her ballet-flat-covered feet on her black footrest, and she nods.

I realize this is the first question I've asked my therapist about her own life.

Maybe I was the one who was rude all along.

As soon as I leave my new therapist's office, I buy a whiteboard on Amazon.

And then I call her.

The Last Story

She wants to see you.

Crushing my cell phone between my ear and shoulder, I shut off the sink and stand at the counter with my hands dripping water and soap on the granite.

Me? Are you sure?

Yes. I'm sure.

I reach for the rag around the oven door. I wipe my hands and then my forearms. Remnants of the garden soil had traveled all the way to my elbows today or, rather, I had been feeling so unsettled today that I had stuck my arms all the way into the dirt as if I could reach the center of the earth and grab hold.

She's dying.

I grip the phone with my right hand. The ache of my torn rotator cuff burning as my shoulder drops down to its proper place.

What? Where is she?

Dragon Island. Well, that's what she told me to tell you. She said you'd understand.

I laugh and shake my head.

Of course. Of course she's there.

It's 12 Pine Walk.

And with that, the woman claiming to be Norma's longtime caretaker hangs up the phone.

———

We were both coffee shop goers. The types of people who craved an artisanal aesthetic to make us feel part of the avant-garde culture. Norma enjoyed sitting there with little to do, looking busy over a chai latte and her laptop. She'd type a few words and then sit back and sip. I, on the other hand, during my lunch breaks went to any coffee shop in the area, whatever area my job shipped me off to that day, to people-watch. This particular day I was in Williamsburg scouting for a new pop-up location.

When I saw her from across the room, I noticed her hands first. The gold rings that adorned them. The way the chunky rings clinked together as her fingers moved unfathomably fast over her keyboard. I watched her type, then sip, then type some more, then pick at her nails or adjust her black bangs so they'd lie evenly over her forehead. European, I thought, surely. Or maybe Middle Eastern. Also, I guessed from her nails and shoes that she was gay. When you're a lesbian, you usually have to guess or, at least, hope. That day in Williamsburg, I guessed right.

Sit with me.

She said while closing her laptop. As I sat down, she asked me the first of many questions she would come to ask me in the coming months:

So, are you a sad happy person or a happy sad person?

I didn't know the difference. She tilted her head to the side. For a moment, I watched her hands waiting for me, her fingers intertwined with one another as if she was praying. I always had an answer or at least a witty response for a stranger, but this time my mind was blank. So instead, I returned the question, and she answered instantaneously, as if she was waiting her whole life for someone to ask her that question:

Sad, Happy. For sure. Like I know somewhere I'm happy. Somewhere deep inside of me. I know it. There's no way I'm not.

Oh yeah?

Yeah. And my plan is to find that happiness one day.

And as she said this, she unclasped her hands, her gold rings glimmering in the light, and I knew then that I was going to fall in love with her and I knew then, without a doubt, that it was going to hurt.

———

I step off the ferry and walk along the boardwalk. I check my phone for directions to 12 Pine Walk. To the right, just like the Airbnb we stayed at that summer. I pause to catch my breath, leaning my hand against the trash can, and take in the smell of the bay. My skin is much paler than the last time I was here. After reaching fifty, I stopped trying to crisp my skin to a mocha brown. When one gets older the imminence of skin cancer or wrinkles eventually overshadows the vanity. For me, it was my father's death. Five years after she left me. Besides, I was naturally tanner than most. Despite my late-bloomed attempts to save my skin, now eighty-two, the thin line tattoos on my forearms from when I was twenty look more like a toddler's "drawings." The images once of a cat, an anatomical heart, and Arabic now a mush of scattered marks and flabby skin.

———

The thing is, we did not meet at a coffee shop. I did not see her from across the room, and she did not invite me to sit with her. I lied to you. But in a way I didn't. There were so many nights when she and I would lie together naked and she would set the scene for us:

If you had seen me at a coffee shop, would you have come up to me?

It was a pandemic! Nothing was open!

I know. I know, but come on.

Then we'd take turns describing the eye contact, the dialogue, the bodily reactions, each of us would have had to each other. She enjoyed indulging in this fantasy meeting. This fantasy and other fantasies, like the one where we met at the park or at Cubbyhole or on Eighth Avenue. She enjoyed these fantasies, because she was the type of person who loved fairy tales. She was always looking outside of us for the story: for a great love.

———

Thirty minutes later, which would have, in the past, taken me less than ten minutes, I arrive at 12 Pine Walk and I am suddenly mortified by my arms and the distorted tattoos. Suddenly ashamed of my wrinkled skin and the crow's-feet that used to signify my smile, now just the permanence of my face. Suddenly acutely aware that I am no longer thirty years old, that I am an old woman now. And suddenly I realize that Norma will not be twenty-seven when she opens the door, but instead seventy-nine.

———

The truth is I found her on a dating app. We matched on the first day of lockdown. For two weeks we FaceTimed. At least forty hours. She did truly ask me if I was a happy sad person or a sad happy person. And I did honestly know I was falling in love with her after our first FaceTime date. When she finally agreed to meet me in the middle of a silent, desolate New York City, we became inseparable. Our relationship began with a mirage of date nights and date days and very quickly sleepovers, which lasted three or four days. During this time, she told me of the rooms in her childhood home that scared her, of the ocean that couldn't heal her, of the attic that terrified her. She told me of the many apartments and neighborhoods in the city she had lived in, her desire, in each of them, to sleep the days away, the pain of opening her eyes every morning. Then she told me of a snakeskin box, a man who was infinite, and the drugs he gave her that brought her closer to oblivion, then of the time she got HPV. In my head, my own memories were strewn across my brain in disconnected fragments. For her, her memories were plot points that connected perfectly to one another. Between her confessions, we made jokes and laughed together. One time I laughed so hard my thumb accidentally ended our FaceTime call, and when I called back, she made me dance around the apartment to a song from Rent as my punishment. As I danced, she sat there on that rectangular screen laughing. Her laugh was like a child's giggle, like it was new and untarnished by the world. Of course, I knew from what she'd told me that this wasn't true. And because of this, I imagined her laugh was exactly what hope sounded like.

The first time she came over to my apartment, I cooked her Chilean sea bass, which I had frantically learned the recipe for the evening before to impress her. Before she took a bite of her food, she told me that she was surprised that I had painted my accent wall pink and that I had so many dried flowers in my apartment. In that moment, I could tell she was reorganizing the character she'd made of me in her mind. Later that evening, we sat on my couch after watching The Notebook, and I told her that love was hard. Love was pain, and I had the scars to show for it. Her large brown eyes glittered as if she was going to let me in on a secret that would change my life:

I know, but love can be something else.

Like what?

Love, the real kind, can take away all the pain. All the ache of the past. The stress of the future. You just have to find *the one*. And when the one comes, all the sadness and suffering fades away.

The one. She was terribly pessimistic and yet, at the same time, naively optimistic. I was reluctant to agree with her about *the one*:

What makes you so sure?

Because love is all powerful. Don't you think?

But look at most people in love, they fucking hate each other.

Then that's not their one. The one is the one who takes the pain away.

She smiled at me and then she jumped up from the couch:

Let's make a list of all the things we want to do when we get out of quarantine. All the places we want to see together.

I took a virgin Moleskine journal from my nightstand, and together we made a list: Pyramids of Egypt. Zip-lining in Costa Rica. The carousels in San Sebastian and in Dumbo. The anechoic chamber in Minnesota. The rowboats in Central Park. The list went on and on. We laughed as we added certain things to the list, like an argument about whether to live in the city or Brooklyn. In parentheses, I wrote, Norma will win. When I wrote this, she smiled so wide, and that smile made the whole cliché of a bucket list worth it to me. When we finished emptying our dreams onto the page, she looked at me.

I think you're my one.

Then she kissed me and I wondered how many people had fallen in love with her before. How many futures she had already planned.

———

She is wearing black. She is not wearing rings. Her fingers are bent and wrinkled like mine. Her house is nothing like I imagined it would be all these years. There is no laptop in sight. No flowers or plants in ceramic pots. No journals or pens. No overflowing basket of blankets. No gold knickknacks, the kind she always placed around our apartment. Instead, there is only white. White empty walls. A white modest sectional. One white armchair. White pillows. White cabinets. A white rug. The only color in the room is the brown of the dining and coffee tables. And of course the blue gray of the bay water outside her windows. She sits in front of me with a white mug in her hands and sips. Though it doesn't look like chai.

Hot honey water.

I had forgotten what it was like to be near someone who could read my mind. Or, rather, someone who had learned my body language so well that they could guess my thoughts. Now, Norma is in front of me again. And now she is dying.

It's cancer.

Her voice has a husky rasp now, and I wonder if she still smokes.

It's like I wrote it into existence.

I still haven't said a word. I had only greeted the caretaker at the door and then, seeing Norma sitting on the couch, was motioned to sit beside her. Norma's eyes are still large and round even though they have fogged from age. I stare into them and try to fit the young woman I once knew into the body before me. It's not as hard as I had imagined it would be.

———

I had always been the loud and extroverted type, the woman who bounced from person to person in a room and walked away from that room with at least two new friends whose names I'd probably already forgotten by the time I got home. The first time we went out together, we had already been together for three months. The world had just started to open again, and everyone was pouring out of their apartments. At the bar, she looked at me in awe. She said she'd never been any good at small talk. And it was true. She was terrible at it. But still, every weekend I begged her to come out with me. At the outdoor bar, she was always quiet, observing her surroundings, perhaps taking notes for her next story. When a friend of mine would come over, I would watch her body shift uncomfortably, as if she'd just lifted a heavy metal shield over her chest as protection. Still she always smiled. She had learned how to smile through discomfort. One time when we were out for Halloween, I introduced her to a guy I had met years ago at a concert and then I was at the bar ordering another drink. Thirty minutes later, I found her and the guy sitting in a booth, and he was confessing some deep-seated fear about his wife leaving him one day because he treated her the same way his father treated his mother. While she was never any good at small talk, there was something about Norma that made strangers feel safe enough to tell her things they had never spoken out loud before. That is, if these strangers were willing to sit with her and her shield long enough.

I don't know what exactly it was about her, but I could feel it too. After our first meeting, one minute I'd be making fun of the old, wobbling dog on the street and the next minute I'd be saying when I was twelve my parents told me their house in Afghanistan had been blown up by a bomb and it was the first time I realized that everything was going to die. One minute I'd be talking about the new tattoo I wanted to get and then I'd be telling her about the first time I kissed a girl and then went home and cut myself with a razor for the first time. Maybe she possessed this power because she had an exquisite ability to listen. Or maybe it was her large brown eyes and how when you looked straight into them they felt like a dangling pendulum, rocking you into a trance.

Despite her public silence and my boisterous presence, in private we reached an equilibrium. I made her laugh. She made me pensive. I gossiped about reality TV stars. She talked about climate change and political injustice. The more we spent time together, the more she let her own thoughts pour out and I, for once, listened. One evening, I asked her about her usual shield and why she felt so comfortable with me.

My heart knows your heart. I don't know how but it just does.

Even though I couldn't understand her obsession with the one, I knew this to be true about our hearts. So five months after we met, I moved into her city apartment. One thing checked off our bucket list. Months later, I took her to Dragon Island, another thing off our bucket list. When we watched the sunset on the dock, I truly felt like everything in the world was perfect; that love truly was what she told me it could be: something that takes away the pain of the past.

————

So how have you been?

She asks this nonchalantly as if we haven't seen each other in a few weeks. I want to say, Seriously? That's your first question? But then I hear myself answer:

You know. Good, good.

Yeah? Good.

Yeah, it's all good. How are you?

Did I really just say "good" again?

Good. I live here now.

How many goods was that? Four? Five? My hand is shaking a little, and I'm not that type of old lady who shakes. I guess it's the nerves. She, on the other hand, looks completely poised. I say:

I can see that. It's nice. Very—uhh . . . white.

It *is* very white. I like it.

I don't think we've ever had such a simple, surface-level conversation before. The awkwardness makes me wish I hadn't come. Maybe I should fake an emergency and catch the three o'clock ferry. She continues:

You know that Airbnb sold only a few years ago. A nice film-maker and his partner own it now. I keep up with the real estate.

Is she really talking about real estate right now? Maybe she has Alzheimer's and has forgotten everything that happened, has forgotten that we haven't seen each other in over fifty years. That would make sense. Either that or she's playing a game. But I'm too old for games now.

I rub her white couch with my hands as if it can pacify the awkwardness between us. I wonder when Fiero died. I wonder if she got another cat when he passed.

So, I looked for your book in every bookstore. Did you use a pseudonym?

She smiles and it's unsettling:

I never finished it.

But you only had one story left.

I still have one story left.

I can hear her caretaker vacuuming upstairs, and I can feel her shield between us as if I'm a stranger in a bar.

Did you stop writing?

No. I've tried writing a thousand different stories with a thousand different beginnings and endings.

She sighs and continues:

I tried writing something about getting old, about my father outliving my mother, about you sometimes. But every time I thought I got it, the story slipped between my fingertips and was gone again.

But you were a great writer. I'm sure you could have come up with something.

She smiles and looks toward the bay.

Come on, let's sit outside. Amy will bring us some tea.

———

The light reflected off the diamond and glittered in my hands. I closed my eyes and imagined getting down on one knee. I could feel the pavement against my bones, but when I looked up at Norma's face, she couldn't say yes. I placed the ring down on the felt cushion. The woman helping me at the jewelry store sensed my hesitation and announced loudly that she'd be right back. Ever since Norma and I had come back from Dragon Island, I hadn't wanted to admit it, but, looking at diamonds, it was hard not to. Norma didn't look at me the same way anymore. She didn't look at anything the same way anymore. She was quiet. She wasn't writing. All the color had drained from her face. She was close to one hundred pounds and wore big baggy clothes to cover the veins and bones that had started to pop out across her body. She was like a skeleton who slept constantly, and she wouldn't tell me what was wrong. She was paranoid when we went out and didn't even fake a smile with strangers anymore. I told her we could stay in more often, but then we'd be watching a movie and I'd look at her from across the couch and her eyes would be blank and staring at the rug. That day, I didn't buy the ring but I told the woman to hold it for me. I'd be back. I was going to propose soon. Just not yet. After we got to the bottom of this, I would.

When I got home that early summer afternoon, she didn't say her usual hello when she heard the door open. Instead, I found her wrapped in a white blanket on the couch. Her laptop wasn't on her lap. There was no book near her. The TV wasn't even on. Her eyes were open and staring out the floor-to-ceiling windows onto Sixth Avenue.

Did you write today?

No.

You've gotta write this last story. That agent is waiting for your manuscript.

I'm not in the mood. Okay? Just leave me alone.

I didn't even recognize her voice. A week later she still hadn't written anything. She had barely showered. Her eyes blinked more slowly. Her bones kept protruding. She stopped going outside altogether. She either paced around the apartment the whole day picking at the skin around her nails or she lay on the couch and didn't move at all. When I asked her if she was depressed, she said oblivion was taking over again. I remembered her mentioning oblivion back when we first met. She'd said that it had gone away because of me, so back then, I didn't think to ask any more questions. Or perhaps I was too naive to know that questions were important. But now oblivion was back, and as she said this, she looked at me blankly as if I were a TV show that she was watching just to pass the time.

During my lunch break sometime in June, I called her mom.

Oh, it's okay, I'm sure she's fine and just missing home. She does this a lot. Eventually she gets over it.

Then I called her sister.

Norm has always been dramatic. I don't know how you do it. I'm sorry.

Her sister's apology was so genuine it made me hate her. I couldn't wait to tell Norma that I finally understood why they never got along.

On my way home, I bought her dried flowers and wrote her a note. For my wildflower. I remembered how that used to make her smile.

Just stop it!

I stepped back.

What? What'd I do?

All you do is treat me like I'm the greatest person in the world. And it's painful. Okay? Like there . . . Right there . . . See! You're looking at me and all I see is love in your eyes and it makes me want to crawl out of my skin.

What? Why is that a bad thing?

Because I can't feel anything when I look at you.

———

We sit outside by the bay in two white wicker chairs with a table between us. She sits quietly as if waiting for me to say something, but I don't budge. I won't be the first to budge. The silence between us is filled with the song of birds and the lapping of the bay. I am reminded of what she once said to me upstate by the lake decades ago now. It was my birthday the first year we were together. With September stars overhead, a blanket beneath us, and the lake before us, she said:

Even in our silence there is sound.

———

For weeks, I begged her to see a psychiatrist. Maybe medication could help. The first time I said this was the night before we went to visit her family for her mother's birthday. She sat on her side of the bed with the covers pulled over her knees, and she looked at me like I had just stabbed her.

Meds? Are you fucking kidding?

Before that night, I never knew her eyes turned black when she got angry.

Why won't you consider it?

Because it's the easy way out. And I'm not weak. I'll just meditate more.

I don't think meditating is helping.

She snapped back:

Look, this is how I've always been. If you don't like it you can leave!

She threw the covers off her, lifted herself from the bed, and came toward me.

Love was supposed to take this away! You were supposed to! And you did in the beginning, but now look at me! LOOK AT ME!

She got closer, shouting, and I thought she was going to hit me.

It's back so you must not be the one.

But then she just brushed by me, her body just barely missing mine, passing by so close that I could feel the wind from her tiny, tiny skeleton. I felt like a ghost that she could walk through, someone who didn't exist, someone who meant nothing to her. I wanted to cry, but instead I got angry. She turned in to the bathroom, and I followed her.

Fuck the one, Norma! There is no "one"!

I threw my hands up in air quotes as she was washing her face.

Yes there is!

No, Norma, this isn't a novel! In real life, there's just a person across from you and you make it work or you don't. And I've been standing here for weeks trying to help while all you do is push me away. Stop ignoring me and listen!

What do you want?!

Love isn't easy. Relationships definitely aren't easy. But this, this right here, is love, and you're trying to throw it away.

She pulls down her pants, her face still soaking wet, and sits on the toilet:

Well, that's not what my head says.

And your head was created from a lifetime of shit. We're not your parents!

This isn't about my parents! It's about us!

That weekend, we still went to her parents' house. She barely said a word the whole car ride. When we got there, her sister was there. She had come alone.

I mean come on, Norm. Do you really want the kids to see you like this?

Norma cried and cried and cried when she found out her nieces weren't coming. I thought she'd never stop. In a way it was a relief to know that she could still feel something. She cried at the dinner table, and her mother yelled at her sister:

See her like what? She's fine! She's perfectly fine!

Her dad didn't even realize someone was crying. He just sat there look-ing at his phone. Norma stood from her chair and ran upstairs. So I said:

I don't mean to be rude, but she's not fine.

See, Mom. She lives with her. She would know. Why would I let her around my kids if she's fucked in the head?

Oh stop it! Don't talk about her like that.

I excused myself from the table and went upstairs. I found Norma lying in bed. Her tears had somehow made a crack in the oblivion that had overtaken her. She grabbed me and held on to me tight as if she hadn't seen another human in years:

I'm sorry. I'm so sorry. I'm so so sorry. I just want to go away until I'm better.

She was back. The woman I knew was back.

You're okay. I'm okay. We're going to be okay.

I'm ruining everything, and I don't know how to stop it!

It's okay. It's okay.

She held me tighter and sobbed louder:

I miss writing. I miss myself. I miss you.

I didn't know what to say. I hadn't gone anywhere. I was right there. So instead of using words, I just wrapped my arms around her and held her in bed. No one else came to check on her. All we heard was yelling coming from downstairs.

———

She cracks first, but she doesn't try another question.

Amy's been with me for four years now. She takes good care of me. I was glad when she told me she found your number. She'll fix us some lunch soon.

Norma, what are you doing? You hate small talk.

Maybe I like it now.

I roll my eyes and stare at her hands. It's so odd to see them without gold rings. It almost makes me nauseous.

Go ahead. Say it.

I look back up at her:

Say what?

What you want to say.

I don't know what you're talking about.

Sure you do.

A man passes by on the bay and waves from his paddleboard. He is young and fit and wearing a Speedo. The bay is his runway. Norma waves back with a large smile on her face as if all is good in the world and nothing at all is wrong. I feel myself get angry so I just spit it out:

Why didn't you call?

Well, Amy was the one that found your—

That's not what I'm talking about.

She goes:

Because it was the best thing for you. I was broken.

And she says this so matter-of-factly that my hands clench.

We're all broken, Norma.

Not like me.

I want to say, "oh come on, you're not special, Norma," but that's not actually true. Norma is special. She's always been special. Just not in the way that she thinks she is.

You know about thirty years back, the G supply ran out.

She says this with a smile on her face as if we aren't in the middle of an argument. God, I forgot she did this. How badly it gets under my skin. She knows this, and yet she continues:

And Labor Day weekend, all the guys finished whatever G they had left. Like a suicide pact or something. G never did come back. I wonder what new drug they take now.

I look at my sneakers and can't believe I'm still wearing Converse after all these years. Suddenly, I am aware that I am attempting, with my footwear, to escape death. I try to hide my feet under the wicker chair so she won't see them, but of course, she already has. She sees everything.

———

A month later she met with a psychiatrist who became her new therapist. And the old woman diagnosed her with depression, depersonalization and derealization disorder, and anxiety from trauma. She put her on medication. She would start with Prozac. The first day that Norma took the pill, she said she had hope, and I thought of her laugh and how I hadn't heard it in so long. Her hand was shaking as she placed the pill in her mouth. I watched her from the island counter and tried to smile.

Norma got much worse before she got even a little better. The depression deepened. Her anxiety multiplied. Her eyes got blurry. The medication made her unbearably tired, but at the same time, her thoughts kept her up at night. Those first months, the ache of that treacherous summer grew to a magnitude I didn't even know could exist. I was worried about leaving her when I went to work. She was worried about going outside because she kept seeing signs and having panic attacks. She sat on the couch rubbing her eyes most of the day:

I can't even see the words on my computer screen. They're so itchy and they're burning! I'm going blind! I know it. I'm going blind. This is why I didn't want to go on medication.

On her bad days, she was furious with me. I had done this to her. I wasn't her one. Look, now she's medicated and it's my fault. She would break up with me every other day, screaming through tears that this was the only way to make the pain go away. I told myself just one more month. One more month and the medicine would take its full effect and the woman I knew would come back to me. I began to believe I deserved the way she was treating me, as if it was really my fault. But weeks later, the sadness still hadn't let up. The doses increased. And with each dosage change, she attacked more. On her bad days, I was to blame for everything that was wrong with her.

But then there were some days when she was completely lucid and completely her. These good days appeared without warning and for what seemed like no particular reason except the right recipe of brain chemistry that day. On these days, we held each other. We added things to our bucket list. On her really good days, we would even leave the apartment *and check some things off our list. On one particularly good day, we sat in the park where we had our first real date, and she looked at me with tears in her eyes:*

This isn't fair to you.

It's okay. I can hold on to the light for us. I know what we are.

I don't even know who *I* am anymore.

I do.

She looked like she was going to cry, but then she held the tears back and said:

Just know you won't have to hold on to the light forever. I'll be there soon. Just a little longer? For me?

I nodded. Of course. Of course I could hold on for longer. Of course I could for her. She would be better soon. I started to cry then. It was the first time I had cried in front of her in months. Before that day, I had reserved all my tears for subway rides to work or in the shower. Any place, really, that she couldn't see or hear me. Any place that I was alone. This was the first time I let her see my pain. She put her arms around me:

Talk to me. I'm here now.

And she was. I could tell from her voice, from the way her body sat on the park bench, from the way her hands held mine and her gold rings shone in the fall sunlight.

I just—I can take it—I can take all of it, except—

What, baby? Tell me.

I just need you to—

The tears kept falling no matter how much I tried to hold them back:

I can deal with everything else, but please—just please—
please stop trying to leave me.

———

Have you gone senile?

Maybe she's referring to my sneaker choice. So I pretend to be oblivious:

Excuse me?

I've been talking to you.

No, you've been changing the subject just like you always did.
Who gives a shit about G?

Norma tilts her chin up and blinks twice:

Did you come here to fight with me or to have a nice time?

To be honest, Norma, I don't know why I came here.

*My tone surprises me. I sound thirty again. Thirty and stubborn. Norma
hears it, but she isn't as surprised. In fact, she seems pleased:*

Oh, there she is.

What's that supposed to mean?

Thirty again.

You never did like being vulnerable. I guess you haven't
changed much either.

I have nothing to say to her, so she keeps going:

I always fantasized that our ending would have just been a stepping stone to your great love. And you'd have grandchildren by now. And a nice penthouse apartment in the city.

I want to lunge toward her but instead I interrupt her:

I live in Brooklyn.

And I can tell from your empty hands that there is no wife. So let me ask you again: did you come here to fight with me or to have a nice time?

I stand up from my chair, pushing it back as I rise:

You wanna know why I came here?

She looks at me with intrigue.

Because I heard you were dying and I thought you should see this.

I reach for my purse and open it. I pull out a black Moleskine notebook:

I thought you should see all the life you missed out on.

She leans forward and takes the book into her hands. She examines it as if it's a meteorite from space, turning it gently in her hands. Her lips are parted. Her eyes are damp.

You kept it?

I didn't just keep it. I checked everything off. I went to every place on that list just like we promised. I keep my promises.

―――

In November on a Friday afternoon, she went to her therapy session and came home with a new Tumi suitcase.

What's that for?

For you.

I had just fed the cats dinner, and I stood there with the can in my hand, waiting for her to explain.

I can't do this anymore.

Don't say that, Norma.

I can't.

Come on. Not again. Please stop.

I'm serious this time. I'm gonna do this my way. And I have to do it on my own. Then I'll come back to you when I'm better.

I asked her what had happened in therapy, but she wouldn't tell me. She was packing a duffel bag, saying she would leave for a few days until all my stuff was gone. I tried to hold her, but she made her body stiff.

It's for your own good. I'm doing it for you.

I don't want this!

Fine. Then I'm doing it for us. Let me do this one thing for us.

Before she left, I reached for her hand:

You promise?

Her wrist was as stiff as a mannequin's:

Promise what?

That you'll call me when you're better?

She looked around the apartment, with a duffel bag hanging on her shoulder, and she took in the space as if she'd never see it again.

Say you promise.

She put her hand on the door handle and opened it:

Promise.

And then she left.

———

The sun is finally going down and the air is cooler. She pets the Moleskine notebook that is still in her hands:

Look, I didn't call, because every story has an ending. I didn't want that for us.

But you did end us. How do you not see that?

Today, I've had to face the reality of what I've done. A premature ending and a short-lived sequel.

Jesus, Norma. I'm not a fucking character in your book. I'm a person.

With her ringless hands, she tosses white, runaway hairs out of her eyes.

Don't get so offended. I always thought of myself like a fictional character too. I'm scared of reality.

I shift the weight in my feet so my right hip stops burning and say:

No, I don't buy it. I think the truth is that your whole *my heart knows your heart* thing was bullshit. And I bought into it. I mean, damn, I believed it for decades. But now I realize I was never like you. I didn't need a fucking meet-cute to make our love real.

The sliding door opens, and Amy walks out with sandwiches on a platter. When she sees our faces, Amy abruptly and loudly announces that she forgot ketchup and walks back into the house.

Fine. You want the truth? I didn't believe we could last.

I almost laugh:

You didn't even try to believe.

She looks up into my eyes and I so badly want to look away, but I know I can't. I have to win. Then she says:

You're right. I didn't. Until now. Can you please just sit back down?

So I do. I sit down and say:

It's too late now! Look at us! We're two old women who can barely walk. You left back then so you could get better, but you never even tried. And now you're sitting here with all these weird philosophical walls up, saying that—that—

I hear myself stuttering and try to pull it together:

That you wish you didn't leave?

She doesn't say anything, so I keep going not because I want to, but because the words just keep coming. I wonder if this was how she felt when we first started talking, like some dam built decades ago had suddenly broken and there was nothing to stop the words anymore.

Why do you wish you didn't leave, Norma? Let me guess. Because then you would've been able to finish your manuscript instead of having it rot in some drawer?

Her jaw clenches.

You were so scared that our love would end and that it would end badly, but sometimes it doesn't end, Norma, and you're just happy!

She cracks, and now she's yelling back at me:

No! Not in a love story! Eventually, there's some deceit or some boredom or, even in the most epic ones, there's death. All love stories are painful!

I'm not talking about stories, Norma! I'm talking about us!

I slam my hand down on the arm of the chair, and I feel my brittle bones rattle underneath. She closes her eyes and takes a deep breath.

When she exhales, her posture adjusts:

Some of us don't feel like we deserve love.

And after she says this, she finally opens her eyes.

Bullshit. I used to be like that. Then you got sick, and I learned that I was capable of staying even when things got hard. That's love. You taught me that.

Isn't there a saying about that? Those who teach cannot do—

Oh shut up! You're just as aggravating as you were back then.

I stand up with all the force I have left in me, walk back into the house, then out the front door and past the gate.

———

Those next two days alone in what was once our home, I folded my clothes slowly, placing piles of denim and cotton on our faux leather couch, hoping that with each minute I didn't put them in the suitcase, she would come to her senses and come home. Sometimes, I could almost hear her laughter filling the room, the late-night conversations we used to have. Amongst the memories, I thought there was no way she wouldn't come back. There was no way she would walk away from what we had. I folded my clothes slowly but she never came. Even after those two days, I truly believed I would see her again. I truly thought she would get better. For us. For me. Or at least for herself.

———

By the time I reach the dock, I wish I'd gone to the bathroom at her house. Without a toilet, I won't be able to hop on the seven p.m. ferry and drive back to the city, which means I'll have to settle for the bar bathroom or go back to her house, which would be pathetic. As I contemplate my bladder, young guys in leather and glitter are beginning to gather for the sunset, throwing their legs over the side of the old dock with an effortlessness I am envious of. I crunch my tired body into a contortion of limbs in the attempt to sit like they are, posting up for the event, but the aches in my shoulder and hip burn. A man in a pink neon muscle tee comes over and offers his chair to me. It is one of those chairs that parents use at soccer games. I hate this young guy for witnessing my crumbling limbs, but still, I want to watch the sunset on Dragon

Island one last time, so I accept. The pink-shirt man smiles at me like I am old, and for the rest of my life, this is how people will smile at me. The sun starts to wane toward the horizon, though there's still probably fifteen minutes to spare.

Hey.

I turn to my right, and Norma is next to me, sitting in a wheelchair. Amy is standing behind her, and then with a gentle nod at me, Amy walks back toward the boardwalk. I can feel my heart beating in my throat when I say:

I'm sorry for telling you to shut up.

Norma intertwines her fingers and places them on her lap as if she's praying:

No. I'm sorry.

For what?

She doesn't say anything, but in her silence, I feel her shield come down and I hear a million apologies. For stopping therapy. For the things she said to me when her anxiety took over. For all the times she blamed me. For every day that she didn't call. For years and years of trying to write me away. I hear her voice in my ears: My heart knows your heart. I feel like I can breathe again, and finally I feel like me again:

Look, I can live with you leaving me. I've done it for decades.
I'll survive somehow. But to leave your work, your writing . . .
I can't.

I can't write the last story.

You could publish the manuscript without it.

Without it there's no through line. The last one was supposed to give the reader meaning.

I look into her eyes and remember what it felt like to be with her all those years ago. How the chaos of life seemed to muster some sort of meaning when we were together. How back then, I didn't have to stick my hands into dirt to feel alive. And then she shrugs:

Don't worry too much about it, though. My manuscript was just fiction. What good is fiction anyways?

I'd asked her this same question on one of our first FaceTime dates. Back then, she answered that fiction holds grief better than reality does, and through it, we know we're not alone. This time, though, she asks the question, and I have no answer for her. We both turn and stare at the sunset. The pink she painted her nails during that first Covid summer. The yellow of the sweatpants she lived in when oblivion deepened. The deep purple, the same color of her favorite plant. The gray blue like her old cat. She says:

This whole thing is a little silly, isn't it?

Her voice reaches my ears from what feels like so far away. I can barely hear her.

Huh?

She turns to face me and the wrinkles on her face begin to move:

We both know by this year, 2070, when we're truly this old, Dragon Island will be underwater from climate change. My white house will not exist. This bay and the ocean will have merged into one, or, rather, the ocean will have consumed the bay. This future only exists in our imaginations. We were never able to predict anything other than what was right in front of us. And any predictions we had were only projections of our past onto the future.

I respond as if reciting a passage from the Quran that I memorized as a child:

A reenactment with old characters. A familiar place with new furniture. A memory as a premonition.

The borders of her body begin to soften into the sunset sky:

The places that we promised to travel to in that notebook, the ones you say you've been to, will probably be uninhabitable in the years to come or ravaged by civil or nuclear war. Maybe they'll be isolated in the attempt to suffocate a new deadly virus, which may, in that future, be much more deadly than the one we met during. We can't know. All I know is that you are sitting in front of me now and my eyes are waterfalls. And my hands . . . all they want to do is hold you, whether your tanned scarred skin is truly as wrinkled as you say it is or as soft as the day we met.

I blink to try to clear the mist that's begun to grab hold of her edges, but it only deepens. I try to speak through it:

The ending of your book . . . will you finish it now?

My time is running out. And I'd rather spend what I have left with you. When I'm gone, you can give it the ending it needs.

But it's your story.

She chuckles gently and it echoes against the sunset sky:

Can't you see what I've been missing all these years? I've abandoned life for an imaginative world. And all the while, I kept hearing the phrase "please stop trying to leave me." But it wasn't your voice saying this. It was my own. Do you get it now?

The mist begins to lift, and her voice gets clearer:

Promise me one last thing.

Her voice has lost its husky rasp and suddenly feels more familiar. She continues:

Promise me that you will write the last story.

I stare into her eyes. Her face is young again. Her brown eyes, unfogged.

Why can't you?

Our bodies are leaning against our faux leather couch. Her hands are adorned with rings again:

Because I never got better.

The taxis are honking outside.

But in the real world, you did. You did get better.

Her lips curl into a smile that I've missed for so long.

THE END

We should not try to "get rid" of a neurosis, but rather to experience what it means, what it has to teach, what its purpose is. We should even learn to be thankful for it, otherwise we pass it by and miss the opportunity of getting to know ourselves as we really are. A neurosis is truly removed only when it has removed the false attitude of the ego. We do not cure it—it cures us.

A person is ill, but the illness is nature's attempt to heal the person.

Carl Jung

Epilogue

When Norma asked me to finish her manuscript, I was hesitant. I thought it was wrong for me to touch her work, to change the narrator after so many pages with the same one. That night after she asked me to finish it, she let me sleep in what used to be our bed even though it hadn't been for months. When I woke to her the next morning, it was snowing, she was sleeping, and it was as if she had never told me to leave. To the sound of the heater that always made our sinuses too dry, I held her damp body until her eyes opened.

Later that morning over chai and coffee, I told Norma my hesitations. She responded saying that readers are smart. They'll be able to follow. Personally, I'm not so sure about readers. I'm not so sure about writing a book or even writing in general. I build things. "Exactly. You build pop-ups. A book isn't so different from a pop-up." I said that they were completely different, and she could tell that I wasn't going to budge. Norma closed her eyes and took a deep breath that sounded like the ocean waves. When she exhaled, she opened her eyes and stared directly into mine.

That morning with her eyes glued to mine and her bare hands tightly gripping her chai, Norma told me why she really needed me to finish her manuscript.

To help me understand, she put it into metaphor:

My manuscript is like a baby's pacifier;

like plastic coverings over furniture in the living room;

like being tired and drinking a cup of coffee in virtual reality;

like training wheels;

like living in New York City but never going outside;

like playing a video game alone in your room while your family is laughing around a board game in the kitchen;

like religion or New Age spirituality;

like SparkNotes for a literary classic;

like sand tray therapy for children.

What Norma meant to say with each metaphor was that her writing was doing what her mind had done for twenty-seven years. Her writing kept her pain at a distance from her. It kept her memories dissociated from her body. It kept her emotions trapped somewhere away from her heart. Writing was her attempt at transplanting her trauma into a character so she didn't have to hold it. And when she transplanted it, she could edit the trauma the way she so badly wanted to edit her memories.

That morning, Norma told me her breakdown came exactly when she needed it, exactly when it was safe enough to come. And according to her, it was safe enough that summer, because I was there. This is the meaning that she's garnered from what she went through. From what she continues to go through. Still, she said she couldn't guarantee either on paper or in her manuscript that we would be together forever, but she said that the only way we stood a chance in real life was for her to start really living. "So now will you finish it for me?"

After I said yes, I realized that to do what she asked, I had to read her manuscript in its entirety. I had to read about all the thoughts in her head that hated me. It wasn't easy, but loving someone is loving the hard parts too. After reading, I'm not sure if Norma's manuscript will get published, and if it does get published, I'm not sure that it won't be banned for having LGBTQ+ characters, because this is the world we live in now. But the truth is: we don't know what will happen. We cannot even guess it, because, like Norma says, we can only predict our past onto the future. All I know is that I have moved back into our apartment. That I wake up to Norma meditating every day and I smile. That one day we will visit Hawai'i together and I won't have to worry about her running toward the crater. That one day this summer and this fall will become, just like everything else, a memory.

Tonight, as I finish writing this final chapter after dinner, Norma comes over to me, wearing one of my old college T-shirts and a pair of period underwear, and she asks me if I can do one last thing for her. I laugh. What more can I do?

Oh, she wants you to know that this is a love story.

Acknowledgments

Thank you to Laurie Sheck for being the first writer, person, and professor to *see* and believe in the soul of this novel. Your mentorship has made me the author I am today.

Thank you to D. S., who helped me "get better" even though you never handed me the answers and, instead, made me work for them (much to my dismay). I can't properly put into words how grateful I am.

Thank you to R. B., who encourages me to keep my eyes open and feel my breath.

Thank you to the neighbor across the hall and to José downstairs, who led me to Mina Hamedi.

Thank you to Mina Hamedi for offering to read my manuscript writer-to-writer, neighbor-to-neighbor, and then for believing in the story. You are an amazing agent, a top-notch fellow cat mom, and a wonderful friend.

Thank you to Ellie Pritchett for being a tireless editor for this wild book and, also, for accepting my awkwardness. You saw the madness I made and helped me polish it to completion in a way that I couldn't have done alone.

Thank you to Mark Abrams and artist Jennifer Allnutt for the cover of this book, which is beyond my wildest dreams. Thank you to the copy editors, designers, and all the eyes and hands this manuscript passed through at Vintage Books and Penguin Random House.

Thank you to Zoé Paddon, who reads every draft of every story I try to write—no matter how unpolished and messy.

Thank you to Anna Duncan, photographer and friend, for making my headshot dreams come true.

Thank you to NYU, Columbia University, The New School, and every professor along the way.

Thank you to all the magazines and journals that published my work before this novel came out: *Epiphany* magazine, *Pank* magazine, *Nailed* magazine, *Eleven and a Half Journal*, Genre: Urban Arts, the *Minetta Review*, and more.

Thank you to my parents, Mark and Elisia Saab, for bringing me into this world, for providing me with a life in which I could learn and explore, and for supporting my dreams even when they weren't looking so promising.

Thank you to my nephews, Lowell and Leo, for teaching me the magnitude of love that I am capable of.

Thank you to my friends, current and past, for accepting me as I am.

Thank you to my ancestors and unseen teachers for bringing us to this very moment.

Thank you to my soon-to-be wife, Frishta Yaqubie, for graciously loving me on my worst and best, sane and insane, ugly and beautiful days. This book wouldn't exist without you (being perfectly you) and without your love.

And lastly, thank you to myself—for everything.

Afterward

Just like the old owners of that house, you can find me in the library.